BLESSED ARE THE DEAD

A MEDIAEVAL MYSTERY

C.B. HANLEY

First published by The Mystery Press, 2023

The Mystery Press, an imprint of The History Press
97 St George's Place
Cheltenham, Gloucestershire, GL50 3QB
www.thehistorypress.co.uk

British Library Cataloguing in Publication Data.
A catalogue record for this book is available from the British Library.

ISBN 978 1 80399 306 5

Typesetting and origination by The History Press
Printed and bound in Great Britain by TJ Books Limited, Padstow, Cornwall.

For B.B.
My friend and partial namesake,
and a wonderful library volunteer.

Blessed are the dead which die in the Lord;
They may rest from their labours.
Revelation, ch.14, v.13

Praise for C.B. Hanley's Mediaeval Mystery Series

'[In *By the Edge of the Sword*] Hanley sets the stage for a page turner with a gentle lady in peril, a heartsick warrior set on heroics, a level-headed detective, and a village and castle filled with said lady's accusers. The game's afoot when floodwaters trap these combustibles in the castle. Highly recommended!'

Candace Robb, author of the *Owen Archer* mysteries

'[*Cast the First Stone* is] brilliantly evocative of time and place, but with themes that are bang up to date. C.B. Hanley brings past and present together in an enthralling story.'

A.J. Mackenzie, author of the *Hardcastle & Chaytor* mysteries

'*The Bloody City* is a great read, full of intrigue and murder. Great for readers of Ellis Peters and Lindsey Davis. Hanley weaves a convincing, rich tapestry of life and death in the early 13th century, in all its grandeur and filth. I enjoyed this book immensely!'

Ben Kane, bestselling novelist of the *Forgotten Legion* trilogy

'Blatantly heroic and wonderfully readable.'

The Bloody City received a STARRED review in *Library Journal*

'The characters are real, the interactions and conversations natural, the tension inbuilt, and it all builds to a genuinely satisfying conclusion both fictionally and historically.'

Review for *The Bloody City* in www.crimereview.co.uk

'*Whited Sepulchres* ... struck me as a wonderfully vivid recreation of the early thirteenth century ... The solid historical basis lends authenticity to a lively, well-structured story. I enjoyed the plight of amiable and peace-loving Edwin, trapped by his creator in such a warlike time and place.'

Andrew Taylor, winner of the 2009 CWA Diamond Dagger and three-times winner of the CWA Historical Dagger

'It's clever. It's well written. It's believable. It's historically accurate. It's a first-class medieval mystery.'

Review for *Whited Sepulchres* in www.crimereview.co.uk

'*Brother's Blood* [is] a gift for medievalists everywhere ... Hanley really knows her stuff. Her knowledge of life in a Cistercian monastery is impeccable. More please.'

Cassandra Clark, author of the *Abbess of Meaux* medieval mystery series

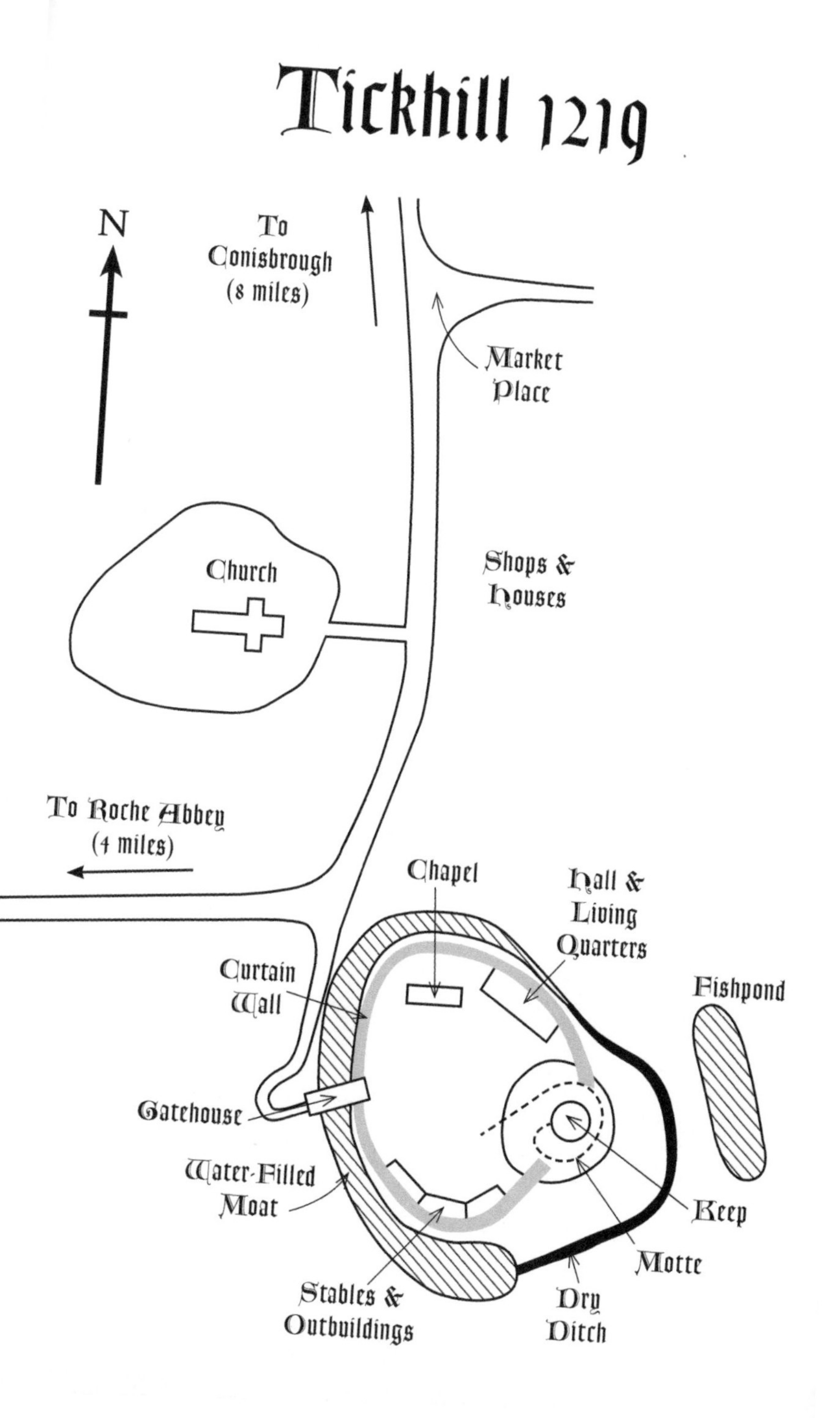
Tickhill 1219
N
To
Conisbrough
(8 miles)
Market
Place
Church
Shops &
Houses
To Roche Abbey
(4 miles)
Chapel
Hall &
Living
Quarters
Curtain
Wall
Fishpond
Gatehouse
Water-Filled
Moat
Keep
Motte
Stables &
Outbuildings
Dry
Ditch

Chapter One

Tickhill Castle, South Yorkshire, April 1219

'Thomas.'

There was a pause.

'Thomas! Can't you hear me?'

It took Edwin a moment – again – to realise that he was the man being addressed. 'Sorry,' he managed. 'My mind was wandering.'

'Aye, well, you've enough to think about just now, I suppose.'

He'd got away with it this time, but he really needed to concentrate harder. These lapses were going to give him away if he wasn't careful.

'Anyway, like I was saying, your horse isn't healing as fast as I thought he would, so it looks like you'll have to stay a while longer.'

'Oh dear,' replied Edwin, trying to sound as if he meant it. 'I hope Sir Robert and Lady Idonea won't mind.'

The stablemaster waved a hand. 'They're known all around these parts for hospitality, and there's always room for one more in the hall. Besides, the lady seems quite taken with your wife.'

The darkness, the foreboding, the crushing fear … it all came rushing back, and for a moment Edwin felt nauseous. That Alys had been put in this situation was intolerable, and he cursed himself over and over again for letting it happen.

He had to pull himself together. 'I'll go and find her now, to give her the news, and then come and see the horse afterwards.'

The stablemaster, with a surprised expression, looked as though he might be about to indicate that he would prioritise the horse, so Edwin nodded to him and walked briskly away to avoid the temptation to snap at a man who was only doing his job.

The bailey was soft underfoot, but not too muddy, at least – the incessant rains of March had tailed off a couple of weeks ago, some time before they'd set off, and the ground everywhere was slowly drying out. Edwin picked his way across with care, trying to find the best places to set his feet; 'Thomas' was a fastidious man and wouldn't want to get his boots dirty.

The motte loomed over him, and Edwin contemplated it as he approached. It was so steep that the path up to the stone keep had to spiral around instead of leading straight up, something he'd never seen before, although admittedly his experience of castles was hardly extensive. It would be exceptionally difficult to attack the keep in such a position, but Edwin supposed that was the point: any men trying to circle the path would be out in the open for some while, making themselves easy targets, but if they tried to force their way straight up the precipitous side of the motte they would be off balance and slipping all over the place, and thus equally vulnerable.

Edwin already knew that he wouldn't find Sir Robert inside the building, for he had carefully noted the knight riding out with a few of his men around the middle of the morning. *Where was he going?* was the question that immediately sprang to mind. *What was he going to do while he was out?* Was it anything to do with … and how would Edwin find out without giving himself away?

And then, the thought catching him so sharply that it almost brought him to an abrupt, winded halt in the middle of the bailey, *Why was I just thinking about the keep being attacked?* Unfortunately, he already knew the answer to that question, and the longer it took him to do what he was here for, the more likely a prospect it became. Edwin felt a cold sweat break out on his forehead.

A very youthful guard stood at the bottom of the motte, looking proudly and keenly about him as he blocked the path, and Edwin allowed himself a brief smile at the thought that the most junior members of the garrison getting the most tedious jobs was not a practice confined to Conisbrough. Did the path really need 'guarding' when the only people inside the castle enclosure had every right to be there, and would one boy stop any malefactors anyway? Still, the Tickhill sergeant-at-arms would no doubt be glad of the youth's enthusiasm until it eventually wore off. The bright red hair was easily recognisable, and Edwin recalled that the boy's name was Theo, and that he had already, over the last few days, chattily let Edwin and Alys know that he was a local, from Tickhill town, and that he was proud to have been taken on at the castle and hoped to progress in Sir Robert's service. Someone so junior was unlikely to have any information that Edwin needed, but he listened very carefully to anything that anyone said to him just in case some small detail might come in useful. It hadn't so far, but he had to live in hope.

Edwin greeted Theo by name, reminding himself to concentrate on who he was supposed to be and assuming the rather hearty manner that was part of his disguise. 'And do you know if my wife is up in the keep, young man?'

Theo's face immediately took on the expression of a lovesick puppy. 'Yes, master, she is. She and Lady Idonea seem to be able to spend all day talking about cloth and suchlike, or so Margaret says – how do they do it?'

'Ah, well,' said Edwin, tucking his thumbs in his belt and rocking back on his heels in the way he'd seen real merchants do, 'Fabrics are a fascinating subject, of course, with all sorts of different qualities and textures …'

Theo's eyes began to glaze over. 'Well, I'm sure it's fine if you go up to find her, master.' He stepped aside.

Edwin made his way up and around until he reached the keep's entrance, which was directly above where Theo stood, pulling himself even straighter to attention when any of the more senior members of the garrison passed. Edwin explained his business to the older and rather bored-looking guard lounging at the door, and was admitted.

The keep was multi-sided, like the one at Conisbrough, with the stair running around the outside of it in the thickness of the wall; however, the building here was much smaller, with just the ground and upper floors and then the roof. There were no hidden nooks where a person might hide unobserved to eavesdrop on conversations, as Edwin had already discovered, so he didn't bother pausing on his way up. However, with Sir Robert definitely out of the way, and Lady Idonea's attention on Alys, might now be a good time to run up to the roof and have a quick look around? If he was noticed then it might be a little tricky to explain what a respectable cloth merchant was doing up there, but he could surely bluff his way through an excuse about wanting to see the view, or looking out over the road he would take to get 'home' once his horse had recovered.

The chances were that nobody was going to see him anyway, for he'd already observed while gazing up at the keep that there was no guard currently on the roof. He decided to risk it, making his way up the final flight of steps and emerging into the daylight.

In one respect it was disappointing: there was absolutely nothing to be seen except the conical wooden roof and the empty path that led all the way round it, just inside the stone crenellations. And nor could Edwin see, as he peered through one of the embrasures, which direction Sir Robert had taken that morning, for he had been gone for some while and his party was out of sight, even allowing for the far-reaching clear view afforded by the double height of both keep and motte. The fish-pond directly under his current position looked very far down indeed, and Edwin was glad he didn't get dizzy when up high, as some men did.

He completed his circuit of the path and reached the top of the stairs again. Nothing. Still, in one sense the emptiness of the roof was at least of some use to him, for he could rule it out: what he was looking for certainly *wasn't* hidden up here.

He was still unobserved as he made his way back down to the keep's upper storey and reached the door to the chamber. He entered after knocking, needing to pause in order to adjust his eyes: despite the bright spring day outside, the room was dark and dull, there being no windows other than narrow slits. However, there were candles enough lit for him to make out three women over by the fireplace, surrounded by rolled, unrolled and draped bolts of cloth.

They all turned as he entered.

'Lady Idonea.' Edwin inclined his head in respect and remembered to put on his rather pompous manner. 'I apologise for interrupting, but I bring the sad news that our horse is not yet sufficiently recovered to travel. I hope and pray that we may trespass on your kind hospitality for a day or two longer.'

The lady made a gracious reply and turned to the plainly dressed girl beside her. 'Margaret, run and tell the kitchens that, happily, our guests will be staying a few more days.' She pointed at a dish on the table that contained some pieces of marchpane and other sweetmeats. 'And you haven't had any of these yet – take one with you as you go.'

The girl happily selected something and slipped out. As she passed him Edwin murmured, 'He's at the bottom of the path, so you'll get the chance for a quick word,' and received a smile in return.

He sighed as he turned back to the room. Margaret was nice, Theo was nice, Lady Idonea was nice, everyone was *nice*. He and Alys had received nothing but a pleasant welcome from all at Tickhill, and it just made Edwin feel ever more guilty about being there under false pretences.

Still, he had his duty to do, and the sooner the better – although his determination was for Alys's sake more than the lord earl's. Keeping her safe was the most important duty of all, and he would sweep everything else aside if necessary, no matter what the cost.

Edwin could feel the throbbing in his head as he looked at her now, the constant anxiety pushing its way to the fore despite his attempts to contain it. She was radiant, as always, smiling back at him over the enormous swell of her belly, and his breath caught in his throat as he thought of the danger she was in, just a couple of weeks – if that – away from her confinement.

He wanted to talk to her alone, and, as ever, she knew exactly the right thing to say. 'Oh dear, poor Kit. Should we go to the stable to see him together?' She began the laborious process of getting to her feet.

Lady Idonea put out a hand. 'Surely, my dear, there can be no need for you to put yourself to the trouble? The men can deal with these things without our help, and you'll be more comfortable remaining here.'

Alys exchanged a glance with Edwin. 'Thank you, my lady – you're so kind – but actually I do find myself in need of some movement and air. Sitting so long in one attitude is becoming increasingly uncomfortable.' She made it upright, a little unsteadily, and Edwin rushed forward to help.

'As you think best, my dear,' said Lady Idonea. 'I wouldn't know about these things.' A shadow flitted across her face, but Edwin barely noticed as he concentrated on Alys.

Alys attempted a brief curtsey, which didn't work very well. 'I'll be very happy to go through any further requirements you might have later, my lady.'

'Very well. There will be ample time now you're going to be staying a while longer.' Lady Idonea smiled and then turned to take up a psalter, adjusting her position to gain the best of the meagre light and allowing them to escape.

Edwin ushered Alys over to the stair. 'Can you manage? We can go as slowly as you like. And then there's the motte afterwards, but I'll keep hold of you so you don't slip.' He held her hand and put his other arm about her waist.

'I'll be fine as long as we don't rush,' she replied, out loud. And then, under her breath, 'Anything?'

'Not yet,' he whispered. 'Though I have bought more time. You?'

She made a face. 'All she wants to talk about is babies.'

There wasn't much light in the stairwell, so Edwin couldn't see her exact expression, but he felt her fingers tighten on his. She was putting on a brave face for his sake, he knew. 'I really don't want to keep you here longer than necessary. We need to get you home, where it's safe.'

Alys sighed. 'Well, it looks like quickest way to do that will be to carry out the lord earl's instructions.'

Now it was Edwin's turn to tighten his grip.

'You will,' she said, soothingly. '*We* will.'

It took them some while to reach the bailey, but they managed it safely, Theo advancing a little way up to them on the steep path to walk on Alys's other side as she negotiated the final stretch. Once they reached the flat ground Alys thanked him, making him blush.

Margaret was just returning across the bailey, singing to herself, and she stopped for a moment to chat. Edwin had noticed her closeness to Theo, but frankly thought that Theo was a little young to be walking out with a girl, especially one who looked to be two or three years older than him. Still, it wasn't his business, was it?

Alys was engaging in conversation, always comfortable in talking to new people in a way that Edwin wasn't. 'Very fortunate for you both to be here together,' she said, brightly. 'And have you got any other brothers and sisters?'

'Yes,' replied Margaret. 'Or, sort of. We're the eldest and the only ones from Mother's first marriage, but she remarried after Father died and had three more. They're all still at home.' She pointed vaguely in the direction of the town.

Edwin kicked himself for not seeing it before.

'Oh, how lovely,' said Alys, though Edwin could see a shadow cross her face. 'I have younger ones of my own, thr— *two* brothers and a sister, and I miss them sometimes. I'm surprised your mother doesn't prefer to keep you at home to help look after them.'

Theo, who was just licking the remains of a piece of marchpane from his lips, stifled a snort of laughter.

Alys gave him a quizzical look, and he was glad to elaborate, his cheeks turning as fiery as his hair as he addressed her directly. 'Not one for looking after babies, our Margaret. She much preferred running around and coming out with me to practise our archery.'

Margaret drew herself up and assumed a superior air. 'That was a long time ago, before I grew up properly – and anyway, someone had to keep an eye out for you and pull you out of trouble, rascal that you were.' She couldn't keep the affection out of her voice, despite her effort to appear ladylike.

She turned back to Alys. 'And we were both lucky to be taken on here, Mother said it was an opportunity not to be missed. Lady Idonea is so kind to me, and Theo's going to go up in the world, just you wait and see.'

'I'm sure he is,' said Edwin, in Thomas's best indulgent tone. 'But you'd both better get back to your duties, and my dear wife and I need to go to the stable to see our horse.'

'Oh, of course,' said Margaret, remembering herself. 'And we shouldn't keep a lady in your condition standing about, mistress, sorry.' She curtseyed, gave Theo a playful poke and told him to behave himself, and started up the path.

'They don't look much alike,' said Edwin, as he and Alys moved across the bailey. 'But I still should have spotted it. Something about their expressions.'

'Yes, families can have shared looks or habits,' said Alys, and Edwin suspected that the fondness in her voice was not just for Margaret and Theo. 'But it's more the way they talk to each other – that tone where you love your brother but you can get exasperated by him at the same time.'

'Well, I've never had a brother, so I wouldn't know,' replied Edwin, sighing once again with worry.

Alys squeezed his hand as they entered the stable.

There was nobody else in there, so they could be sure they were unobserved and would not be overheard. Finding their horse, Edwin did what he had already done a couple of times before: he unwound the bandage, wiped off most of the poultice with some straw that he then pushed into the middle of a dung heap to hide it, and retied the linen around the horse's leg. 'Sorry,' he murmured. 'I do want you to get better – just not yet.'

Suddenly a great weariness threatened to overcome him, the exhaustion of being permanently on edge. How in the Lord's name was he supposed to succeed in his duty *and* keep Alys and their unborn child safe? He'd been set difficult tasks before, but this one seemed impossible.

She seemed to know what he was thinking, and touched his hand. 'We'll be all right.' But he could see that she was afraid, too: afraid of what might befall them if they were found out, afraid of what might happen if she began her labour while they were far from family and friends. Terrified, as he was, for the fate of a baby born away from home and in dangerous circumstances.

Edwin bent his aching head to lay it on the horse's flank for a moment. He had to be strong. For her, for *them*.

It was actually the anger coursing through him, rather than the fear, that gave him the energy to stand upright once more. Indeed, anger wasn't a strong enough word: he was absolutely livid. Furious with the earl and also with himself for not standing up to such an unreasonable demand. And this, in turn, brought two more thoughts to the forefront of Edwin's mind with a clarity so piercing that it made his head throb even more.

The first was that he didn't want to work for the earl any longer. That one was an old wound, like picking at a scab that wouldn't heal – he'd felt it for some while, every time the earl sent him into danger, but this time the overt callous disregard his lord had shown for anything except his own interests had solidified it.

The second thought was newer, more painful, a sharp knife wound that still bled and would probably never heal. There was no escape from it: Edwin felt raw, wrenching, visceral grief to know that he would never, *ever*, be able to forgive Martin for what he'd done.

Martin looked at the two men sprawled on the ground in front of him and wondered why he hated everything.

'Oh, get up,' he said, in disgust. 'Go back and find me someone worth sparring with.'

They scurried off and he kicked the ground while he waited, glaring through the narrow eye slits of his helm. He wasn't even out of breath.

Why was everything so wretched? Why was there no enjoyment in anything any more? He hated his duties, he hated all the talking and the thinking and the *politics* that went with some of them, and he didn't even enjoy the riding and the training these days. Riding just wasn't the same, and as to sparring ... well, there was nobody within twenty miles who could hold a candle to him in a fight, and the fact that the next tallest man in the castle barely topped his shoulder didn't help. They had to come at him in twos and threes to mount any sort of challenge, and he still won easily. It was boring.

Two more of the Conisbrough garrison were soon flat on their backs, and Martin still despised his life and detested himself. But he needed another fight. He needed it because if he stopped moving and concentrating then he might have the time to start thinking about —

'Martin?'

He swung round abruptly, causing Adam to step back out of reach of the sword. Hugh, who was hovering behind him, looked apprehensive, and some of Martin's anger cooled. He would never hit the younger squire or the page who were under his authority, no matter how he was feeling, and he hoped that they knew it.

'Sir Geoffrey says training's over for today, and we need to clean up and attend on my lord while he looks at his letters.'

Martin groaned inwardly, but removed his helm and took in a gulp of the fresh spring air. He passed the sword to Hugh, hilt-first. It was a blunt training one, which meant that Martin's opponents only had bruises rather than cuts: neither the castellan, Sir Geoffrey, nor the sergeant-at-arms, Everard, wanted any of the garrison permanently disabled by 'friendly' sparring. But the lack of any real danger or risk was only making Martin more dissatisfied every time he fought.

He pulled his mind back to his duties. 'Obviously it doesn't need sharpening,' he told Hugh, 'and there's no rust on it, but see these mud flecks? They'll want cleaning off before you oil it.' He wondered when he would next have the chance to face a real opponent over the gleam of sharp steel. His heart surged and his fingers clenched around an imaginary hilt even as he thought of it.

The page nodded, always eager to help. 'Shall I take the helm, too?'

'Yes, if you can manage both.'

Fortunately Hugh, who was now nearly nine, wasn't quite as tiny as he'd been when he'd first arrived in the household. He was still small for his age, though, and made an awkward job of carrying both items as he stumbled over to the armoury.

Everard, who had been organising groups of men and giving them orders, now hailed Martin. 'I'm taking some of the newer boys out on a patrol. Have you time to come? It would do them good to have you along.'

Reluctantly, Martin shook his head. Riding out wasn't quite as pleasurable an activity as it had once been, not with the horse he had now, but it would still be infinitely preferable to listening to letters and politics. 'I have to attend on my lord.'

Everard chuckled. 'One of the perils of rank. There aren't many advantages to being born out of wedlock, but having a good steady position where there's no danger of rising too high and having to think about things is one of them.'

Martin wondered if he might get the time to ride out later, once all the day's talking was over and done with. He did so whenever he could get away, enjoying the peace and solitude, and sometimes dreaming that he might find a nest of outlaws or other malefactors – that would give him an excuse to really let his feelings rip, taking out his anger justifiably on those who deserved it. His fingers clutched around a non-existent hilt once more as he imagined …

He hadn't said anything out loud, and now realised there had been an awkward silence.

'Well,' continued Everard. 'I'll leave you to it. Next time, maybe?'

'I hope so.' Martin watched the sergeant's departing back and then turned to Adam with a sigh. 'Let's get out of this, then.' Now that Adam was sixteen, he'd moved on to wearing full-weight armour for training, but he wasn't quite used to it and was looking weary; Martin helped him out of his mail and gambeson first before allowing Adam to do the same for him.

'*Letters*,' said Martin, morosely, as they stacked everything back in the armoury. 'Here, pass me that and I'll put it up here.' He shoved his rolled-up hauberk on to the top shelf. There was all kinds of jumble up here that probably wanted sorting out, but he just couldn't muster enough interest to want to do anything about it. He'd note it to Sir Geoffrey or Everard later, if he could be bothered, and perhaps one of the recruits could deal with it.

'But don't you think it's interesting?' asked Adam. 'Learning about what's happening in other parts of the realm? How my lord deals with other earls and even the king and his regent?'

'No,' said Martin, shortly. He stared through the roof beams that were at his eye level. 'No, I don't want to think about that sort of thing at all.'

'But when you're a knight …'

'When I'm a knight I'll train my men, follow my orders and fight where I'm told to fight,' he snapped. 'The lord earl will need a strong right arm from time to time, and he's got plenty of others to do his *thinking* for him.'

Adam made no reply, and Martin knew that his mind had turned to Edwin. Adam had been there too, that day.

Martin cleared his throat. 'Anyway. Get some water and we'll wash before we go to the council chamber. Don't let that sweat cool on you.'

Adam left, and Martin checked that Hugh had cleaned the sword and helm adequately, which he had. 'Good lad,' he managed, seeing Hugh's face light up at the praise. There was no need for the boys to suffer just because he was in such a foul mood all the time.

They went outside and Martin hoped that Adam would take as long as possible over fetching the water, because he really, really didn't want to go into the council chamber. However, with his usual efficiency Adam was back almost before anyone might have noticed he'd gone. They all washed faces and hands so they would be presentable before the lord earl, which was enough for the others, but when they'd finished Martin stripped off his shirt, picked up the pitcher and poured the rest of it over his head. The icy deluge was a shock – water from the castle well was cold all year round, and the spring weather hadn't yet taken the bitter chill off it – but he welcomed it.

'Well then,' he said, once dried and dressed, and trying not to sound like a man on the way to his own execution. 'Let's not keep my lord waiting.'

Martin normally took the keep stairs two at a time, but he found his steps slowing as they went up, and by the time they reached the level of the council chamber the other two were in front of him. Adam knocked and opened the door, holding it for Martin to go through first, and Martin did so. He knew what it was all going to remind him of, because it was in this very room that he'd done the stupid, idiotic thing that he was going to regret for the rest of his life.

'Yes, my lady, this burel is very hard-wearing and would make excellent tunics for your household. You want them to look smart, of course, but not *too* fine, and any garments made from this will last a good long time.' Edwin wasn't quite sure how long he could keep this up, and hoped Sir Robert would arrive back soon.

'Hmm … agreed,' replied Lady Idonea. 'Now, at fourpence the ell, did you say? And two ells per tunic …'

Edwin thanked the saints that the conversation had finally turned to something he *did* know about; he could add up more quickly than anyone else he'd ever met. 'Fourpence the *yard*, my lady, not the ell, so two and a half yards per tunic for two dozen men is sixty yards, which makes exactly one pound of silver.'

Clearly, Edwin didn't actually care whether she bought this fabric or not; but, partly to stay in character and partly to prolong the conversation, he pretended to consider. 'Of course, given that the bolts are thirty-two yards long, I would be happy for you to have two whole bolts for that price, with my compliments.' He stuck his thumbs in his belt again. 'Indeed, if you and your needlewomen are careful with your cutting, you might save enough fabric for four or even six additional tunics – rather a bargain, if I do say so myself.'

He was beginning to flag again, and was grateful to be interrupted by the arrival of a small boy, who waved something at Lady Idonea. 'A letter for Sir Robert – Father said to bring it up.'

Edwin was immediately on the alert, but the parchment was of no great size and carried no seal, and the boy's next words were 'About the new supplier of ale, he says.'

Lady Idonea smiled. 'You can leave it here for him.' She ruffled the boy's hair as he placed the letter on the table, then picked out a piece of marchpane from the dish. 'Here.'

The boy's eyes widened. 'Thank you, my lady!'

'And how have you been getting on since you started working with your father? Is everybody treating you well?'

'Oh yes, my lady.'

The words were addressed to her, but his eyes were on the marchpane in his hand, and she laughed. 'Very well then – off with you.'

He departed and she smiled after him before turning back to Edwin and Alys. 'Our steward's eldest son – he's just started working here. He's very young, but they take care of him and he doesn't do any of the heavy work.'

'Good for him,' said Edwin, heartily. 'Boys need to be brought up in their trade.'

'Now,' continued Lady Idonea. 'Where were we?'

Edwin, who certainly hadn't been brought up in the fabric trade, had run out of conversational gambits about it. He cast a meaningful glance at Alys.

Thankfully, she took the hint and chimed in. 'Oh yes, my lady. As my husband was saying, there will be plenty of the burel to spare, especially given that some of your men are young and slight.' She smiled in an encouraging manner at Lady Idonea and, on receiving a nod, continued in an easy tone. 'Very well. Now, as to your own personal requirements, perhaps my husband wouldn't mind if I showed you the fabric while he stands by to discuss price. It's nice to speak of such things with another woman, don't you think?'

Edwin heaved a sigh of relief and just about managed to restrain himself from blowing her a kiss as she started to go into the sort of technical detail that could only come from being genuinely a member of a merchant family. Lady Idonea seemed to be relaxing a little, and perhaps she might begin to gossip, or to let slip something – anything – that might help him. Listening to Alys demonstrate her expertise, Edwin could almost begin to appreciate … but no, he wasn't going to go down that route. Forgiveness would not be meted out so easily. He would much, much rather be here by himself, however many knots he tied himself in, if only Alys could be safe at home.

The two of them were engrossed, and Margaret was listening with interest, so Edwin eased away from them, trying to make himself as invisible as possible and hoping that Lady Idonea would eventually forget about his presence altogether.

'And, pardon me for asking, my lady,' Alys was saying, 'but do you need authorisation for this spending? Should my husband speak directly to Sir Robert about the cost, or perhaps to your steward?'

'I discussed it with him yesterday evening.' Lady Idonea smoothed down her skirt, and a slight edge came into her voice. 'It's some time since I ordered new gowns, so your arrival was most fortuitous and he was happy to set aside a budget, particularly as it would mean not having to travel to Pontefract or York.'

'You would travel, normally, my lady?'

'Oh yes. Not, perhaps, for the household fabric, which can be sourced locally, but nobody here in town can produce anything to match the quality of these.' She picked up one of the more expensive fabrics – Edwin couldn't remember what it was called – and rubbed it between her thumb and forefinger. 'But you're not from north of here, you said? You've travelled from Lincoln?'

Her question set Edwin on edge a little, but it seemed a natural one with no particular undertone. And it was obviously a safe subject for Alys, who had grown up in the great city before leaving her family behind and moving to Conisbrough to become his wife.

He hoped she wasn't going to live to regret it.

Alys was agreeing, and sliding a few specific details into the conversation that would certainly allay any suspicions that she didn't know Lincoln.

Lady Idonea was nodding. 'I have never been there myself, but I hear that the cathedral is a wonderful sight – comparable even with York.'

The women's talk was general for a few moments, before Alys returned to the cloth. 'So, my lady, you have a sum set aside for your own gowns, and one for Margaret in the plainer twill.'

She bestowed a smile on the girl, who had been sitting silently all the while, and whose face now brightened at the treat in store for her. 'And for the burel for the household? Did you also agree this with Sir Robert?'

'Yes. To begin with he tried to say that new tunics wouldn't be needed this year, but back in my father's day the Tickhill household and garrison was known for being smartly turned out, and I've been determined not to let standards slip since the duties of castellan fell to me.'

Edwin listened with greater attention. This was new information, and although it might not be relevant in any way to his investigations, he was so hopelessly stuck that at this point he'd take anything. He was by now almost directly behind Lady Idonea and facing Alys, so he indicated that she should continue the subject.

'I didn't realise, my lady.'

'There's no reason why you should. But yes, the castellanship here is hereditary, and as I was my parents' only child it came to me as heiress. To be held by my husband, of course, so the marriage was arranged for me, but he's a good man.'

'And …' Alys hesitated. 'You have no children?'

Edwin saw the lady's shoulders tense. 'None. Though I am still of an age … I pray every day that the Lord might grant us our wish.'

Alys placed a protective hand over her stomach.

'Don't worry, my dear, I'm sure you'll be fine,' said Lady Idonea. 'There's plenty of time for your horse to recover and then it's what – four or five days' travel to Lincoln, if you take it steadily? You'll be home and with your family when the time comes for your confinement. Will your mother be with you? Sisters?'

Alys shook her head and made no reply, and Edwin winced. Alys had watched her mother die of childbed fever when she herself was just a girl, and that was not something she needed to be reminded of just now. Edwin, of course, was hoping that Alys would be home – in Conisbrough, less than a day's travel even in the slow cart – long before her time came. Home, where she could be looked after by his own mother and aunt, as well as the experienced village midwife.

Oh Lord, if he started thinking about Mother as well, and how he'd left her at this time of need, he really was going to cry.

Fortunately, it was at that moment that footsteps were heard on the stairs and Sir Robert entered. He was a breath of fresh air, bouncing over to his wife to kiss her and enthuse about the hunting he'd had – 'We've only brought back hares for the kitchen today, though we saw the first roe buck of the season and marked its position ready for next time' – while remembering to ask about her day so far. 'Lovely, these materials, but then you'd look lovely in anything, of course.' He nodded to Margaret and Edwin, and asked Alys how she was.

He, like everyone else in the castle, was just so *friendly*. That was the major problem Edwin had encountered since he'd been here, trying to work out what was going on and how the deception might have been practised. There seemed to be no hint at all in the man of low cunning, so how could Sir Robert possibly have done what the lord earl was accusing him of?

Chapter Two

Conisbrough Castle, a week earlier

Martin didn't know why everyone had to be so ostentatiously *happy* all the time, but it was irritating him beyond measure.

He watched Edwin and Alys laughing together and had to turn away to hide the raging jealousy that kept threatening to erupt. Not, of course, that he wanted Alys for himself; she was the perfect wife for Edwin, and Martin had been overjoyed when they'd wed. No, it was the fact of Edwin having the woman he wanted, the one he'd yearned for, the one he couldn't live without, when Martin didn't. And there was no respite up at the castle, either, for Sir Geoffrey – that renowned, elderly bachelor – had married none other than Edwin's widowed mother, whom he had apparently loved silently for years, and they too were sickeningly blissful. Martin, meanwhile, had been turned down, rejected. Nobody wanted *him*, and probably nobody ever would.

'Oh, hurry up, or we'll be late,' he growled, watching as Edwin kissed Alys and then put a gentle hand on the swell of her belly. 'You can bear to be parted for an hour, I'm sure, and my lord wants to see you.'

Alys looked a little hurt by this, and he was sorry that he'd said it – well, sort of. Oh, he didn't know how he felt, except that he wanted to get out of here and hit something until it all went away.

He strode through the village and up the path to the castle, deliberately setting a pace that Edwin, with his much shorter legs, couldn't match. Edwin was breathless by the time they reached the outer gate, and Martin knew he should slow down, but he didn't; instead he hurried him on through the ward and up to the inner gate. Unfortunately Martin then found that luck was against him once more – or rather, as he thought of it these days, Lady Fortune spat in his face – for there in front of him was Sir Geoffrey, also taking leave of a beloved wife before heading up to see the earl, with that exact same mawkish smile on his face. And, astonishingly, just to top everything off, *a wife whose belly was also swollen with pregnancy*.

It had been considered a miracle when the news broke. Lady Anne had kept it quiet from everyone except Sir Geoffrey, Edwin and Alys for as long as she could, fearing some mishap, but eventually her condition could be hidden no longer. Then Sir Geoffrey had been obliged to break it to the earl, who was bound to be displeased: after so many years of thinking that Sir Geoffrey's manor would eventually revert back to him – for the old knight had no other heirs – he would now have to face up to the idea that it would pass to a new generation upon Sir Geoffrey's death. Happily (and there was that blasted word again), the right moment had been found, the earl in a good mood for some other reason, and the news had been given without material damage to either people or furnishings.

The villagers seemed split over whether this pregnancy was something malign and to be feared, or a sign of God's favour. Edwin, of course, thought the latter, and he had patiently explained a number of times that it wasn't all that miraculous: although he was twenty-one, his mother was only in her late thirties, and many women were still giving birth at that age.

Except, as he'd confided to Martin, that these were normally the women who already had many children, who birthed easily time after time. He was worried that the number of years since his mother's last confinement – that is, his own arrival more than two decades previously – would be against her. Martin had nothing to say to that, knowing very little of the business, and anyway his own birth had managed to kill his mother so it wasn't a subject he wanted to broach.

And so, as he reminded himself sometimes in the dark, he had no mother and no wife while Edwin had both, and would likely soon have a son and a brother to boot. Martin didn't need much more proof that he was not in God's favour.

Edwin had stopped to talk to his mother, who was apparently even nearer to her confinement than Alys was, although they both looked equally huge to Martin. Sir Geoffrey was getting more and more anxious as the weeks went by, his barked instructions to squires and garrison getting shorter along with his temper. He was fussing around unnecessarily, and had even summoned a girl, Joan, from his own manor ready to act as wet nurse, on the rather illogical reasoning that his heir's first milk should come from his future home.

She, in turn, was creating nuisance; not through any fault of her own, Martin had to admit, but because the sight of a buxom young woman, even one known to be married and with her own baby already at her breast, was causing the castle men to fall over themselves gawping instead of getting on with their work. Martin had already had to administer more than one cuff to the back of the head when he noticed some of them getting familiar enough to make Joan uncomfortable.

Honestly. Women? They were nothing but trouble, and he was better off as he was. The sooner all this baby business was all over, the better, though Martin didn't want to think about how much his own loneliness was going to be rubbed in once Edwin's happy family was enlarged.

'Oh, come *on*,' he urged Edwin, who was still speaking to his mother. 'My lord had something particular he wanted to talk to you about, and he won't want to wait much longer.' Secretly, Martin hoped it was going to be another mission, one where he could accompany Edwin to look after him. Anything that took him away from here for a while would be fine, and if it were dangerous, then so much the better.

He finally got Edwin away and hustled him into the keep. Sir Geoffrey, whose knees increasingly found the stairs an enemy, followed more slowly. Some small part of Martin remembered his manners, and he waited outside the council chamber until the knight had entered, before giving Edwin an unnecessarily hard shove and then following him in. He kicked the door shut behind him, took up his accustomed place by the wall and prepared to be bored.

'You remember my youngest sister, Maud?'

That was an unexpected start, and Edwin couldn't keep either the surprise or the bitter tone out of his voice. 'Only too well, my lord.'

The earl looked at him in puzzlement for a few moments before his face cleared. 'Yes, of course, that. But never mind that now. Her present husband is her second; she was formerly married to the count of Eu, in Normandy.'

Thanks to Edwin's drilling from Sir Geoffrey in noble family lineages, Edwin knew that. 'They had one surviving daughter, my lord.'

'Yes, Alice, my niece. Well, this is about her.'

Edwin wondered how this could possibly concern him. Surely the earl wasn't about to send him to Normandy? Martin certainly hadn't given him any hint of such a thing, not that he'd given Edwin any information at all as he'd hurried him up here.

'She was widowed at the beginning of this year, so I'm taking charge of her interests in England.'

'Her interests in England, my lord?' This was not something that had been included in Edwin's lessons, and he was beginning to feel lost.

'Yes. The manor and castle of Tickhill were granted to her some years ago, along with a few other properties, but her husband neglected to pursue her rights and it was never handed over to her. This can't be allowed to continue, so I have taken steps.'

As ever, the earl seemed to expect Edwin to understand exactly what he was talking about from very minimal information. Edwin glanced over at Sir Geoffrey and at Brother William, the earl's clerk, who had already been in the room when Edwin had entered it so unceremoniously, but the knight looked as puzzled as Edwin felt and the monk merely shrugged. Adam and Hugh were also present, standing in Martin's shadow, but none of them would have a clue – and besides, Martin had been in such a foul mood recently that Edwin could hardly get two words out of him even on a subject that interested him. He was now staring resolutely at a patch of wall about a foot over the earl's head, and Edwin couldn't get his attention at all.

He'd have to do it himself. Clearing his throat, he said, 'I'm sorry, my lord, but I'm not quite clear on what you're asking me to do.'

'I'm coming to that,' snapped the earl. 'Hugh.'

Once Hugh had passed him a full goblet – more to have something to toy with rather than because he wanted to drink it, as Edwin noticed – the earl continued. 'Tickhill is in the hands of Sir Robert de Vieuxpont. I told him to give it up, but because he holds it from the crown he said he wasn't prepared to do so until he had specific permission from the lord regent.'

'Er … that sounds reasonable?' ventured Edwin, wondering if something would shortly be flying at his head.

'Yes, yes, to start with – not that he should argue with me, but he owes allegiance to the king, not me, so it was fair to want the authorisation. But,' – and here the goblet was banged down on the arm of the chair – 'this was in the second week in January. And now we're in Holy Week, with Easter this coming Sunday!'

'That seems like quite a long time, my lord.'

'Exactly. And there's more.' The earl flicked his fingers at Brother William, who passed him a piece of parchment. 'I have it in a letter today that the lord regent is ill, and you know what that might mean.'

Edwin had encountered William Marshal, the man who ruled the kingdom on behalf of the eleven-year-old king, a couple of times. Edwin didn't know how old he was, but elderly, certainly – in his seventies at least – so any illness would be dangerous. And if he were to die …

'You see my problem?'

'Yes, my lord. If the regent dies then a new one will be appointed, and you might have to start this whole process over again, with a man who might be less well disposed towards you. It would be much better for you if Tickhill were already under your authority before that happens.'

The earl nodded. 'Sharp as ever. That's why I want you to go there. Find out what Sir Robert knows, what he's hiding.'

Edwin considered that for a moment. Tickhill wasn't far, but to leave Alys at this time would be dreadful. Could he possibly get out of this?

'Thoughts?' The earl's glance encompassed not only Edwin, Sir Geoffrey and Brother William, but also Martin – who, as he neared the time when he would become a knight, was being obliged against his will and inclination to offer opinions on such matters.

'Can I go with him, my lord?' Martin's voice was eager.

'Hardly,' came the earl's dismissive reply, 'given that you're the most recognisable man in the county. Anyone would know that I'd sent you.'

Martin managed to look both crestfallen and angry, but he'd given Edwin an idea. 'As you say, my lord, to arrive openly as your liege man, as I am, would be of little use,' was his first, cautious attempt to track away from the plan. 'Perhaps someone else, maybe from one of your other estates …' he cast a significant 'help me' glance at Sir Geoffrey, who surely must understand his worries.

Brother William, who was oblivious to the concerns of a man with a wife and a child on the way, was giving the matter his full attention. 'But Tickhill doesn't come under the jurisdiction of the Conisbrough bailiff, so there would have been no reason for you to go there with your late father? And you haven't been there more recently, since his death?'

Edwin was reluctantly forced to concede that he hadn't visited Tickhill since he was a boy.

'Well then.' Brother William sounded convinced, and only belatedly realised why Edwin was looking at him with such an agonised expression. He grimaced an apology and continued in a more offhand tone. 'But, of course, as you say, maybe someone else might do just as well.'

The earl was shaking his head. 'No, no, it has to be Weaver. He'll be able to find out what's going on much more quickly than anyone else.' He paused. 'You're right that declaring yourself my man wouldn't help, though. Some kind of pretence …' he tapped his fingers on the goblet that he still hadn't drunk from. 'A travelling merchant?

You certainly look more like a trader than a soldier, and that would give you an excuse to be a stranger who appears at the gate.'

Edwin was starting to feel very agitated indeed. Could he – did he dare state his real reason out loud?

The earl was now taking a first sip of his wine, which was a sure sign he considered the matter closed. 'But, my lord, my wife …' Edwin began.

'Your wife? What about her?'

'She's very near her confinement, my lord.'

'So?'

'I would really prefer not to leave her, my lord …'

'Oh, take her with you, then, if you can't *bear* to be parted.'

It was Martin who had burst out with these words, and Edwin gaped in shock. Had he just —

'She knows everything there is to know about cloth, doesn't she?' continued Martin, his tone bitter. 'The perfect disguise, if you want to be a merchant, and then you don't have to leave her at all.'

'Excellent!' That was the earl.

Edwin stood frozen in horror, unable to believe what he'd just heard. Surely Martin hadn't just thrown a heavily pregnant woman into the path of danger? A woman he knew and liked, the wife of his best friend?

Sir Geoffrey was looking daggers at Martin, and slowly the squire's expression changed: from petulance to realisation, from realisation to dismay, from dismay to outright horror. 'No! No – my lord, I'm sorry, I don't know what I was saying, I didn't mean —'

The earl cut him off with a wave. 'It's the ideal solution.' He turned to Edwin. 'We'll get you a horse and cart, as much cloth as we can find, and the two of you can set off in a couple of days. If you arrive the day before Easter Sunday then it would be natural to stay for the feast – or maybe we can arrange to lame the horse, though that would be a shame.'

That was what tipped Edwin over the edge. That the earl should be showing more compassion for a *horse* than for Alys filled him with rage.

The word 'No!' was out of his mouth before he could stop it, but he wouldn't have stopped it anyway.

'What did you just say?'

The earl's tone was dangerously level, but Edwin didn't care. 'I can't take my wife into danger like that! What if something happens to her? What if her labour begins while we're away?'

Sir Geoffrey, with real concern, joined in the pleading. 'My lord, please consider! Of your goodness … to place a pregnant woman in such a situation.'

The goblet hit the wall, the wine it still contained dripping down the stones like blood. 'Enough!' The earl pointed an accusatory finger at Sir Geoffrey. 'I knew it was a mistake to let you marry that woman. You've gone softer and softer ever since. Now, get out of my sight and make the arrangements.'

Sir Geoffrey could do nothing but bow in silence, though the look on his face indicated that anyone other than the earl, speaking to him thus, wouldn't live very long.

The earl turned to Edwin. 'And as for you – you remember who you are. Go, prepare, get yourself to Tickhill and send me back news once you've found what Sir Robert is hiding. The sooner you sort this out, the sooner you and your wife can come back. And I don't want to see your face again until you've succeeded, is that clear? I want that castle and I mean to have it.'

Edwin, too, seethed; but Edwin, too, knew that he had to submit. He followed Sir Geoffrey out of the room, refusing to look at anyone else as he left.

He just about managed to control himself until they got outside, and then his anger burst out again, an incoherent sound of impotent rage escaping him.

'I can't, Sir Geoffrey, I can't,' he gasped, when he was able to make himself at least semi-coherent. 'I'll have to leave, we'll have to go somewhere else, I can't …'

The knight, accustomed to having to make life-or-death decisions at speed, had recovered himself to a greater extent. 'Stop that. Leaving the earl's service and fleeing to another part of the realm while Alys is so near her confinement won't do her any good, either.' He took a couple of paces away and then back. 'We have to think.'

'I can't,' said Edwin, and realised that he really meant it. He was so afraid for Alys that he couldn't force his mind to work. He couldn't see a way out.

'Well,' said Sir Geoffrey, grimly. 'The earl might believe I've gone soft for considering the opinions of women, but I think the best thing now is for us to sit down with our wives and ask them what they think.'

Edwin began to nod and then stopped. 'How am I going to tell her? How am I going to explain that I couldn't protect her?' Then, bitterly, 'And how will I tell her whose idea this was?'

'I'll deal with that boy later.' Sir Geoffrey's voice was cold in its fury. 'But for now, let us fetch your lady mother and see if she's well enough to walk down to the village. This conversation would be better held outside of the castle.'

As it happened, Mother wasn't in the castle quarters she shared with Sir Geoffrey – modest household rooms rather than the great chamber, for the earl's reluctant permission for their wedding had not extended to any other privileges – and the porter at the inner gatehouse said that she'd already gone out. As it was unlikely that she'd be in any of the workshops or household buildings in the outer ward, they headed straight for the castle's main gate.

The thickset figure of the guard on duty there was unmistakeably Willikin, whom Edwin knew well, and he was able to inform them that 'Lady Anne went out earlier, saying she was going to see her sister, Sir Geoffrey. I asked her, was she going to be all right on the path, it being steep, but she said she'd be fine. Anyway, the bailiff came past just then so he took her arm, so she'd be sure to get there safe.' He paused. 'I'm not sure now whether I shouldn't have gone with her.' His honest face looked pained, and Sir Geoffrey took a moment to assure him he'd done the right thing in not leaving his post.

They found the two women together in Cecily's cottage. This was a busy place these days: the widowed Cecily had remarried, being now the wife of Crispin the smith, and they fostered four orphaned children.

Mother was watching the noise and the chaos with pleasure, but her expression changed as soon as she saw them come in. 'What is it?' She began to struggle to her feet. 'Is it Alys?'

'No, it's – I mean yes, it does concern her – can you come home for a few moments?'

Cecily, catching his tone, made her way over. 'Do you need me? Or do I need to fetch Agnes?'

Agnes was both Crispin's mother and the village midwife. 'Not yet, thank the Lord,' said Edwin. 'I'll explain later.' He and Sir Geoffrey accompanied Mother out.

Home was normally Edwin's place of refuge. The cottage, with its familiar hearth and furniture, Alys's loom, the bedchamber they shared, and above all the air of calm, of welcome and of love, was so far removed from the cold stone and even colder attitudes of the castle that he couldn't wait to come back each evening to sink into its warm embrace. And now here he was, about to bring doom and despair inside his sanctuary.

The news, when it was explained by Edwin and Sir Geoffrey constantly interrupting each other, came as something of a shock, and for a few moments both Alys and Mother sat in silence. They reached out to hold each other's hands.

It was Alys herself – dear, beautiful Alys, whom Edwin couldn't love more if he tried – who spoke first, putting a brave face on the situation. 'At least this time I won't have to sit and worry about you while you're away. We won't be apart.'

Edwin felt tears coming to his eyes. 'You … you think we should go ahead with it?'

'I don't think we have a choice,' she replied. 'So let's try to stay calm. The lord earl only wants you to find some information, doesn't he?'

Edwin nodded.

'So, it's not like some of the other things he's asked you to do. Nobody has been murdered. There is no killer on the loose. The worst that might be said about this …' she waved.

'Sir Robert,' Edwin filled in.

'Yes, that was it. I don't know where my mind's got to these days. The worst that might be said against this Sir Robert is that he's concealed some information.'

'Yes, but we don't know – there might be so much more to it than that. I just don't like putting you in a situation we know so little about.'

'I don't like it either,' said Mother, firmly. 'This is Alys's first child, and she needs to be here where we can all take care of her. Me, Cecily, all her friends.'

Edwin couldn't speak through the tears that were now pouring openly down his cheeks.

Sir Geoffrey cleared his throat, and everyone looked to him. 'The only way I can think and talk about this is if I compare it to a military campaign, because that's what I know about. So you'll all excuse me if I use the wrong words.'

Edwin wiped his face on his sleeve and tried to concentrate.

'As I see it, we're trapped between two hostile forces.' Sir Geoffrey took on a brisker tone. 'On the one hand, you and Alys are facing an unknown danger if you travel to Tickhill. But on the other, the lord earl has been very clear that he expects his orders to be obeyed. If you don't go, the only alternative is to be cast out of his service – to lose your position and your home as well. Where would you go? What would you do? This would also be putting you in danger, but with the added disadvantage of being in my lord's disfavour.' He swept them all in a glance, his air of effortless authority resuming. 'There's never an ideal time and place for battle, but you must always choose the lesser of two evils. So what we have to do now is decide which one of those options is which.'

Edwin could see the sense in this, even though he didn't want to. 'But there must be another way, something else …'

'I don't think there is. Now, we can all have our say, but a decision must be made one way or the other.'

'If Edwin and Alys have to leave Conisbrough, and go into exile, then I'm going too,' said Mother, firmly. She looked at Sir Geoffrey with eyes that were glistening as much as Edwin's. 'I'm sorry, my love, but they're my children.'

He took her hand. 'I know. And if you go, I go too.'

Edwin gasped. 'But you've been in the lord earl's service for …'

'More years than I care to remember,' finished Sir Geoffrey. 'And that was my life, then. But now I have family and responsibilities, and a man must do what is *right*.' He paused and closed his eyes before venturing the most critical comment Edwin had ever heard him make about the earl. 'And knowingly putting a pregnant woman in danger, when it could be avoided, is not right.'

Edwin's anger began to resurface. 'That part of it wasn't his idea, though, was it?' He still couldn't understand why Martin should have said something so terrible, so cruel. It was a betrayal of all their years of friendship, and Edwin felt his blood rise and start to thump in his head. That Martin – *Martin* – should have put Alys and the baby in such danger —

It was at that exact moment that a knock, an instantly recognisable pounding, sounded at the cottage door.

There was a moment of silence while they all looked at each other. 'Do you want me to …' began Sir Geoffrey.

But Edwin shook his head. With fury surging through him he strode to the door, flung it open and propelled Martin backwards out on to the path before he could even open his mouth.

Normally, attempting to shove Martin physically would be a pointless exercise, but he was caught by surprise and almost overbalanced. 'Edwin,' he began. 'I had to come and see you.'

'Oh, did you? Why? To crow about how you've finally got your own back on me for being happily married?'

'What? No! I came to say I'm sorry. I didn't mean —'

'Didn't mean to what? Didn't mean to put my wife and our child in danger of their lives? How *could* you! How *dare* you come here after what you've done?'

They were attracting an audience of interested villagers, returning from the fields now that the sun was setting.

Martin tried a placatory tone. 'Can we go inside? If you would just let me explain ...'

Edwin snorted. 'Explain? As if I got the chance to do any such thing earlier. And no, you can't come in. I may have to follow the orders of my *betters*' – he almost spat out the word – 'but my home is my own and I'll say who sets foot inside it.'

'But —' Martin put out a hand.

Edwin did something that would have been foolish in the extreme under normal circumstances: he struck Martin, knocking his arm back. 'No! No, you don't get to come here and try to deflect the blame from yourself, not when we'll have to go through with this idiotic, reckless plan. You did this – *you*. The lord earl would never have thought of sending Alys if you hadn't opened your stupid mouth, and nothing will ever change that.'

Martin made as if to speak, but Edwin cut him off, jabbing his finger into Martin's chest. 'If anything happens to Alys or the baby, I will kill you, do you hear me?' He heard a sharp intake of breath from the onlookers, but he didn't care. If he lost Alys, his life wouldn't be worth living anyway. 'I will find you and I will challenge you and I will kill you, right here in public. And in the meantime, leave us alone. In fact, *don't ever speak to me again.*'

Martin drew himself up to his full height, his fists balling, and Edwin braced himself for the blow that would knock him senseless. He didn't care. He wouldn't back down.

But Martin only stood for a moment before turning on his heel and striding off, the villagers scattering hastily out of his way.

Two days later it was Good Friday. It was a sombre time of year at the best of times, and Edwin felt his heart weighing heavily as he stood in the church along with the other villagers. He reached out to take Alys's hand, but clutched at empty air – somehow in his distraction he'd managed to forget that she was seated over on the bench by the wall, placed there by a kind priest for the benefit of those parishioners who were elderly, infirm or heavily pregnant. At least *someone* cared for such people.

Thankfully, he thought to himself as the service ended, he hadn't been obliged to see or face either Martin or the earl, for the castle-dwellers would have their own service up in the chapel there, and didn't need to attend the village church. He didn't want to encounter any of them.

Hugh was waiting outside when Edwin emerged, darting forward to catch his attention. 'If you please, Sir Geoffrey says can you come up to the stable.'

Edwin was arm in arm with Alys, who – despite all her protestations that she'd rather come with him to Tickhill, that it was better than him leaving her on her own to worry – was starting to feel the strain as the day of their departure drew near. She slipped her hand out from under his elbow. 'I won't come up with you; you can tell me what's been arranged when you get home.'

He kissed her cheek. 'Yes, there's no point you having to face that hill.' He looked around, grateful to see that both Cecily and Alys's friend Rosa, a girl of about her own age who was already married with a baby, were nearby. Rosa lived on a farmstead a few miles outside Conisbrough, but everyone came into the village to attend church on Sundays and holy days – indeed, those who lived in the outlying districts were glad to do so, for it might be the only time in the week they spoke to anyone outside of their own families. Rosa's husband was dawdling outside the church chatting to Crispin and his assistant, Ned, who was Rosa's older brother, and they seemed in no hurry to get on. Rosa cast the men a glance and rolled her eyes; she came over to Alys with a smile, her own sleeping infant tightly bound to her. Edwin was pleased that Alys would have cheerful company for a while, and he watched them set off home. How good it was to have family and friends who could be trusted.

Edwin followed Hugh up to the castle, his stomach rumbling. The timing of having a fast day just before they had to leave was not ideal, but he would make sure Alys had a good meal in the morning before they set off.

Sir Geoffrey was waiting for him at the stable, along with a groom, a horse and a cart. 'We'll load it up with all the cloth we've managed to find later,' he began, wasting no time on pleasantries. 'But you need to practise harnessing and unharnessing the horse, so you're familiar with it. It needs to look like something you do every day.'

For two days Edwin, Alys and Sir Geoffrey had been planning every detail that might possibly make the mission safer. The key thing, they had all agreed, was to make absolutely sure that nobody would suspect that Edwin had been sent to Tickhill by the earl, which meant that the 'merchant' ruse had to be as convincing as possible. Alys had been drilling him on the names, prices and types of cloth they were to bring. Fortunately the Conisbrough steward had just bought a large consignment of something or other – *burel*, must remember to use the proper name – in order to make household tunics, so when that was added to a few bits of finer stuff that were in storage in the castle plus Alys's own excellent homespun, there was enough to make a creditable showing. Any lack of quantity or range could be explained away by them having been on the road for some time and having already sold most of their merchandise.

Edwin was going to be 'Thomas of Lincoln', which was the name of Alys's eldest brother, who was indeed a cloth merchant in that city. Edwin had visited the shop and Alys had grown up there, so she would be able to describe it and its location very precisely if needed. Edwin thought it was extremely unlikely that they were going to run into anyone who had been to Lincoln at all, never mind being familiar with one specific street of traders within it, but it was best to be on the safe side. Alys wouldn't need to disguise her name for, as she pointed out, who was going to know or be interested in the name of a merchant's wife? Women were just background to most men, like hangings on the wall.

Finally, Sir Geoffrey and the groom were happy with Edwin's handling of the harness.

'Now,' the knight went on, 'as to the horse. I've picked this one out specifically to help with your excuse for staying.'

Edwin nodded. The earl's initial idea that 'Thomas' and Alys would be invited to stay for Easter Sunday had been a good one, but the natural course of events would see them leaving again the day afterwards, and even Edwin didn't think he was going to be able to find out everything he needed in one day, especially when it was the most important feast of the Church year.

'He's slightly lame already,' Sir Geoffrey was saying. 'Aren't you, Kit?' He stroked the horse's nose. 'And by the time he's gone eight miles on these roads he'll be too sore to go on. So you pull up at the castle, say you're there to show your wares, and ask if the stablemaster can look him over while you're resting up for a day. If he's worth his job then he'll want the horse to rest.'

'And what if he doesn't? I mean, what if the horse isn't lame enough?'

Sir Geoffrey stroked his beard. 'You'll have to play it right. If you get near to Tickhill and he's still not too bad, get off the wagon and sit on his back – the extra weight will do the job.' He patted the horse apologetically. 'On the other hand, if the roads are too bad and he starts pulling up before you get there, get out of the wagon to reduce the weight, and lead him. That should see you safely there, and all the better if you arrive like that.' He paused. 'Not Alys, I mean – she shouldn't get out and walk at all, never mind what state Kit is in.'

Edwin was glad to find that there was one man in the castle, at least, who thought more of the comfort of a pregnant woman than of a horse. 'And at least we'll be loaded with fabric. I can arrange it in the back there so she can sit in comfort, or even lie down all the way, if she wants.'

Sir Geoffrey only nodded without speaking, and Edwin realised how overcome the knight was about the situation, though he wouldn't say so, not out here in the open where anyone in the outer ward might hear him.

Saturday's dawn arrived sooner than Edwin wanted.

They didn't light the fire when they got up, but Edwin made sure that Alys ate plenty of bread to line her empty stomach before they set off. He had some himself and, realising that it would be stale by the time they got back, wrapped the rest to bring it with them. He had to remind himself firmly not to use the word *if* about their safe return, even in his head.

The sound of horse and cart outside made them look at each other. Wordlessly they moved forward into an embrace, Edwin holding Alys as tightly as he dared. 'I'll bring you back safely,' he murmured into her ear. 'I promise I will.'

'I know,' came her voice. 'I wouldn't have married you if I didn't trust you with my life, and I love you.' She paused and Edwin hoped that neither of them was about to burst into tears. 'Just think,' she said, eventually, 'in as little as a week we might be back here as though none of this had happened. Back home, ready to start our new lives as parents.'

Edwin clasped her to him a moment longer and dropped a kiss on to the top of her head. He inhaled the fragrance of flowers that always surrounded her; the scent of comfort. 'That is the thought that will sustain me.' Then, reluctantly, he stood back, taking both of her hands in his. 'Now. Are you ready?'

He felt his fingers being squeezed. The familiar smells of the cottage were all around him as he gave it a farewell glance. He shook his head. Why was he acting as though he was never going to come back? He'd been on more dangerous missions than this one, and travelled much further away – why did have this overwhelming feeling of foreboding this time?

A small group was gathered outside. Most of the villagers only nodded or waved as they made their way out to the fields, but Mother had come down with Sir Geoffrey, as had Willikin, who was holding the horse's head. Cecily and Crispin were there too, the children standing about them in an unnaturally subdued manner.

Two figures hovered a little further off. One was Hal, the younger brother of Alys's friend Rosa, who had once worked for Edwin before being called back to help his own father in the fields. He looked a little uncertain at joining the family circle, especially in Sir Geoffrey's presence, but Edwin waved him over.

Hal went straight to Alys. 'Rosa says she couldn't come all the way in this morning, but I was to give you her … her *love*, she says, and she'll be waiting to help you with anything you need once you get back.' Sheepishly, he produced a hedgerow flower. 'She's thinking of you, she says.' He then added, somewhat hastily, 'This is from her.' Edwin watched as Alys took the flower, Hal now blushing scarlet. He had noticed that his wife had this effect on many of the youths about the place, but he didn't mind – it was all innocent and she *was* very beautiful, after all. Who could blame young lads for being tongue-tied in her presence?

The second figure standing further off was Martin. Edwin deliberately turned his back and addressed Sir Geoffrey. 'Everything's ready?'

'Yes.' Sir Geoffrey seemed on the verge of expressing an emotion, but he suppressed it. 'Now, remember what I said about the horse.'

'I will.' Edwin hesitated. 'I hope that I'll see you again within the week.' He looked over at Mother, who was embracing Alys. 'And certainly before …'

Sir Geoffrey gripped his shoulder. 'I hope so too. Now, get on with you, so you're on your way before the sun's much higher.'

While they'd been speaking, the children had scrambled up into the back of the wagon, and they now displayed the nest they had managed to form out of bales and bolts of fabric. Willikin came round, lifted Alys as though she were a baby and placed her gently inside. 'You stay comfortable in there, mistress.'

And then it was time for Edwin to climb up to the driver's seat, take the reins and set off.

The road to Tickhill was well travelled, so it was easily wide enough for the wagon, but Edwin wasn't used to driving one, the horse was already lame and the way was rutted with drying mud. Still, trying to keep themselves upright and moving was at least something that required concentration, so Edwin didn't have too much time for fretting as they inched their way through the countryside, other than calling back to Alys in alarm every time there was a particularly bad jolt.

It was nearly noon by the time the town came into sight; their journey had been slower than one made on foot on a good day.

Edwin pulled up the limping horse. 'We're nearly there.'

Alys's head poked out of the wagon's cover behind him. 'What do we do now? Do you need me to get out?'

'No, you stay there. I *think* the horse has done this exactly right, but if he struggles any more then I'll get out and lead him, like Sir Geoffrey said. Especially if it's crowded in town.' He wasn't confident in his ability to look like an experienced driver if the horse was going to shy at noise and traffic, and Tickhill was a much larger place than Conisbrough.

'Well then, Thomas,' said Alys. 'I'm ready to face it if you are.'

Edwin wasn't prepared to do this, not at all, but there was no choice, was there? 'Yes, I'm ready too,' he lied. 'Let's do this together.' He shook the reins and they started again on their road into the unknown.

Chapter Three

Martin sat bolt upright.

His breathing was laboured, he was sweating and there was blood everywhere. Blood oozing from the corpses round his feet, blood dripping from the severed head he was holding high in the air. There was blood on his hands.

He shook his head to clear it. There was no blood; his hands were pale in the darkness. But he really was sweating and breathing heavily, sitting up on his sleeping palliasse with his blankets kicked and strewn about the floor.

The chamber was silent. Little Hugh was slumbering over near the fire, and the sounds from the curtained bed indicated that the earl was still asleep, thank the Lord. Martin tried to breathe more easily and calm his heart, but then gave a huge start when he saw Adam's open eyes glinting at him from across the room.

Adam put one finger to his lips and then stood and padded over to Martin, his bare feet making no sound on the wooden floor. He picked up one of Martin's scattered blankets and draped it over his shoulders. 'A bad dream. A dream, only.'

Martin clutched the scratchy wool close and shivered as Adam fetched another and whispered again. 'Though you do seem to be having them a lot recently.' Martin made no reply. Adam understood, returning to his own palliasse and wrapping himself up. 'Still a good while until dawn, I'd say.' He turned over so he was facing away, leaving Martin to his own thoughts.

But Martin didn't want to be left alone with his thoughts – not now, not ever. He sat for a short while, hoping they would go away, then tried lying down again, but sleep would not come. Tossing and turning didn't help, so eventually he got up, feeling about him for his hose, tunic, boots and belt, and crept out of the room.

There was no guard on the keep's door overnight; there was no need, not with the outer and inner gates both firmly locked and a patrol on the walls. It was still not yet dawn, so the only signs of life were the night porter's brazier over by the gatehouse, and the first sounds of movement and light coming from the kitchen.

What Martin needed was some physical activity, so he headed for the woodpile that lay between the stone kitchen building and the curtain wall. There was always work to be done there, and as Sir Geoffrey considered wood-chopping to be a good strengthening exercise for squires, Martin had spent many hours of his youth in this exact spot with an axe in his hand, blisters on his palm and aching shoulders. He was excused such duties now, though he knew Adam had to endure it, and Hugh tried his hardest.

The kitchen hand just emerging from the dark corner, his arms full of wood, got the fright of his life as Martin suddenly loomed in front of him, so Martin had to help him pick all the dropped logs up again before he could send him off and try to see what was what in the murky half-light.

The axe felt comfortable in his hands, a familiar weight. A reminder of what life was like before everything got so *complicated*. The rhythm soon came back to him.

The next thing he knew, it was full light and Sir Geoffrey was calling him for training. Martin realised with a lurch that he hadn't been present when the earl awoke – what if he'd been needed? But the others had managed without him, and Martin promised himself he'd do something nice for them next time he got the chance.

Training kept him occupied for the first part of the morning, despite its unfulfilling nature these days. Then it was into the hall to make sure all the arrangements for the earl's late-morning dinner were in train, and Martin fussed about everything much more than he usually would, in order to keep the nagging thought out of his head that had taken up residence and would not leave. Edwin had left

Conisbrough on Saturday morning. It was now Wednesday and they had heard nothing from him – what was happening?

The meal itself was not a happy occasion. The earl sat at the top table with only Sir Geoffrey on his right and Father Ignatius on his left, and the priest had only been invited so that the other two wouldn't have to sit on their own. Lady Anne was strictly forbidden from eating at table with the lord earl, so she apparently only made an appearance in the hall when he was absent – something Martin never saw, of course, for when the earl went anywhere Martin went with him.

Given that serving such a group was very easy and didn't need all three of them, Martin whispered to Adam during the meal that he should slip out and see that Lady Anne had everything she needed, wherever she was, and to take some of the delicacies off the sideboard in case she didn't have them. Nice food like that would be good for a woman in her condition, wouldn't it? And some of the fine wine. Martin might not be able to do anything about Edwin or – oh God, he'd thought of it again, hadn't he – Alys, which was all his fault, but Edwin's mother should be taken care of while they were away.

Adam had barely reached the sideboard and picked up a dish when a messenger burst through the main door, causing several onlookers to pause with spoons halfway to their mouths. He made as if to hurry right up to the top table but was intercepted on his way by Brother William, who was sitting with the men in the lower part of the hall. The monk spoke to the newcomer and took the proffered letter; after a glance at the lord earl for permission, he broke the seal straight away and scanned the contents.

Martin expected that Brother William would then take his seat again, but instead he made his way up and around the back of the top table in order to murmur something in the earl's ear. The earl's expression changed and he stood up abruptly.

All movement in the hall ceased.

The earl addressed the company. 'All is well. Continue with your meal.' Then he turned, and with a glance that encompassed knight, page and squires, said, 'Council chamber. Now.'

Edwin stared at the ceiling.

He'd been awake for some time now, but he didn't want to move in case he disturbed Alys, who had finally dropped off. Her condition meant that every sleeping position was uncomfortable to her, and she also needed to get up to pass water numerous times every night; she wasn't getting much rest. Apparently this was normal for women so near their confinement and nothing to worry about, but he wished she could have a night's deep, peaceful sleep so that she would be stronger for the travails to come. Labour could take days, and it wasn't unheard of for women in the village to simply die of exhaustion even if they managed to avoid any of the other serious complications.

And they were still here. They had arrived at the castle on Saturday afternoon and been welcomed, but Sunday, Monday and Tuesday had all passed without Edwin discovering a single useful piece of information, and he was starting to wonder whether there was anything to find out at all, or whether he'd been sent here on a fool's errand. But why would the lord earl wish to waste everyone's time like this for no reason? Why would he send Edwin here if there was nothing to find?

Alys sighed and shifted uneasily in her sleep. They were, fortunately, not on the floor in the hall along with the garrison and servants, but in a tiny guest chamber in the same building. So Alys at least had a bed to lie down on, and Edwin wasn't so afraid of her being accidentally stumbled upon or kicked in the middle of the night.

She hadn't woken, so Edwin remained where he was and tried to think. It was impossible that an urgent request from the earl, made to the regent in January, had not yet been seen and dealt with. So why had there been no reply? There was always the possibility that a message had gone astray, he supposed, but the royal couriers were surely reliable – and, besides, if the regent had, in turn, received no reply, he would have sent another. In which case …

Wait, wait. He was getting ahead of himself. He needed to take a step back and consider matters in greater detail and from an earlier point. There were, logically, three possible options: that Sir Robert had been told that he should retain control of the castle; that he had been told to give it up; or that he had not yet received any instruction at all. Each needed to be examined separately.

The first seemed the most implausible. Knowing that the earl was impatient to wrest control of Tickhill from him, Sir Robert would surely have communicated any royal order to keep it as soon as he had received the information. He would then be protected, for the earl would have to go against the regent's will himself if he wanted to argue the point, and Sir Robert would have the full authority of the crown behind him. And in any case, if such an order had been given then a communication would surely have been sent to the lord earl as well, to explain why his claim had been denied. He had made no mention of any such thing to Edwin, and it would have been pointless to send Edwin to Tickhill if that were the case.

The third possibility, to take them out of order for a moment, could have two causes: no letter had been sent, or a letter had been sent that had not arrived. For it would certainly be written down, an order of that gravity; written and with a royal seal appended, rather than just being given as a verbal message. It would be relatively easy to hide one letter. Or, of course, to destroy it: Edwin might be here looking for something that didn't even exist. But it wasn't just about one letter, was it? The matter wouldn't rest there – there would be serious repercussions later on for Sir Robert if he ignored an order that came directly from the regent. Such disobedience could not be overlooked, and an army might even be sent to take the castle from him by force.

Edwin shivered at the thought of that. He'd seen far too much violence in the last couple of years to want to be near any armed conflict ever again, especially with Alys here. She was fidgeting in her sleep now, and he shifted to stroke her brow and smooth her hair. He could hear the first sounds of waking from the hall, and long habit told him he ought to be getting up, but he had no household duties to attend to here, did he, so he decided to wait a little longer. Besides, he didn't like to go out and leave Alys on her own while she was sleeping in a room just off a hall full of men they didn't know.

He settled back with one arm behind his head. The second possibility seemed to be the most likely of the three, but if Sir Robert was concealing something then he was doing it very well. There was no hint in his manner – or, at least, not that Edwin or Alys had seen – that he was in any way apprehensive about having taken the first steps towards rebellion against his king. And surely nobody contemplating such a thing could be quite so insouciant about it?

The whole situation, of course, was complicated by the regent's illness. Even if he didn't die now, the confusion caused by his indisposition – when coupled with his great age – was enough to send all the self-interested nobles in the kingdom into a feeding frenzy. And he couldn't last all that much longer in any case, so the current state of affairs would either be prolonged or repeated whenever he next fell into a dangerous illness. Which naturally led to the question, would any orders given by him now still be valid if he died? Edwin wasn't quite sure how that worked. But trouble seemed to be brewing in the realm on a much greater scale than most people realised, and he didn't want Tickhill, or Conisbrough, or any place associated with his friends and family, to be the eye of the storm.

Which meant, of course, that he had to get on with finding out what had actually happened. He had discovered very little so far, but it was time to get up and begin afresh.

Once Alys was ready, they had an excuse to go up to the keep again, for she had deliberately left her discussions with Lady Idonea about new gowns unfinished. Edwin hoped that Sir Robert might be there too, and indeed he was; his voice could be heard as they neared the top of the stairs. He was talking to —

Edwin stopped dead on the threshold of the chamber and so, for a moment, did his heart.

Sir Robert was standing just inside the room in conference with a white-robed Cistercian monk. Edwin didn't recognise him but he was surely from Roche Abbey, only four miles from here and a place where Edwin had stayed for some while only a year and a half ago. But if he didn't know the monk, then he might be safe, because the monk wouldn't —

The man turned, saw Edwin, greeted him with a wide smile of recognition and opened his mouth to speak.

It was all over, surely. In desperation, Edwin tried to think how he might —

But, just this once, the saints smiled on him. Sir Robert, who was standing further away and who could therefore not see the monk's expression as he faced Edwin, broke in before the latter could say anything. 'Ah, let me introduce you to our guest, Master Thomas of Lincoln, a merchant. And his wife – do come in and sit down with my wife, mistress, no need to stand there on ceremony – they arrived just before Easter and Thomas will be able to share other news he's picked up on his travels, though it won't be as recent as yours.'

The monk was staring at Edwin with a puzzled expression, but either the introduction or the look of panic Edwin couldn't keep off his face gave him pause. He sketched the sign of the cross in the air, smiling as Alys made her way past him. 'And soon to be the recipients of God's blessing, it seems,' he said.

Edwin still couldn't place him, but there was something about the voice …

'Thomas,' continued Sir Robert. 'This is Brother Richard – I beg your pardon, *Prior* Richard now – of Roche Abbey. It's quite near here: you'll probably pass it on your way home once your horse is sufficiently recovered to enable you to leave.'

That was it! Brother Richard. The last time Edwin had seen him, his face had been hugely swollen by a tooth abscess, which is why Edwin didn't recognise him now that he looked normal. He, meanwhile, was aware that he looked almost exactly the same as he had done when he'd prayed over the monk's bed; the cares of the last eighteen months had been great, but they hadn't managed to age him out of all recognition. Still, the monk seemed content to say nothing for now so Edwin prayed he'd go along with the deception at least long enough for him to explain in private.

'Let us sit,' said Sir Robert, still seemingly oblivious to the undercurrents in the room. 'We'll leave the ladies near the fire so they can be comfortable and move over here.' He waved them to the table in the opposite corner, politely indicating that Prior Richard should take the chair at the head, an offer that was declined with equal civility as the monk took a lower stool.

When they were all seated Edwin glanced over towards the fire. Alys and Lady Idonea appeared to be deep in discussion, with Margaret listening in silence. He couldn't hear what they were actually saying, but perhaps it was better for now if he and Alys each concentrated on one conversation and conferred later.

'The abbey, like all such places, is a hub for travellers and news,' Sir Robert explained to Edwin, 'and Abbot Reginald is kind enough to keep me informed when any important tidings come his way.'

Edwin already knew that, just as he knew that the abbot was also in frequent communication with the earl via Brother William, who had been cloistered at Roche before being attached to his lord's household. But of course he wasn't about to say any of that, so he merely nodded.

'And it now appears —' Sir Robert broke off. 'But, Prior Richard, it would be better for you to speak for yourself. Tell him what you've already told me.'

Unfortunately whatever news the monk was about to impart remained unspoken, for it was at that moment that hurried footsteps were heard on the stairs and a figure appeared in the doorway.

It was Theo, the young guard. 'Begging your pardon, Sir Robert, but I've been sent to tell you that some men from the town have brought in a riderless horse that turned up this morning.'

Edwin was immediately alert. A riderless horse meant that somewhere there was a horseless rider – an accident, at the very least, and possibly worse.

'I'll come down.' Sir Robert rose and followed Theo out. Edwin was desperate to go with him, to see this horse and try to glean what information he could. He had no official standing to request such a thing, of course, but surely it would be no more than normal curiosity for someone in his position to wander down and see what was going on? Maybe …

'Edwin.'

'Yes?' he replied to Prior Richard, his mind still on the horse.

And, as easily as that, he'd given himself away.

'The regent is dying.'

From the earl's tone that sounded serious, but Martin couldn't think how it affected their present situation, or why it was important enough to have dragged them all away from the hall before he'd had the chance to eat anything. Being hungry never helped his temper.

'Is there any doubt, my lord?' Sir Geoffrey was asking.

'Not according to Arundel, who is on the spot,' replied the earl, waving the letter.

Martin felt Hugh fidget beside him. The earl of Arundel, their own lord's close ally, was Hugh's father, although as Hugh was his second son he wasn't in line to inherit anything – he'd have to take his chances with service and patronage, the same as the rest of them. Noble life was all about fighting for what you could get, unless you were one of the lucky few whose birth gave them everything. And even they were in constant competition with each other, as the lord earl's never-ending ambitions demonstrated.

Sir Geoffrey was continuing, and Martin tried to pay attention in case he was going to be asked for an opinion on anything.

'So, there will be a struggle to succeed him – someone will certainly need to rule in the king's name for a few years yet, until he's of age – and there will also be a scramble for the favour of the man who is chosen.'

'How will they choose a new regent, my lord?' interjected Martin, hoping this was an easy way to look interested without having to be too knowledgeable.

The earl continued pacing. 'Who knows? Surely they won't make it hereditary and pass the kingdom into the hands of his fool of a son. And the bishop of Winchester already has control of the king's person and education, so not him – it would be too much. De Burgh, maybe? Or someone else?'

'Whoever is appointed, my lord, might choose either to continue his predecessor's path of patronage and favour, or to strike out on a new one.' That was Sir Geoffrey again.

Martin was just beginning to see how this might affect them here, and the earl's next words confirmed it. 'Yes. And if he has a different opinion about my niece's claim to Tickhill ...' he stopped and slapped one hand into the other, crumpling the letter. 'If only we knew what was happening there! If the new regent, whoever he is, thinks that the matter is still up for discussion then he might reverse the decision. But if it's *already* been decided – if there's a document out there somewhere with the present regent's seal on it, he might think that the matter is best left untouched. After all, he'll have plenty else to deal with.'

Martin and the others watched as the earl continued to wear a groove in the floorboards. He looked frustrated and thus imminently about to lose his temper, which was never a good thing for anyone close to him. Despite the fact that he was called Warenne, after his mother's line, the earl was on his father's side a Plantagenet, a family said to descend from the devil, and when he let his anger loose Martin could well believe the old tales.

'Oh, what is that man doing!' the earl burst out, eventually. 'How long has he been there now? He's always been useful before but maybe he's losing his touch.'

Martin cast a glance at Sir Geoffrey but didn't dare say anything – not to either of them. His tongue had got Edwin in enough trouble as it was.

'Well,' said the earl, halting abruptly in the precise centre of the room and letting the anger show in his tone, 'I can't wait much longer.'

That jerked everyone to attention.

'My lord?' Sir Geoffrey sounded cautious.

'I'll need to set off for London within a week. If we hear nothing from Weaver by the end of today, we'll muster as many men as we can find locally tomorrow and the next day, and move on Tickhill in force on Saturday.'

Martin gaped.

Brother William attempted to interject. 'But, my lord – armed conflict? At such a time? Is that … wise?'

The earl stared him down in silence, and Martin wondered if Brother William knew how lucky he was.

Sir Geoffrey, ill-advisedly in Martin's opinion, tried. 'My lord, surely – some caution …?'

Martin saw the earl's anger a fraction of a moment before they all heard it burst forth, giving him just enough time to signal to Adam and Hugh that they shouldn't move. Anything that drew the earl's attention towards one individual was to be avoided, in case they ended up bearing the brunt of his rage for something that wasn't their fault.

It was Sir Geoffrey, thanks to his words, who was on the receiving end, the earl bellowing at him that he was turning into an old woman these days. 'And what good has it ever done to wait and hide? Do you think my father – a bastard, no less – got this earldom without taking direct action when it was needed? Have you gone soft in your old age?' His finger was jabbing perilously close to Sir Geoffrey's face and Martin was terrified that he was going to call the knight a coward out loud, and then all hell really would break loose.

However, 'And did we get Prince Louis out of the kingdom without a fight? No we did not!' was the earl's next roar, which turned Martin's thoughts in an entirely different direction. With a stab he was reminded of the carnage, the bodies at his feet and the blood that had taken so long to wash off.

That should probably have been a warning to him. However, far from feeling it all a nightmare, as he had in the middle of the night, the images and the recollection gave Martin energy and purpose. *Battle.* He almost took a step forward.

The earl noticed the tiny movement, but when he swung round to Martin it wasn't in fury. Or, at least, not at him. 'Ha! At least there's one man in here who agrees with me.' His glaring eye met Martin's. 'Are you ready for a fight?'

'I knew it was you as soon as you came in,' murmured Prior Richard, taking care not to disturb the women, who were still passing fabrics to and fro between them over by the fire.

'There is a good reason for the deception, I can assure you,' began Edwin, in a similarly low tone.

'I hope so.' The monk sighed. 'I owe you my life – and indeed I have often thought of you and prayed for you – which means that I at least owe you the benefit of the doubt, but you must know that I can't become involved in lying or duplicity.'

Edwin hesitated. He couldn't tell Prior Richard everything, but … 'If I told you,' he said, carefully, 'that I was pretending to be someone I'm not in order to find a peaceful solution to something that might otherwise end in violence, would that satisfy your conscience?'

Prior Richard looked torn, but eventually he nodded. 'Violence should be avoided if possible, for it is always the innocent who suffer. And although I can't tell a falsehood and call you by this name, I can leave to return to Roche without telling anyone your real name or your purpose, for now.'

Edwin nodded gratefully.

'And … is there anything specific I should tell Father Abbot about the matter?'

Edwin hesitated. 'Only to ask him to pray for continued peace.'

'That might soon be in short supply.'

'Why? Oh – I never asked you, did I? What was the news you were about to tell me when Sir Robert left?'

'That the lord regent is on his deathbed. Unlikely to last more than a couple of weeks, if that, according to the abbot who sent the tidings.' He crossed himself.

It didn't take Edwin more than a count of three for all the many implications of the situation to hit him. If he didn't act swiftly, if he didn't do what he came here to do and then get out, things might turn very nasty indeed. *And it is always the innocent who suffer*, he thought, looking over at Alys and the other women.

Prior Richard was getting to his feet. 'I wish you success in your peaceful endeavours, and will pray that violence can be avoided.' He, too, glanced over at the fireplace. 'And is that lady really your wife?'

'She is, and I give thanks to the Lord for my good fortune.' Edwin paused. 'If it's not too much to ask, might you remember her in your prayers too?'

'Of course.'

The monk moved to say his farewells to the ladies. 'And the Lord's blessing be upon you, and His mother watch over you, when your time comes,' he added to Alys, in a kind tone that almost made her face crumple.

She recovered and thanked him, and Edwin approached the group. 'I'll go down with Prior Richard, and see if I can be of any assistance to Sir Robert,' he said, keeping his voice casual but giving Alys a significant glance that indicated Lady Idonea. 'There's no need for you to come.'

Lady Idonea broke in. 'Of course she must stay here!' She gestured at Alys's swelling form. 'You can't keep going up and down that steep hill – you're my guest and your safety is my responsibility, so I must insist on you resting whenever you can.'

Her tone was odd, somehow, but Edwin didn't have time to consider it. He gave Alys a parting smile and followed Prior Richard down the stairs and then around the spiral path into the bailey. On the way he enquired after a few of the other monks he'd met while he was at Roche, but he stopped the chat as soon as they came near to other people. He'd already given himself away once today; best not do it again.

There was a group of men outside the stable, so that was a natural direction in which to bend their steps. Prior Richard disappeared inside the building to seek out the mule he'd arrived on, while Edwin lingered to catch a glimpse of the riderless horse, which had by now been unsaddled and was being looked over by the stable-master. It didn't appear to be injured, and to Edwin it seemed to be in quite good condition, but he was well aware that he was hardly an expert in equine matters. He was fairly certain it wasn't a war horse – which would be unlikely anyway, in the circumstances – but that was about it.

Anyone might gossip in circumstances such as this. 'Come far, do you think?' he risked asking the man next to him, keeping his tone as casual as he could.

'A fair few miles, I'd say, though how much of that was before he lost his rider and how much was after, I couldn't tell.'

'Been out overnight?'

'Maybe. Looks tired enough.'

'I wonder what happened.'

The man shrugged. 'Bolted? Thrown his rider? Or maybe footpads or outlaws, who knows.'

I'd very much like to know, thought Edwin. He edged nearer to where the animal's saddle was leaning up against the stable wall. It was not decorative or embellished in any way, but it looked to be of fine construction. It was certainly not new; even Edwin could see that it was worn smooth and shiny from years of use. A man accustomed to riding up and down the land? A messenger, perhaps?

A pair of saddle bags had also been put by the wall, and Edwin was itching to open them so he could examine the contents. Was it just possible that the document he was seeking might be in one of them? Or at least some information on who the rider had been?

The temptation was almost overwhelming, but he had to fight it. Yes, the contents of those bags might be the means to get him and Alys out of here; but being seen to look through them with too much curiosity would arouse suspicion.

Sir Robert was speaking. 'Which direction did it come in from? We'll send out a search party – there might be an injured man lying somewhere, or footpads and thieves about.' He nodded his head at the garrison's sergeant, who began to shout names and organise men. 'I'll come too,' continued Sir Robert. 'The safety and security of this castle and its manor are *my* responsibility, and I won't shirk it. If there are outlaws about, we'll find them.'

Edwin had noticed the slight emphasis on the word *my*. Was this the first indication that Sir Robert might be aware that the castle wasn't, in fact, his responsibility? Or that it wouldn't be for much longer?

All the men around him were starting to be in motion, and Edwin edged even closer to the saddle bags. But even amid the activity somebody would be sure to notice if he started rifling through them. Perhaps he could drop a few hints that they should be searched, or offer to carry the bags up to the keep? He would be in full view out here, but a bit of dawdling in the keep's stairwell while no one was looking …

Prior Richard emerged from the stable, leading his mule. He nodded to Edwin without speaking and made his way over to Sir Robert, who was waiting for his own horse to be made ready. 'I'll be on my way back to the abbey. If we have any further news from London, Father Abbot will no doubt let you know. And perhaps you'd have the courtesy to do the same. Best if we all stay as well informed as we can in uncertain times.'

'You're likely to hear of any important tidings sooner than me, Prior – news always seems to take an age to get here, whereas you Cistercians have your spies everywhere up and down the land.'

Prior Richard was shocked. 'Not spies, my lord. But all our abbots keep in touch with each other for the good of the whole Order.'

'My apologies. I misspoke. Yes, I'll certainly let you know if I hear anything, and I hope everything is settled peacefully by the time we meet again.'

Prior Richard sketched a benediction in the air and mounted, leaving Edwin to wonder whether everything being settled peacefully referred only to the impending change of regent, or to something else.

The mule had hardly taken its first step when a small party of men Edwin didn't recognise rushed through the gatehouse and into the bailey. Prior Richard pulled up and Sir Robert went to meet them. Townsfolk, Edwin assumed, or men from the outlying parts of the manor. He couldn't hear what they were saying, but there was a lot of gesticulating and pointing, as though they were giving directions.

The content of the conversation soon became evident as Sir Robert turned away from them and shouted to his sergeant. 'Anselm! Never mind the search party, but bring a few men and find a litter of some sort. They've found a body.'

Chapter Four

Everard was already in the armoury when Martin and Sir Geoffrey entered, anxiously pushing weapons and pieces of armour around on shelves and muttering to himself.

'You don't like this any more than I do, do you?' Sir Geoffrey didn't bother with a preamble, knowing that the news had gone round the castle like fire already.

'It's not for me to say, sir.' Everard was trying to keep his voice steady, but even Martin could spot the uneasy tone.

'But, if you *were* to say ...?'

Everard twisted his hands together and looked past them to check that nobody else was about to enter. 'Well, if I may ... you know we've taken on a few new lads recently, Sir Geoffrey. They're hardly trained and not ready for this sort of thing, not yet.' He rushed on, words starting to fall over themselves. 'What I mean is – I'm not questioning their courage, not that – they're good lads. But a lot of them are very young, and I worry ...' he trailed off.

Sir Geoffrey nodded. 'And some of the men, not just the new ones, have family round these parts.' He paused. 'In the Tickhill direction, for example.'

Everard nodded without speaking.

Sir Geoffrey turned to Martin. 'You?'

Martin didn't want to lay bare his very mixed thoughts. 'Edwin and Alys are in there,' was his only reply.

'Well, that's another thing,' broke in Everard. 'The castle and the garrison, that's one thing, but are there other women in there? Or visitors like Edwin? And then there's the town.'

Sir Geoffrey shook his head. 'The lord earl wouldn't attack the townsfolk.' Martin thought to himself that he'd like to believe that, but he'd heard Edwin's tales of what had happened to the citizens of Lincoln after a battle there that was not of their making.

'And it's customary, if a stronghold is going to resist, that women and other unconnected non-combatants are allowed to leave first,' added Sir Geoffrey. 'Which, we might hope, would include both Edwin and Alys.'

There was a long pause before Martin risked asking, 'And you, Sir Geoffrey? You don't like it either?'

He jumped as the knight banged his hand down hard on a shelf. 'Of course I don't like it!' Sir Geoffrey, it appeared, was as tense as the rest of them, though after the uncharacteristic outburst he made an effort to pull himself together. 'I'm not sure the lord earl has fully thought through the possible consequences of this action,' he managed. 'And of course I'm afraid for Edwin and Alys. How I will tell my wife about this, I don't know.'

'Won't she have heard already?' asked Martin. 'Everyone else seems to know.'

'I'm not sure. She hasn't been feeling well since they left, and this morning she was so out of sorts that I told her to stay in bed. Her sister is with her.' He paused for a moment. 'Perhaps I'll go and tell her now, so she doesn't hear it from anyone else. You two start looking through everything in here, and check it all against the inventory. I won't be long.'

He made a move towards the door, but was stopped from leaving by the appearance of a small figure silhouetted against the brighter light outside.

Martin recognised the boy who ran errands for the steward, one of those who now lived with Edwin's aunt. 'If you please, Sir Geoffrey, I'm to tell you that Lady Anne's labour pains have started, and she's shut up now with the women. Mother says she'll send news as soon as there is any.'

Sir Geoffrey stuttered, fell over his words, then finally managed to thank the lad and send him away. Then he stood so completely still and silent for so long that Martin and Everard exchanged glances.

'It's a difficult time,' said Everard, to nobody in particular. 'Lord knows I was in pieces every time my wife was confined. But most women come through it fine.'

'You have children, don't you?' asked Martin, trying to keep the conversation cheerful and wondering how soon he could leave.

'Yes, four, all grown up now, and two grandchildren to boot.'

'But you had six to begin with, didn't you?' Sir Geoffrey's voice was toneless as he turned to face them. 'You've got four grown up, and another two in the churchyard.'

Everard pulled at the neck of his tunic. 'Aye. It happens. But that's no reason to suppose …'

'These hauberks will need cleaning,' said Sir Geoffrey, suddenly, poking with one finger at some of the rolled mail stacked neatly on the shelves. 'Make sure you see to it.'

And then he walked out.

Martin exhaled. 'As if all this could get any more difficult.'

Everard's face was still strained. 'I don't like it, Martin, I tell you I don't.' He hesitated. 'Of course, a man has to do his duty, so if it comes to it then the new boys will have to manage alongside the others. But I don't suppose there's the least chance of the lord earl changing his mind?'

'Not unless we hear anything from Edwin by tonight.' Martin couldn't remain cooped up in the windowless space any longer. 'Anyway. I'll leave you to start in here – I'd better go and fetch the earl's own armour and give it a proper check.'

He stepped outside and gulped at the air. But it was no good – he was immediately surrounded by men wanting to know what was going on, by the steward waving pieces of parchment and saying something about food, by Humphrey the marshal tugging his arm and wanting to know about the lord earl's planned travel arrangements, because he hadn't managed to see him in person to get his orders … there was so much noise.

Martin shrugged them all off and stalked back to the keep.

Edwin was still in the bailey when the body was brought in. It was lying on a litter swung between two horses, and was covered by a cloth so he could see nothing of it.

He heard Sir Robert give the order for it to be placed in the castle chapel – a small stone building on the opposite side of the bailey – and he drifted over in that direction, slipping behind Prior Richard. On hearing the tidings the monk had decided to delay his short journey back to the abbey, partly so he would have a fuller account of the news to bring his abbot, and partly because, like some other senior monks, he was also a priest and could therefore say the prayers for the dead over the corpse, whoever it was.

Prior Richard gave Edwin a sharp look as they made their way across. 'Is this the violence you were hoping to avoid?' he asked, in a low voice.

'I don't know,' murmured Edwin, 'but I'm very much afraid that it might be.'

The monk's mouth set in a line and Edwin could see that he was displeased, though whether this was with Edwin personally or with the situation in general he couldn't tell. Still, the fact that they were conversing made it easy for Edwin to follow Prior Richard into the chapel without making a fuss about it.

Sir Robert was already inside, watching as some of his men lifted the corpse and placed it on a board they had balanced on two trestles. Then he folded back the top part of the cloth to reveal the head and shoulders.

The body was that of a man, as Edwin had known it would be. He didn't look at it too closely to start with, as he wanted to be able to gauge Sir Robert's reaction, but there was no flicker of recognition on the knight's face. Edwin wondered again if he could possibly be as innocent as he seemed, or whether he was simply a very cunning dissembler.

Prior Richard began to intone prayers over the body, and Edwin lowered his head respectfully. As the Latin continued, however, he edged closer to the corpse, facing Sir Robert over it. He mouthed, 'Anyone you know?'

Sir Robert shook his head and whispered. 'No. Certainly not anyone from the castle, and I don't recognise him from the town either. Besides, nobody was reported missing, and that horse wasn't one of ours.' He paused. 'I don't suppose you recognise him? Not seen him on the road anywhere during any of your travels?'

Edwin took advantage of the question to lean forward and study the dead man's face carefully. The eyes were closed, so he couldn't see the colour, but he would guess that they were blue based on the shock of white-blond hair and the pale skin and beard. Not an overly unusual complexion, but relatively distinctive nonetheless; that might be useful in finding out when and where anyone had last seen him alive. The clothes, insofar as Edwin could make out from looking only at the neck and shoulders, seemed to fit well with the style of the riderless horse and its equipment: the man was dressed in plain garments suitable for travelling, but they were of fine fabric, well made and not cheap.

'No,' replied Edwin, finally. 'No, I've never seen him before.' He hesitated, wondering how to prolong the conversation. 'At least, not that I can think of. Perhaps if we draw back the rest of the covering so I can see his clothes? If he's wearing anything particularly eye-catching then it might have attracted my attention if I'd passed him anywhere …' He began to reach out a hand.

'There's no need for that.' It was Prior Richard who had spoken. He'd finished his prayers and now opened his eyes. 'I know who he is.'

Edwin couldn't restrain his gasp, and he heard Sir Robert make a similar exclamation. 'Why didn't you say so straight away?'

'Because his soul, and the prayers for it, are more important than the identification of his mortal remains,' retorted the monk, more sharply than Edwin might have expected. On seeing their surprised expressions, he relented. 'Of course, as men of the world,' – he gave Edwin a hard stare – 'the two of you would be more interested in finding out who he was. But he's known to God, I'm a man of the cloth, and the sooner prayers are said after the soul has departed the body, the better.'

He paused, and they waited for him to continue. When he didn't, Edwin prompted him. 'But you know who he is? His name?'

'Not his actual name, no, though our guestmaster would, for he's sought our hospitality more than once. But I know *what* he is.' There was another pause. 'He's a royal justice.'

Edwin's throat felt tight. 'Are you sure? An actual justice? Not just a messenger?'

'I'm sure,' replied Prior Richard. 'And now I really must be on my way so I can take this news back to the abbey.' He looked at the others. 'The death of a royal justice is a very serious matter, as I'm sure you're both aware. I must warn Father Abbot of the upheaval that will no doubt be visited on the region once this becomes more widely known.' He inclined his head and left the chapel.

Sir Robert had turned completely white. 'A royal justice …' he murmured, faintly. 'And on my land?' He shook his head as if to clear it. 'But, an accident, surely?' His voice took on a tone that was almost pleading. 'If we can show it was an accident … after all, we don't actually know how he died.'

'I'm afraid we do.'

'Do we?'

Edwin didn't want to look like too much of an expert, but it was so obvious that there could be no harm in pointing it out. 'There. It's easy to see the blood because of the very light colour of the hair, though perhaps you didn't notice it because you're standing on his other side.'

Sir Robert stepped round and Edwin indicated what could be seen of the back of the dead man's head on the right-hand side, where the white hair was matted with dried blood and what looked like splinters of bone. 'The back of his skull has been smashed in.'

Sir Robert staggered back.

'Perhaps we should uncover the rest of him, just to see if there are any other wounds.' Edwin knew he was pushing his luck now, but he hoped that Sir Robert was too dazed to notice.

The knight nodded and Edwin carefully removed the covering. There was no more blood anywhere – no stab wounds or anything

– though the right hand was at an odd angle where it joined the wrist. Tentatively Edwin picked it up, replacing it hastily on the board with a gulp of nausea when he felt the bones grinding under the skin. Something broken there. Defending himself, perhaps?

But the really key point, as far as Edwin was concerned, was the belt pouch. It was a large one, with plenty of room for – say – a letter or parchment scroll with a seal. But the pouch was both open and empty. 'He's been robbed.'

Sir Robert managed to pull himself together sufficiently to take a closer look. 'Not just empty anyway? Or the contents fallen out?'

'The strings have been cut.' Edwin pointed to the leather thongs used to secure the pouch, with their neat severed ends.

'Footpads?'

'Perhaps.' Edwin didn't want to give too much away. It was evident to him what had happened, and if he could just look through the saddlebags as well, he could confirm it.

'Anyway,' he continued, belatedly remembering Thomas's brusque merchant's tone. 'I'll leave you to get on. No doubt you'll want to confer with your men and so on.'

'Wait!'

Edwin turned back.

Sir Robert put out an imploring hand. 'You don't understand … well, of course you wouldn't … what I mean is …' he took a deep breath. 'Please – you have to help me.'

The earl's mail armour was always kept in good repair, but now it gleamed. Checked, cleaned, oiled, everything. There was nothing else Martin needed to do, but he sat buffing it all again and again, unnecessarily, because if he stopped he'd have to go out and face it all.

He was sitting in the earl's council chamber in the keep. The earl himself was down at the stables, having taken Adam with him, so Martin had enjoyed having a silent space in which to work. Once or twice the marshal had come up, but a growl had been enough to see him off, temporarily at least.

'Martin?'

Martin had forgotten that Hugh was in the room. He was over by the window looking over the earl's surcoat to see that there were no rips or loose stitches – no easy task with all those tiny squares of blue and yellow sewn together. He hadn't said anything for a while, and it now struck Martin that he wasn't sure exactly what they'd do if the surcoat did need mending: there was only one woman resident in the castle, and she was in labour. He supposed they'd have to find some girl from the village who was handy with a needle, though he had no idea who. Alys would kn— 'What is it? Does it need mending?'

'No, I don't think so.'

'Well, what then?'

There was a pause. 'I just … what's it going to be like?'

'What?'

'You know – when we go to Tickhill.' Hugh swallowed. 'Is it going to be like when we were at …'

Martin recalled that Hugh had witnessed some of the horrors of Sandwich a couple of years back, and that he'd only been seven years old at the time. He put the chausses down, placing them carefully on the blanket he'd laid on the floor so the oil wouldn't get scratched off.

Hugh looked pale. 'I'm not scared,' he said, his voice wavering, 'but I'm not sure I could fight a grown man even if he wasn't a knight.'

'Nobody will expect you to,' said Martin, trying to sound reassuring. 'What happened then … well, that was different. There are rules about this sort of thing, as I'm sure you've learned from Sir Geoffrey, and boys your age aren't expected to take part in the combat.'

'You think there will be combat, then?'

'I certainly hope —' he looked at the boy's pale face. 'Well, perhaps. You never know, seeing the might of our lord earl coming towards the castle might make them surrender straight away.'

Hugh looked doubtful.

'And besides,' added Martin, firmly, 'even if we do have to make an attack on the castle, you won't be part of it. Nobody wants children to get hurt. Or women.'

There was a moment of silence before Hugh asked, 'But what about Edwin?'

'What about him?'

Martin's reply had been rather more angry and defensive than he intended, and Hugh shrank back a little. 'Well – he's not a child or a woman, but he is inside the castle that we might attack. What will happen to him?'

What indeed? As if Martin had been able to put that out of his mind for one single moment since the lord earl came up with this idea in the first place. And since Martin himself had made it infinitely worse.

'I'll make sure he's safe,' he said, and forestalled any further questions by sending Hugh off to see if he could find Sir Geoffrey.

He was just starting to roll up the earl's hauberk when the marshal appeared in the doorway again.

'Oh, *what*?'

Humphrey was not by any means a pugnacious man, but he stood his ground. 'I have a job to do.'

'Yes, yes, to make the travel arrangements – I know. I don't see what that has to do with me.'

'The lord earl is too busy to speak to me, and Sir Geoffrey is … distracted. Everard doesn't have the authority or the knowledge to tell me what's what. If I'm to plan properly – and if John Steward is to manage efficiently here while you're away – I need to know how many men from the garrison will be coming, how many will be mustered from the surrounding area, of what ranks they will be, horse or foot, how long we will be away, what sort of rations will need to be organised —'

Martin cut him off. 'Of course. But why me?'

'Who else is there?'

'What?'

'You're the next most senior man in the castle, after the lord earl and Sir Geoffrey. If not them, then it has to be you.'

Martin looked at him in shock.

'Martin, you have to get used to being in charge.'

It was a headache-inducing hour or so later that Hugh finally reappeared. 'Where have you been?' growled Martin, who had been hoping all the while that the page would be back and he'd have an excuse to get away.

'Sorry,' said Hugh, not sounding even vaguely apologetic. 'I was on my way to find Sir Geoffrey, like you said, when my lord saw me and said to come to the stable. He says the old pony is no good for going on a campaign, and I can have a different one to ride, a bigger one!'

Martin didn't have the heart to shout. He would have felt exactly the same excitement at that age, and the news had evidently driven away some of Hugh's fear, which was all to the good. Besides, if the earl had wanted his page then that had to take precedence over any task Martin had given him. 'So you didn't find Sir Geoffrey?' he asked, aware that Humphrey was still hovering.

'Oh, yes, that's what I came to tell you – as soon as my lord said I could go, I went to look for him, like you said. He's out in the tiltyard giving extra training to some of the new men.'

'Excellent,' replied Martin, standing up. 'Sorry, Humphrey, I have to go and see him about … some important things.'

He heard the marshal's sigh as he left the room.

Sir Geoffrey was still in the tiltyard on the flat ground behind the castle when Martin reached it. The knight looked exhausted.

Martin hailed him. 'Have you been out here all this time?'

Sir Geoffrey pulled off his helm, and Martin could see the sweat running down his face. 'They need the practice,' was his terse response.

And you're trying to keep your mind off everything else, thought Martin. *I know the feeling*.

They stood in an awkward silence for a few moments before Martin cleared his throat. He didn't have anything in particular he needed to say to Sir Geoffrey – he'd just used the errand to get rid of Hugh, and then to get away from Humphrey. 'Shall I help you disarm, if you've finished?'

'I suppose so,' came the grudging reply. 'I seem to get stiff and sore more easily these days.'

Dealing with armour, mail and padding was something both of them had been doing all their lives, so the familiarity made things easier.

'Any news about … you know, from the chamber? From the women?'

Sir Geoffrey extracted his head from the soaking gambeson. 'Not yet.' He stroked his disarranged beard, which these days was not so much grey as almost completely white, back into place. 'Does it always take this long?' he burst out, in exasperation.

'No point asking me,' replied Martin, kneeling down to lay the hauberk out flat so he could roll it properly.

'I haven't seen her, so I haven't told her about the lord earl's plan to move on Tickhill. And I don't suppose any of the women have either, with so much else to worry about.' Sir Geoffrey pulled on his tunic and looked directly at Martin. 'So she doesn't know how much danger Edwin and Alys are in.'

Martin's buried anger began to surface again. It was rage at himself, he knew that – this whole mess was of his making, and nobody else's – but now some of it was strangely directed at Sir Geoffrey for reminding him of it. 'You worry too much about Edwin,' he muttered, looking at the hauberk on the ground rather than the knight's face above him. 'He's a grown man and he can take care of himself.' *Lies.* Martin knew that Edwin needed looking after – he was just too innocent, too nice, for the world he lived in, and he needed people like Martin and Sir Geoffrey to watch over him. And as for Alys … 'Anyway,' he continued, not really knowing what he was saying but desperate to try to push the guilt back down again, 'he's only your stepson, not your real son.' He finished rolling the mail and shoved it away. 'Or is he?' he added, malevolently. Stupidly.

'*What* did you just say?'

It was too late to back out now, or to pretend he hadn't said it. 'Well, honestly, the way you fuss about him, anyone would think he was your real son.'

The next thing Martin knew was that he was staring at the sky.

He took a moment to realise that he was lying flat on his back and that his jaw hurt.

The sun was still bright, despite the lateness of the afternoon, but now it was blotted out by a looming, furious Sir Geoffrey. 'If *any* other man had insulted my lady wife in that way, he would be planning to fight for his honour and his life by now.' His voice was actually quivering with rage. 'She was a good and faithful wife to her first husband, Edwin's *father*, and I will challenge and defeat any man who says otherwise.'

'I …'

'*You*,' said Sir Geoffrey, contemptuously, 'are a boy who needs to grow up. Yes, you're bigger than every man in the county, and in the whole kingdom for all I know, but you seem to have no more wit or intelligence than you did when you were seven years old. I will spare you the challenge because you are a foolish youth, and because I know the lord earl expects better things of you.' He took a step back, and the sun burst into Martin's eyes again, forcing him to look away. 'But I will not forget. And unless you mend your ways, I will not forgive.'

Sir Geoffrey turned on his heel and left.

Martin remained where he was. He was aware that some of the men were staring at him, probably pointing and either mocking him or whispering in hushed tones about what they'd seen, ready to spread the gossip everywhere. The huge, terrifying Martin, the knight-in-training, put flat on his back by a man in his sixties. He would be a joke for weeks in the hall.

Martin put a hand up to his jaw. Sir Geoffrey might be old, but he had muscles and sinews like whipcord and a fist of iron. He knew how to throw a punch and Martin, kneeling as he had been, was an easy static target.

Of course, he shouldn't take this lying down – ha – what he should do was get up and challenge Sir Geoffrey, fight him, punish him for daring to strike. *If any other man* … but he wasn't going to do that. Of course he wasn't.

As he gazed at the uncaring sky, Martin remembered a monk he'd met when he and Edwin had stayed at Roche Abbey. Brother Guy had told him that knights fought with their heads and their hearts as well as their strong right arms. Well, he'd failed on two of those three counts, hadn't he? He'd acted and spoken without thinking and he'd caused pain to those nearest to him, to those who deserved better. Nobody liked him, nobody wanted him, and it was all his own fault.

Martin lay on his back on the cold ground and wondered if things could possibly get any worse.

'Help you with what?' Edwin paused in leaving the chapel and turned back to face Sir Robert.

'Look,' said the knight, still gazing at the body, 'none of this is anything to do with you, but explaining it to someone who isn't involved might help. You strike me as an intelligent man, a man of the world, and they're in very short supply around here.' He looked up. 'Will you listen, at least?'

Edwin tried to rein in his excitement and sound neutral. 'Of course.' He indicated the makeshift bier. 'Should we perhaps …'

'Oh, yes.' Sir Robert picked up the discarded cloth and they laid it once more over the corpse.

Once that was done, the knight looked about him. There were no chairs or benches in here, but there was a step just in front of the rood screen, where the main body of the chapel was divided from the chancel and the altar. Sir Robert sat on it and gestured to Edwin to join him.

'Now, where to start?' he murmured, before reaching a decision and nodding to himself. 'Yes, from the beginning.' He ran a hand through his hair. 'You know, of course, that there is a much larger castle near here, at Conisbrough?'

That was safe to answer. 'Yes.'

'It belongs to Earl Warenne.'

Still common knowledge. 'Yes.'

'Well, some months ago I received a message from the earl saying that he was claiming this castle, Tickhill, in the name of his niece, and that I was to hand it over to him straight away.'

Edwin feigned surprise. 'How astonishing!' He thought quickly. 'But evidently you didn't comply with his request, or we wouldn't be sitting here now.'

'That's correct. I hold this castle from the crown, and therefore I would never give it up unless ordered to do so by the king – or, in this case, his regent.'

'So what did you do?'

'Well, naturally I wrote to the regent to ask for further details of Earl Warenne's claim and to ask for his orders.' He tapped a finger repeatedly on his knee in what Edwin thought was an anxious gesture. Edwin was nervous, too, but trying not to show it. Was he about to get the answer he sought, the one that would enable him to take Alys home? They could be out of here in —

'I don't know what I was going to tell my wife if we'd been ordered to give up the castle,' continued Sir Robert, oblivious to everything except his own concerns. 'It's been our home for many years, for all that we don't actually own it. Indeed, she's been here all her life.'

'If? You said, *if* you were ordered to give it up? Is that not what happened?'

Sir Robert made a sound of frustration. 'That's just it! I've never had a reply. I mean, I know the regent must have plenty of matters that require his attention, but surely the castellanship of a royal castle must be of at least *some* import?'

'You've heard nothing? Nothing at all?'

'No. And in the meantime the earl has been sending me ever more pressing demands to cede Tickhill to him. But I can't, can I? If I surrender to him and then word comes from the south that I should have held out? It doesn't bear thinking about. I would be in gross dereliction of my duty – why, it might even be treason.'

He could sit no longer, getting to his feet and beginning to pace up and down. Edwin remained where he was, thinking. What would Thomas say now? What level of knowledge was safe to display?

'And,' said Edwin at last, 'you think that if this dead man is a royal justice, his presence in the area might be related to your situation?'

'Yes, of course – why else would he be here? It's the wrong time of year for the courts of king's justice to be up this way.'

'And his death complicates matters.'

'It certainly does.'

Edwin let the silence develop. So far the conversation hadn't been as useful as he'd hoped, but there was always the chance that Sir Robert might give something away. He seemed so sincere in his protestation that he'd heard nothing, but sincerity could be faked. If he would only give the slightest hint that he'd been hiding information that might benefit the earl ...

'The thing is, he might have been killed by footpads. That would be the simplest solution, of course – I might be in some trouble for the lawlessness happening in my jurisdiction, but it would be a simple matter to send out patrols and find the perpetrators.' He halted his pacing abruptly. 'But I can't help thinking there's more to this.'

'Oh yes?'

Sir Robert came to sit down again, so he could whisper his next words closer to Edwin's ear. 'What if Earl Warenne is behind all this?'

'What?' This time Edwin's surprise was genuine.

'What if this justice has been sent here to tell him that he has no claim on the castle – you'd need somebody quite important to tell an earl that – and he's had the man murdered, so nobody else can find out?'

Edwin was in such shock that he didn't know how to respond.

'You see, you're surprised. Of course you are. Honest merchants don't go about committing murder, or even contemplating it. But these great men ... you never know what they're capable of.'

Edwin's mind was beginning to race, and not in a good way.

'Think about it,' continued Sir Robert in his urgent whisper. 'If the regent was merely sending a letter to me, he'd employ a messenger. A trusted one, maybe, but a messenger nonetheless. He wouldn't need to send a royal justice! But if he needed to tell Earl Warenne to back down, he'd need a representative with more authority.'

Edwin acted as though he was only belatedly understanding. 'Like a royal justice?'

'Exactly.'

There was silence for a few moments before Sir Robert spoke again. 'So, you must see the danger this puts me in. And not just me – my wife, the garrison, even the townsfolk.'

'How so?'

'Earl Warenne is a very powerful man, and he is also a very determined man who is used to getting what he wants. If he's decided that he's going to have this castle – and maybe to take it now, when there is turmoil with the regent being ill or dying – then he will use all the means at his disposal. Which, I need hardly add, are much greater than my own.'

'You can't believe that, surely?'

The knight nodded, pulling now at Edwin's sleeve. 'Earl Warenne might already have committed – or *caused*, at least, I don't suppose he did it himself – one murder. If he's decided he wants Tickhill, he'll do anything and he won't care who he puts in danger.'

Edwin made no reply. This was all ... he knew that he, as the earl's man, should disregard any such suspicions. He was here to serve his lord and he had to do his duty. His loyalty had to lie with the earl.

The problem, and the main reason for Edwin's shock and churning stomach, was that he had very little difficulty in believing that Sir Robert might be right.

Chapter Five

Edwin had lain awake all night, or so it seemed. Now it was nearly dawn, and Alys was stirring.

'We need to talk,' he whispered. 'About what to do next.'

She manoeuvred so her head was in the hollow of his shoulder, his arm about her, and he placed his other hand on her swollen stomach. Up until a week ago they had liked to lie thus for a short while every morning before getting up, feeling safe and secure in their bedchamber at home. Edwin hoped they would be there again before many more days had passed, and no sooner had the thought crossed his mind than he was answered by a kick from their child.

'He's awake too,' he said.

'He's been fidgeting most of the night – for some reason he always wants to be up and about while I'm at rest.'

Edwin kissed her hair, uncovered as it was while she was in bed. 'It's tiring for you, but surely it means he's healthy and strong.'

'I hope so.' She sighed. 'Anyway, let's talk about more immediate matters. Do you really think there's any truth in what Sir Robert said about the lord earl? Or is he throwing accusations around just to hide his own guilt?'

'If I knew that, we could probably be out of here today. The thing is – I just don't know. And not only do I not know what's happened, but now I'm not even sure whether I'm actually here to find out the truth, or for some other purpose.'

She shifted position again so she could see his face. 'Do you really, honestly believe that the lord earl would have sent you here deliberately as some kind of bluff?'

Edwin's head was beginning to ache again. 'I don't *believe* it, not exactly – but the problem is that I can't altogether disbelieve it, either.'

It was a terrible thing to say about the lord he had sworn to serve, he knew. But if he couldn't reveal his innermost thoughts to his wife, who could he confide in? It wasn't as if he had too many friends he could trust completely.

He decided to change the subject. 'Let's think practically. This man was murdered somewhere out on the road, and within the last day or so.'

'So the culprit must have been someone who was known to be out and about at the time.'

'Whatever time it was, yes – and it would be easier if I could get a clearer idea of that.'

'Well ...' Alys tapped her fingers thoughtfully on Edwin's chest. 'Is there anyone who we know *hasn't* been out of the castle at all in the last couple of days?'

Edwin ran through in his mind all the people he'd met since his arrival. 'Lady Idonea hasn't. Although she couldn't possibly have done this anyway – I'm sure this is a man's crime.'

'Why? Because it was violent?'

He smiled. 'You're about to tell me that women can be violent as well, aren't you? And I know they can, especially if they've got something to protect, but in this case I just don't think any woman would have had the strength. A grown man, an experienced man, knocked off his horse and then battered, his wrist broken in the fight? No.'

'All right. So not Lady Idonea, or Margaret, or indeed any merchant's wife who happened to be on the road.' She paused. 'Sir Robert has certainly been out.'

'Yes. With most of his garrison, at one time or another.'

'Which only narrows it down to several dozen men who are used to fighting and bearing arms.'

It was Edwin's turn to sigh. 'Yes. Plus any merchants, townsmen or traders who might have business on the roads.' He paused. 'Or monks, of course, though surely we can rule them out along with the women.'

There was silence for a few moments. Edwin knew that Alys was still thinking, because her fingers continued to tap idly.

'I suppose,' she said, at length, 'that we have no way of knowing who from Conisbrough might have been in the area at the right time.'

'No,' replied Edwin. 'And of course it's the same thing – patrols going out all the time, as well as messengers.' A thought struck him. 'Although, of course, we can be sure that no group led by Sir Geoffrey would be responsible. He wouldn't murder a royal justice even if the lord earl ordered him to directly.'

Alys nodded. 'I agree. But a group … that would be much more difficult to hide. How often do the garrison men ride out on their own?'

'I can't say exactly, but I would think it's rare.'

'The lord earl himself?'

Edwin shook his head. 'He would always have someone with him.' He stopped abruptly halfway through the thought of who would be attending on the earl, because it reminded him that there *was* someone from Conisbrough who rode out alone quite frequently. Someone who wasn't afraid of taking on a fight or even provoking one. But Martin would never …

'What is it?' Alys could feel that he had tensed.

'Nothing.' Edwin wasn't ready to share that thought just yet. 'I'm getting too suspicious in my old age.'

'So am I. Perhaps we're both getting old.'

Edwin smiled at the idea of his beautiful, fresh-faced wife feeling old. 'What are you suspicious about?'

'You'll say it's foolish.'

'I won't, I promise. Nothing you say could be foolish.'

'Well … it's Lady Idonea.'

'What about her?' Edwin took her hand. 'Has something happened?'

'No, nothing particular – it's just that she makes me very uneasy. Especially when she starts talking about the baby, which she does quite a lot.' She paused. 'I told you you'd think it was foolish.'

'Not at all.' Edwin realised that he'd had similar thoughts somewhere at the back of his mind; all Alys had done was confirm them. 'I agree. So, the sooner we get you out of here, the better.' *And how are we going to do that?* asked the inconvenient voice within him.

Alys made a move to sit up. 'Let's see what today brings, then, shall we? It does sound like you made some progress yesterday, so perhaps you can talk to Sir Robert again to see if you can draw out anything else.' She made a face. 'While I concentrate on her.'

Edwin put out an arm to stop her getting out of bed. 'How worried are you about her interest in you and the baby? Shall I tell her you're not well enough to go up to the keep today, and you've stayed in bed?'

With some reluctance, she shook her head. 'I think she'd just end up coming here, to see how I was.' She made a frustrated noise and waved her arm. 'Oh, perhaps I'm just imagining it. Strange things can go through your head at this sort of time, that's what your mother and Rosa have both said to me. After all, everything Lady Idonea has said and done is just about how I should take care of myself, how she'll make sure I'm safe here, that sort of thing. Perhaps she's just being kind and I'm misinterpreting.'

Alys, as Edwin well knew, had something of a gift for reading people, so if she felt uneasy then he was inclined to take it seriously. 'You're more important to me than anything else in my life – you and our child. If you say the word then we'll go and hitch up the horse and the wagon right now and just leave. I don't care what happens afterwards.'

For a brief moment she looked as though she was considering that. 'No. Equally, you and the baby are the most important people in the world to me. I can't have you throw away your position, your career, our child's future, just because I've got some silly idea in my head about Lady Idonea.' She looked him in the eye. 'We'll go when we've got to the bottom of this matter, and not before. And then you can return in triumph to the lord earl and everything will be fine.'

'All right. But,' he added, 'if you change your mind, tell me straight away.'

As he got out of bed, Edwin reflected that 'triumph' might mean different things to different people. To him it would be finding out the truth. To the earl, he was fairly sure, it would mean winning his dispute at any cost.

This feeling of unease hung about him as he and Alys left the hall building and crossed the bailey, not helped by Edwin happening to notice that there were more guards posted at the castle's gate than there had been previously. They passed Theo and Margaret standing in a patch of sunshine, the former apparently giving the latter a detailed shot-by-shot account of the archery practice he'd just finished, and then began the slow and laborious task of ascending to the keep. Edwin's disquiet didn't dissipate on the way up, and the feeling grew more ominous when they entered the upper chamber to find Sir Robert and Lady Idonea deep in conversation.

Sir Robert loomed out of the darkness of the badly lit room. 'Ah, just the man I wanted to talk to. And do come and sit down, mistress.'

Something in Edwin's mind was trying to tell him that he should leave, now, and one glance at Alys showed him that she had also picked up on the undercurrent of alarm. But it was too late for that.

Edwin spotted something and tried a distraction. 'Are those the dead man's saddlebags?'

Sir Robert, who was already ushering Alys to a seat by the fire, glanced at them. 'Yes. I've had a look through but there's nothing that adds to the identification we already have.'

'Do you mind if I have a look?'

'Please do.'

It didn't take Edwin long to scan the contents. And, thank the Lord, now he finally knew *something* for sure.

He dawdled over poking the bags around, trying to work out what was going to come next. Eventually, though, he had to put them down and turn back to the others. *Remember to be Thomas*. 'So, what was it you wanted to speak to me about? More purchases, I hope?'

'Alas, no, though what I have to say might be of some financial interest.'

Edwin's puzzlement increased, as did his sense of apprehension. He took the proffered stool by the hearth and waited to hear more.

'Now,' began Sir Robert, as soon as he was seated. 'I've been thinking about the conversation we started yesterday. About you helping me in my … current predicament.'

'Yes?' said Edwin, warily.

'Well, you know that I have my suspicions about Earl Warenne.'

'Yes.'

'You don't need to worry about speaking of this in front of my wife,' said Sir Robert, misunderstanding Edwin's reluctance to engage. 'She and I have discussed it all, and she is in agreement with what I'm about to suggest.'

The unease was now screaming very loudly in Edwin's head. 'Which is?'

'As I said yesterday, you're an intelligent man, a man of the world who travels widely. If you were, for example, to head to Conisbrough with your wares, nobody would think it suspicious.'

Edwin exchanged a sharp glance with Alys. 'And why would I want to do that?'

'I thought, if you went to Conisbrough, you could maybe ask around, find out if there was any talk about Earl Warenne having heard from a messenger or royal justice. Nobody would suspect you.'

Edwin could hardly believe he was hearing this. 'And then I'd come back here to let you know what I'd found out?'

'Exactly.' Sir Robert paused. 'I'd make it financially worth your while, of course. You're a man of business, and I could pay you for doing this small thing, more than enough to make up for whatever you might lose from missing out on another few days' trading.'

Edwin could hardly believe his ears. His anxiety faded a little. Was it to be this easy? They were to be sent home, out of danger, perhaps even today? The circumstances would provide the perfect excuse when he came back to the earl – 'I'm sorry, my lord, but to refuse to do so might have aroused Sir Robert's suspicions, so we just *had* to come away' – and then he could talk through the murder and its repercussions with Sir Geoffrey and with Brother William, who might have further news from Roche. And then, even if he had to return to Tickhill himself, he could leave Alys at home and safe.

Relief washed over Edwin in a tide, and his main concern was now not to look too keen. 'I suppose …' he began, pretending to weigh it up carefully.

'Your horse is almost recovered,' added Sir Robert. 'I've already checked with the stablemaster. In an ideal world he'd want to have it rest another couple of days, he said, but it's not all that far to Conisbrough and it should manage.' He laughed. 'Indeed, if you turn up at the gate with a lame horse it will be a good excuse to stay there for a couple of days!'

How much did he know? Was he actually now mocking? Or perhaps was this was all just a huge coincidence, or even a mark of God's favour on Edwin.

In any case, there was only one thing for it. 'I'll have to speak to my wife, Sir Robert, if you'll give us leave to have a private conference for a few moments, but I'm sure we can —'

'Of course, of course,' interrupted Sir Robert, who was in turn interrupted by a loud cough from his wife, who then threw him a significant look.

'That is to say …' he began, and then tailed off.

The alarms in Edwin's head started to sound again. Alys was evidently hearing them too, for she reached out to take his hand, her face suddenly pale.

'What my husband means to say,' said Lady Idonea, with a smile, 'is that you will be going to Conisbrough alone. Your wife will stay here.'

The earl was swearing profusely.

News of the murder had reached the castle that morning, via a lay brother who had been sent from Roche Abbey at first light. He was still in the ward somewhere, waiting to see if the earl had any message to send back to Abbot Reginald, though Martin didn't think his lord had yet said anything that that would bear repeating to a man of the cloth.

His own thoughts were also not worth a silver halfpenny, for they mainly consisted of *What in the name of God have I done?* as he considered the situation Edwin and Alys were now in.

He didn't think there was any possible way in which he could feel more guilty. It was he who had put his friends in danger, he who had spoken and acted so thoughtlessly. And if he hadn't opened his big mouth again yesterday to Sir Geoffrey, he might be in a better position to ask the knight for help and advice on how to fix the mess he'd made. But as it was, Sir Geoffrey was staring blankly at – or possibly *through* – the earl, and seemed almost not to be in the chamber at all.

Of course, that wasn't all to do with Martin's stupidity. Sir Geoffrey had spent the night on the floor of the hall along with the men, because Lady Anne was still labouring in their shared quarters. And although the knight liked to think or pretend that he was still young, sleeping on a hard floor wasn't as easy to recover from as it had once been. Not that he looked like he'd slept much, in any case. Martin was desperate to apologise to him, willing to abase himself if necessary in order to gain forgiveness. He would take the first opportunity as soon as this council was over.

Realising he was going to get no reaction from Sir Geoffrey in the meantime, Martin tried to catch Brother William's eye, but the monk's gaze was fixed on the lord earl. No help there either. So, it was going to be up to Martin to work out how he was going to get Edwin and Alys out of Tickhill. The problem was, this would no doubt require some clever stratagem, whereas Martin only knew one way to go about achieving his aims.

'Right!' bellowed the earl, eventually, causing Martin to start. 'Never mind Saturday – we'll go today.'

'What?' Even Sir Geoffrey was jolted out of his stupor.

'I won't have it said that I allowed lawlessness on my lands. A royal justice!'

Even Martin could spot the mistake in that, but he left it up to someone else to point it out. 'Er, the murder appears to have occurred on Tickhill lands, my lord?' ventured Brother William.

'And they're mine,' retorted the earl, sharply. 'Or they soon will be.' He stabbed a finger at the monk. 'And I won't lay myself open to accusations of inaction when a serious crime has occurred. There are some in the realm who would seek to use that against me, and I need to make sure I keep my standing in the eyes of whomever is the new regent.'

'But —'

'The only possible explanation for all this,' continued the earl, without pausing to acknowledge the interruption, 'is that this man was bringing Sir Robert the orders to hand the castle and manor over to me, and that he had him murdered to stop the truth coming out.' He glared round the room, daring any of them to contradict him, but wisely nobody did.

Martin was just wondering if he dared to mention Edwin – and, if so, whether this would do Edwin any good or just harm his cause further – when Sir Geoffrey interjected. 'My lord, the muster is not yet complete. It will take time to assemble those men you've summoned who need to come from further afield.'

The earl brushed away the issue. 'Never mind that. We've got enough here to make a decent show of force, and the others can make their way straight there to join us.' He gave Sir Geoffrey a direct look. 'See to it.'

'Yes, my lord,' was the only possible reply, and Sir Geoffrey left the room.

The earl turned to Brother William and began to dictate messages, the monk's quill flying across pieces of parchment as he tried to keep up with the rapid instructions.

Martin waited a few moments and then cleared his throat.

The earl paused in mid-sentence. 'What?'

'While you're busy with Brother William, my lord, I wonder if the rest of us might not be better employed elsewhere? If we're leaving today there will be much to organise …'

An arm was waved. 'Yes, fine. Be off with you and make ready. Tell Humphrey I want to leave as soon as possible after noon. I don't care if all his arrangements aren't finalised – just get a tent and some food on the move and the rest can follow.'

Martin ushered Adam and Hugh out and down the stairs. Once outside, they all paused to catch their breath and Martin crouched. 'Are you all right?'

Hugh looked as though he was imminently about to either cry or vomit, but he swallowed, rubbed his sleeve across his face and managed 'I'm fine,' without sounding too wobbly.

'Good lad. Now, the thing to do is to keep busy. Run to Humphrey now and tell him what the lord earl said. You remember it?'

'Yes.'

Martin watched the boy depart and turned to Adam. 'My lord's own gear is all standing ready in the keep, and our helms are there too. Find two men to bring it all down now, and then supervise personally as they load it. I'll get the rest of ours from the armoury and check Everard knows what's happening.' He looked around the ward. 'And I need to find Sir Geoffrey.'

Adam ran off, and Martin wondered where to start. The armoury was right there in front of him and Sir Geoffrey was nowhere to be seen, so he guessed it would be better to do that first.

Everard was already in there, reaching up to a high shelf, and he jumped and knocked a pile of swords to the floor when Martin ducked through the doorway. Fortunately they were all in scabbards, or both of them might have been invalided out of the forthcoming campaign before it even started.

'You've heard, then?'

'Yes.' Everard stooped to collect the swords and then straightened.

Even in the gloom Martin could see the strain on the sergeant's face, but that wasn't a conversation he wanted to have just now. 'There's not much light in here,' he said, briskly. 'And it will get too crowded to issue gear. Not to mention that we're in much more of a hurry than we thought we would be.'

Everard nodded. 'I'll have it all brought outside and loaded, and we can issue it from there or even on the way.' He precariously balanced another sword on top of the pile he was holding. 'Or, rather – not all. Sir Geoffrey will need some for the men who stay here with him.'

'Good. I'll take my gear and Adam's now.' Martin slung a hauberk over each shoulder and then hesitated. 'Surely my lord will keep Hugh out of the way, but I'd better bring him some kind of protection.'

Everard, his hands full, indicated with his head. 'That's the padding he normally wears – no armour, though.'

Martin gathered it up, along with his own and Adam's. 'Helmet? He wears one when he trains. Leather, not metal.'

'Yes. There.'

Martin balanced it on top of the gambesons and stepped backwards out of the armoury, not wanting to turn round in case he knocked anything else flying. Lord, but he hoped Hugh wasn't going to need this in earnest. How was he to protect them all? Hugh, Adam, Edwin, Alys? And all at the same time as he had to carry out his duties for the lord earl as well.

It was just one more thing to worry about, and he tried to think through it as he lugged everything down to the outer ward, saw it safely packed and watched the lay brother from Roche leaving. Well, he'd have plenty to tell his abbot as soon as he got back. Martin noticed Humphrey trying to catch his attention from the middle of a group of men all talking at once, so he pretended he hadn't noticed and turned to go back up.

Sir Geoffrey was in the inner ward. Martin had never seen him look so harried, not even when there had been a band of outlaws in the area a couple of years back. He looked like he was being pulled and stretched beyond endurance and would soon snap.

Martin strode over to him. They met near the bottom of the stairs that led up into the keep, and over Sir Geoffrey's shoulder he could see Everard, outside the armoury now and supervising the counting and carrying of piles of equipment.

At first Sir Geoffrey looked as though he might not stop, but Martin blocked his path and began straight away. 'Please, Sir Geoffrey.

Please – I know it's not the best time, but I have to apologise, I have to say sorry for what I said to you yesterday, and not only that – for how I've been behaving for a long time now. I should never have put Edwin in such a position, and I'll regret it until the day I die. Please, Sir Geoffrey, please help me to put it right.'

It might have been Martin's imagination, but he *thought* that the granite features might have softened ever so slightly. 'Being sorry is a start, I suppose.'

'I need to get them out of there.' No need to explain who he meant, or where 'there' was.

'You do. But I can't think how.'

'Maybe once I get there I'll be able to find a way —' Martin paused, his attention caught by a new arrival at the armoury. It was the steward's boy, and he was in floods of tears. He picked his way through the piles of gear to reach Everard, and then pulled at his sleeve. Once he had the sergeant's attention he said something that made Everard's face collapse.

Martin watched the sergeant's gaze sweep the ward. He was looking for someone, and it was with a deep, lurching sense of inevitability that Martin saw the eyes finally fix on him and Sir Geoffrey.

Everard pointed them out to the boy, who immediately backed away and began shaking his head. Everard put out a hand to stop him, but then dropped it, nodded and sent him off. He squared his shoulders and took a deep breath. Martin watched his every step as he made his way over with aching slowness, recognising the walk of a man who didn't want to reach his destination.

Martin exchanged a glance with him over Sir Geoffrey's shoulder and then put out a hand to grip the knight's arm. 'I think Everard wants to speak to you,' he said, as gently as he could manage.

'What is it?' He hadn't seen what Martin had seen. He didn't realise, not yet.

'Sir Geoffrey …' Everard didn't know how to begin, and Martin didn't envy him.

'Well, what? You need me for something?'

'It's not that, Sir Geoffrey. It's … news.'

'From the birthing chamber? My wife? The child has arrived?' He was almost in motion already, but Martin's increasing grip on his arm held him back.

Everard stood in helpless silence.

The old knight's next word came out in a voice that was markedly less steady. 'What?'

Everard shook his head. His face creased, and a tear rolled down his cheek. 'I'm sorry, Sir Geoffrey. I'm so, so sorry.'

'This is totally unacceptable.' Edwin was trying hard to remember to be Thomas – because matters would be infinitely worse if they found out who he really was – but the rage building inside him was making it very difficult.

'Come, now.' Sir Robert was still trying to be conciliatory. 'Your wife will be perfectly safe and well looked after here – and surely you'd prefer that to having her out on the roads during this present uncertainty?'

'This "uncertainty", as you put it, is nothing to do with me.'

'My dispute with the earl isn't, admittedly, but we still don't know for sure that this man died because of that. It may well turn out that he was killed by footpads or outlaws. Surely you'd rather have your wife safe here behind our walls rather than out in danger from them.'

Edwin folded his arms and said nothing.

'Look, all you have to do is what we agreed a few moments ago: travel to Conisbrough, ask for hospitality, and then see what you can find out. It's a big castle – there will be plenty of men in it ready to gossip. Then return here to me, accept your payment and you can both be on your way.'

Edwin opened his mouth and then belatedly realised that Alys was throwing him looks of increasing significance. 'As I said, Sir Robert, we'll need some privacy to discuss this between ourselves.'

'Of course, of course. Idonea and I will take a turn about the bailey and return in due course.' He held out an arm to his wife and they left the room.

As soon as they were gone, Edwin dashed around looking for possible avenues of escape. There were none. The windows were mere slits. A curtained-off area contained a bed but no way out. There was only one door, the one leading to the stairs and the keep's entrance. In one corner of the chamber there was an opening in the wall, but it led only to a private garderobe. In his desperation Edwin even inspected that more thoroughly than he might otherwise have done, but the exit pipe was too narrow to allow for any idea of escape.

He returned to the chamber and sat down heavily. 'There's no other way out. We couldn't possibly fight our way past the guards, and I suspect that Sir Robert is even now giving orders that we are not to be permitted to leave together on any pretext.' He reached out a hand but dared not look Alys in the face, recognising how badly he had failed her again.

He felt her fingers on his own. 'I think you should go.'

He almost leapt to his feet. 'What? No!'

'Think about it —'

'It's out of the question. I won't leave you, and that's final.'

And that was the message he gave to Sir Robert when he and Lady Idonea returned, and the one he repeated at intervals throughout the long afternoon.

Sir Robert, of course, tried different tactics to get him to change his mind – without ever straying into the realm of outright threats – but Edwin remained firm.

'Very well,' said Sir Robert, at last. 'And although you won't help me, we'll be happy to offer you further hospitality until you change your mind, or until all this is over.'

'Am I to understand,' said Edwin, still heroically giving his best impression of a spluttering merchant, 'that you intend to keep us prisoner?'

'Not at all. But there are clearly criminals or footpads operating in the area, and until I can guarantee your safety on the roads I can't in all conscience allow an unarmed civilian and a pregnant woman to leave the shelter of our walls. Why, we'd never forgive ourselves if anything happened to you.'

Edwin was too furious to reply; he simply held out his arm to Alys and they left the chamber together.

By the time they were down in the bailey she was pale and gasping for breath. 'I'm sorry,' he said. 'But I didn't want to leave you in there with him – with them – and I was too angry to stay. I'd have given myself away if I hadn't walked out. Let's go to our room now and you can lie down while we think.'

As they made their way across the open space towards the building that housed the hall and the guest quarters, a man rode in through the main gate at speed. He threw himself off the horse, shouted for the sergeant-at arms, and then said something to him that caused immediate consternation.

'Run and tell Sir Robert!' the sergeant instructed the nearby Theo, who hared off. 'And shut the gates!'

This was serious. Edwin needed to find out what was going on – this couldn't be a result of the conversation he'd just had with Sir Robert, because the news had come from outside. Edwin had no doubt that it was connected to the matter at hand, and it must be important if the castle gates were to be shut during the daytime; the sun wouldn't go down for hours yet.

Alys was drooping on his arm. He must get her back to rest before he did anything else; she was his first and only priority.

Once they were inside their room he helped her on to the bed and made sure she had her feet up. 'Can I get you anything? Do you need to eat or drink, or a cool cloth?'

She shook her head, her eyes closed. 'No. I'm sorry, I just came over a little dizzy for a while, but I'll be fine once I've rested.'

'And … the baby? It's not starting yet?'

'No.'

He sat by her side, holding her hand. Her breathing slowly steadied, and eventually she opened her eyes again. 'Now. To return to the conversation we were having this morning.'

Edwin was already shaking his head. 'You're going to be in danger here whatever happens. And I'd rather you were in danger with me by your side than without me.'

'Let's think calmly. Sir Robert seems to believe that it might only be footpads, but you don't, do you?'

'He's *definitely* lying about that.'

'How so?'

'The dead man's bags had two purses of coins in them – Sir Robert must know that because he said he'd already looked through them. Any footpad who had killed him and robbed his belt pouch would certainly look through the bags and steal the money. Indeed, they'd probably take the clothes off his back as well.'

'So Sir Robert knows as well as you do that this man's death is something to do with the control of the castle, and not just an ordinary crime.'

'Yes.'

'And both Sir Robert and the lord earl suspect that the other has intercepted a document that rules in favour of the other.' She yawned. 'That didn't come out right, but you know what I mean.'

'Yes. And if I could just find that document, or find out that Sir Robert knows more than he's letting me see, that would help. So I need to stay here in any case, to see if I can locate it.' He rubbed his aching temple. 'If indeed it exists, and if it's only been hidden and not destroyed.'

She was just starting to doze off, and mumbled something. 'I didn't quite catch that, my love.'

'I said,' she managed, a little more clearly, 'What if it's at Conisbrough?'

Edwin sat with her until he was sure she was fast asleep, and then ventured out into the hall. The temptation was to march over to the locked gate and demand to know what was going on, but he suspected that word had already been passed round that he was now a figure of some suspicion, so that probably wouldn't work. Besides, he didn't want to move that far away from Alys while she was asleep and defenceless, so he just drifted into the hall, which was the scene of activity as the tables were being set out for the evening meal.

'I don't like it,' one man was saying to another, as they laid a board over two trestles. 'My brother works fields in between here and there – what if they decide to destroy the crops or burn the houses on their way?'

This was even more serious than Edwin had thought. Had a royal army been sighted on the march? Because Sir Robert had not responded to an order to hand over the castle?

'The earl wouldn't do that, would he? Conisbrough and Tickhill have always been on good terms.'

'Who knows what these great men will do?'

Wait. Conisbrough? It must be the earl who was on the march. On his way here, with armed men, causing the gates to be locked against him and men to worry about their families. Edwin felt sick.

The second man fetched another trestle. 'My sister's husband is in the garrison there. What if he's in this army and ends up getting killed? Or if he and I have to fight each other? What will we do then?'

'Are they bringing everyone? Did Anselm say?'

'I don't know. Just that the lad out scouting said there were armed men on the road from Conisbrough and he reckoned they'd be here before dark. With the earl's banner flying, he said, though I don't know if that means he's there himself.'

Edwin's mind began to work. This changed his situation and Alys's drastically. He would have to …

'Well,' continued the man who was worried about his brother-in-law, 'all I can hope is that he's one of those who stays with Sir Geoffrey at Conisbrough. They can't take everyone – someone has to stay there to defend their own patch.'

'Ah, well, *he* certainly won't be coming,' replied the other, 'because I did hear some talk about him, and fresh from the horse's mouth today.'

Edwin's ears pricked up.

'What's that, then?'

'Well, you know he got married?'

'Aye, daft old fool. At his age!'

'Ah, he wasn't past it, though – he managed to get his wife with child.'

'Did he now? Come to think of it, I reckon I did hear something about that. Has she gone into labour, then, and he won't leave her?'

'No, it's not that. Well, yes, what I mean is, she did go into labour. But this morning she died.'

Chapter Six

The earl was in the outer ward issuing some last-moment instructions, but Martin could see that Sir Geoffrey wasn't listening. Indeed, he hardly even seemed present; his mind had travelled so far away that it was almost as though his body had followed, and Martin wouldn't have been surprised to see him dissolve and float away like feathers on the wind.

Once the earl had moved on to speak with someone else, Martin pushed his way through the throng to reach Sir Geoffrey. He knew he was never exactly eloquent, but words now failed him completely as he gripped the knight's shoulders and tried to resist the impulse to embrace him.

He looked down into Sir Geoffrey's bleary and bloodshot eyes. 'You have to stay strong.'

'Why?'

'Because … because we all need you. Your *daughter* needs you.'

Martin had caught a glimpse of the tiny scrap earlier, swaddled and in the arms of the weeping wet nurse. The word was that she was likely to survive, though of course nobody could be sure of such things for the first few days and weeks; perfectly healthy-looking babies could simply die, drifting off into a sleep from which they would never wake. The child did not yet have a name, because Sir Geoffrey had been too distraught to consider the matter and nobody had the heart or the courage to press him. Martin hoped that 'the daughter of Sir Geoffrey of Rochford' would be enough to identify her at the gates of heaven if that was where she was going to end up before the week was out.

'Yes,' came the distant reply. 'But then, so did my wife, didn't she? She needed me, and she died. She died because I was over-proud enough to want a son, and then I wasn't even with her when it happened.' His eyes bored into Martin's. 'We had such a short time together. And now she's dead and I'm left behind, and I know which one of us is better off.'

Martin felt a large lump come to his throat, and he tried to swallow it. 'Time, Sir Geoffrey,' he choked. 'You need time.'

'Time?' the knight's voice was hoarse. 'Who knows how much time we have? Any of us? My wife was so much younger than me, I thought my only worry about time was that I needed to make provision for her to live without me before it was too late. I never thought it would happen the other way round.' He too started to choke, and then suddenly he gripped Martin's hands with an astonishing force. 'Bring them back, do you hear? Whatever it takes, bring back the rest of my family. My daughter lost her mother today – don't let her lose her brother as well.'

Martin nodded, no longer trusting himself to speak, and Sir Geoffrey turned and walked away without another word.

The outer ward was teeming, but over everyone's heads Martin could see the lone female figure over by the forge. Once more he shoved his way through the crowd, but Cecily saw him coming and fled inside. Crispin stepped forward to bar Martin's path, his huge arms folded across his chest. Other than Willikin, he was probably the only man in the castle who could hope to overpower Martin, but Martin wasn't about to try the truth of that today and didn't attempt to get past him. 'Please, tell her I'm sorry for her loss,' was all he said.

Crispin's rough and spark-pitted face creased in concern. 'She's very upset.'

'As well she might be.'

Martin didn't know what else to say, and they stood in an increasingly awkward silence amid the bustle in the ward.

After a while, Cecily emerged. She was clearly making an enormous effort to remain composed, though her eyes were so puffy and swollen that she could barely see out of them, and her chest was heaving.

Martin took in a breath, but before he could say anything she held up a hand. 'Don't speak.'

He shut his mouth.

'I know you're sorry. But I can't forgive you, not yet. And especially considering what happened today. My poor sister' – her voice wobbled – 'it might have been her time to die anyway, for that was in God's hands, but to have her unable to see her beloved son before she was confined in the chamber …' she broke down in sobs.

Martin was going to start crying himself soon. 'I'll bring them back, I promise. Both of them. *All* of them.'

'You'd better do.' Cecily's ravaged face tilted upwards so she could look directly at him, and her voice came more strongly. 'If anything happens to them as well then you'd better hope God will forgive you, because I never will.'

Martin watched her walk away and wondered if he'd just been cursed.

The earl's courser was now being led from the stable, so Martin went to hold the stirrup while his lord mounted, keeping his face turned down and away. Then he boosted Hugh up on to his pony – the bigger one he'd been promised – and swung into his own saddle.

He looked across at Adam. 'Here we go, then.'

Riding towards military action as part of the earl's retinue should have made Martin happy – it was what he'd been longing for all this time, wasn't it? But he didn't feel the way he ought to. Instead of pride and anticipation there was guilt and worry, and the gnawing sense that he was not going to be able to achieve what he'd promised. He was desperate to get Edwin and Alys out of the castle, but *how* was he going to do it? The only way he would get in there himself was if they were to launch a direct attack, and he didn't want that as it would put them in even more danger. Besides, if they were fighting inside the walls, the earl's priority would be to secure the castle, not to rescue Edwin and Alys. Still, as long as his lord didn't issue Martin with a direct order *not* to help them, he would be able to do something.

His other worry, of course, was that they wouldn't be able to defend themselves until he got to them. Once he was physically beside them he would be able to fight off all comers and get them out, but what if they were attacked before he could reach them? No Conisbrough man would do such a thing deliberately, of course, but in the heat of battle and with panicked armed men everywhere anything could happen, and Edwin would be hopeless – he just didn't have the training.

The question occupied Martin's full attention for the first couple of miles, at which point Adam called to him that a rider was approaching. Martin tensed, but he could soon see that it was Turold, one of the earl's most trusted messengers, who had been sent with the vanguard led by Everard.

Turold reined in as the earl's personal party approached, and the earl indicated that Martin should see what he wanted.

'They're going to have advance warning that we're coming,' were his first terse words. 'I didn't see anyone, but Everard shouted that he'd spotted a scout and sent everybody flying after him. They're just regrouping now, but the man got away.'

'I'll tell my lord.'

Turold rode off and Martin went to make his report. 'That's a shame,' was the earl's response, 'but it's not a disaster. They would have seen us in time to shut the gates anyway – this has just given them the chance to do so earlier, though hopefully not early enough to start laying in extra stores.'

Martin raised the other point that had been lurking at the back of his mind. 'And, the townsfolk, my lord? Some of them might try to flee inside the castle, but there will surely be plenty still left outside. What are your intentions towards them?'

'If they cause me no trouble, I will make none for them. We'll have it proclaimed when we get there that they should stay inside their homes.'

Martin's relief was palpable. 'Thank you, my lord, that's generous of you.'

'Generous? Think, man.'

This was one of those times when he was supposed to have picked up on a nuance, wasn't it? 'Um …'

'It makes no sense,' continued the earl. 'These lands are mine, and when they come rightfully into my possession, I'm going to want to collect what is due to me. If I start burning the fields and the town, and the shops and houses in it, nobody will be in a position to pay up, will they?' He shook his head, to indicate that Martin should have been able to think of something so obvious for himself.

Martin allowed himself to fall back a little from the earl as he rode. His lord was now occupied in speaking to the only two knights who had made it to Conisbrough in time to join the muster, Sir Baldwin de Hersey and his brother, the one-eyed Sir Malvesin, so he could do without Martin for a while.

Whatever the earl's motivations, the promised safety for the civilian population meant that Martin had one less thing to fret about. Actually, two things: their safety and his own conscience. He had never yet decided what he would do if he was ever given a direct order to kill women and children, and he was glad to know that the point was not going to be tested today.

All of this gave him leisure to begin worrying again about Edwin and Alys, and he was soon sunk in his thoughts once more.

Alys awoke from her afternoon doze to see that Edwin was sitting on the end of the bed. He had his back to her and was bent forward, his arms clutched tightly around himself.

'Edwin?'

The sound of her voice made him jump, and he turned. She could see that he had been crying. 'What is it?'

He rubbed his eyes. 'Nothing. No – that is to say – not nothing. Something has happened.'

She struggled to sit up, needing him to help her. Lord, but she would be glad when this baby was born and her body felt like her own again. *But not yet!*, she added, both as an afterthought and as a prayer. 'Tell me.'

He took a deep and shuddering breath. 'The lord earl is on his way here with armed forces. They've locked the gate and they expect him here before dusk.'

She gasped. 'There will be fighting?'

'Not if I can possibly stop it.' He took her hands. 'And that means I might have to go out, I might have to leave you here. I don't want to leave you in danger, but this has changed things, and the danger to you will be less if I can persuade the lord earl in person not to attack.' He paused. 'Do you see? Can you forgive me if I go?'

Earlier, Alys had been trying to convince him to leave, torn between his safety and having the comfort of his presence. She had been disappointed but also relieved when he had refused, knowing that they would be together. But now ... she wished she felt more awake, less tired and less stupid, so she could think through all of this properly. But her immediate, visceral reaction to the news had been a vision of sharp swords coming towards her and the child in her belly, and that was the thought she needed to escape from.

Edwin was gripping her hands more tightly. He was shaking. But think – if he went out now, he would be safe. He would meet the lord earl on the road, before the army arrived. The force would be men from Conisbrough, they would recognise Edwin from a distance, and they would welcome him back to them. He would be protected. And if anyone was able to persuade the lord earl to change his mind ...

'Of course you must go.' She hoped her voice sounded steadier than she felt.

Edwin now ran his hands through his hair. 'But to leave you! And at such a time.' His voice was cracking, and it made her heart break. 'And here!'

Alys could hear the sounds of men assembling in the hall. 'Lady Idonea will surely find me somewhere safer to sleep while you're away. Don't forget – they still think I'm a merchant's wife from Lincoln, so their hospitality should hold.'

Edwin nodded. His eyes were closed and he seemed on the verge of adding something, but he didn't. Tears squeezed out from between his lashes, and Alys felt such a deep and abiding love for him that she was almost overcome.

They spoke for some while before she started to raise herself off the bed. 'There's no point in putting it off – we'd best go and tell Sir Robert about your change of heart. The sooner the better, as you'll be able to meet the lord earl before he gets too close.'

He nodded without speaking, still dazed himself, and helped her up.

By the time they had wound their tortuous way round the motte and then up the stairs to the keep's chamber, Alys was exhausted again, though she wasn't sure whether it was just physical, or whether the additional worry had weakened her. She gratefully took the proffered seat while she listened to 'Thomas' explaining that he had changed his mind and was now happy to take up Sir Robert's offer. 'But,' he added, 'there is one firm condition.'

'Which is?'

'If my wife is to remain here without me, she must be lodged up here in the keep, and not on her own in the guest chamber off the hall.'

Sir Robert and Lady Idonea exchanged glances. 'Agreed, of course. Every courtesy will be shown to you, mistress.'

Alys could do no more than nod, though she didn't really like the eager look that had come into Lady Idonea's eyes.

'Well,' said Sir Robert, 'Now that's settled, we may as well move straight away. No sense in wasting time.'

Edwin came to kneel by Alys's side, and they embraced for a long moment. Now that the moment of parting had come, Alys didn't feel quite so brave. She kept reminding herself that Edwin would be safe, and that avoiding violence and bloodshed would be best for everyone, even if it meant their separation. And she would do everything she could to help him.

'I won't come down,' she murmured in his ear. 'If they all leave I might be able to search the bedchamber for the document.' Alys couldn't read, of course; but, as she'd mentioned to Edwin in their room, she thought that a document with an official seal on it ought to be fairly easy to recognise. And Edwin had said that everything would be much easier if only he could find it.

'Don't do anything risky,' he whispered back. Then he pulled back a little so that his words were more audible. 'Take care of yourself, my love, and rest. I'll be back as soon as I can.'

He kissed her, and then was gone. She wouldn't cry. She *wouldn't*.

Sir Robert accompanied Edwin out of the room, but unfortunately for Alys's plan Lady Idonea and Margaret both remained. A search would have to wait until another time, but they would surely leave the chamber at some point.

Alys managed to stand up and make her way over to one of the window slits. She stood there, the cool draught of air playing on her face, as she watched Edwin reach the bottom of the motte's path and head over to the stables. Sir Robert gave some orders, and soon the horse and wagon were being hitched and Edwin was taking his place in the driving seat. He flicked the reins and drove over to the gatehouse; at another word from Sir Robert, the gates were hauled open and the wagon passed through.

Edwin was gone.

'Don't worry,' came Lady Idonea's voice from behind her. 'We'll keep you safe here.'

Alys didn't answer, partly as she had nothing to say in reply, and partly as her attention was now caught by a different stir in the bailey. After Edwin left, she expected that the gates would close straight away, but they did not. The reason for this soon became apparent when a party of three monks rode in on mules; they must have crossed paths with Edwin and called out for admittance.

They were all in Cistercian white robes, and therefore presumably came from Roche. Yes, one was the monk who had been here before: Prior Richard. The second was a very tall man who was completely bald, and the third was being treated with such deference that he must surely be the abbot himself.

Sir Robert was pointing up to the keep, so Alys needed to decide how she was going to behave. She had the advantage that they wouldn't want to speak to her – it wouldn't occur to monks to ask the opinion of a woman on anything. She would therefore be dignified and silent, in the hope that they would forget she was there and say something that might be of interest to Edw—

Tears came to her eyes.

Inconveniently, she now found that she needed to use the garderobe; another part of pregnancy that she would be happy to see the back of. Fortunately there was, at least, one up here so it didn't involve any more stairs. She indicated to Lady Idonea where she was going and then squeezed herself into the narrow passageway, resisting the temptation to turn sideways, which was not a useful manoeuvre when you were temporarily wider from front to back than you were from side to side.

She was still in there when she heard Sir Robert and the monks enter the chamber. There was no need to worry that they could see anything; the passage turned a corner before it reached the garderobe itself, so they would be unaware of her presence until she chose to come out. She did hear what she thought was a brief query from Sir Robert to his wife, but Lady Idonea evidently either answered it in a low voice or simply indicated the garderobe passage, for he did not pursue it.

Some conversation began, and Alys crept nearer the passage entrance.

'… unexpected honour, Father Abbot,' Sir Robert was saying. He sounded a little on edge, which Alys supposed was only natural given that one of the realm's most powerful men was currently marching an army towards him.

'I felt obliged to come myself,' said a voice Alys didn't recognise. 'This dispute must end, now, before violence ensues.'

Sir Robert laughed, an odd, high-pitched sound. 'You'd better tell that to Earl Warenne, Father, not me.'

'I shall. Prior Richard and I will do everything in our power to dissuade him from hasty action.'

'I'm grateful, Father, and to you, Prior. And also to …?'

'This is Brother Durand, our infirmarer. If there are – which God forbid – to be injuries or wounds to be dressed, he will be able to assist.'

'Let's hope it doesn't come to that.'

'Indeed,' said the abbot. 'But, after much careful deliberation and prayer, I also consider it my duty to tell you that a great deception has already been practised upon you.'

'What? What sort of deception?'

Alys hoped he wasn't about to say what she feared.

'Prior Richard will be able to tell you more, though I can certainly confirm his story now I've seen the man myself.'

Oh dear.

The abbot's words seemed to give Sir Robert an idea of where this was heading. 'Man?' he asked, sharply. 'Whom do you mean?'

Prior Richard now spoke. 'I hesitated about saying anything when I was here previously, because I wanted to consult Father Abbot before doing so, and because I thought there was a chance that violence might be avoided. But the discovery of the justice's body, and the earl's subsequent actions, have made the situation more urgent.'

'But what man are you speaking of?'

'Again, I would hesitate if I thought I was putting him or his wife in danger, but now that they have left I can say it freely: Thomas, as he told you he was called, is not a merchant and he is not from Lincoln. His real name is Edwin and he is a member of Earl Warenne's personal household.'

Alys closed her eyes as she heard Sir Robert and Lady Idonea's exclamations of horror and anger. There was no point in hiding: they both knew where she was and she had no desire to be dragged out bodily. So, telling herself to be strong for what was to come, she stepped out into the chamber.

Edwin cursed to himself as he drove past the monks riding the other way. He tried to keep his head down, but he knew they had seen him: not only Prior Richard but also the abbot and the man he recognised as the infirmarer. All would be able to identify him – what would this mean for Alys?

He had to resist the urge to turn around and go back to the castle. He must. Alys's safety would be best assured by preventing any physical assault on the castle, and by him discovering what in the Lord's name was going on – who had killed the justice, who had hidden the document, if there was one, and who was in the right of the dispute. But he knew that the earl was going to be in a hurry to get the Tickhill question settled before he went to London, so he had to *think*. Which was difficult when the whole of his mind was taken up with anxiety and raw, shredding grief.

Mother. Poor, poor mother. What had she been through, before she died? How had she suffered, and he not there? Of course, he wouldn't have been at her side in any case, as no men were allowed in a birthing chamber, but she could at least have had the comfort of knowing that he was nearby and praying for her. Instead her last days and hours had been spent not only in agony but in worrying about him.

He drove up Tickhill's deserted main street, past the shuttered and bolted houses and shops, past the church. Mother was with God now; that must be his comfort. And presumably also the child with her – Edwin would pray for it and find out later if it had lived long enough to have a name, and whether he had briefly had a brother or a sister. And he would pray for Sir Geoffrey, whose grief must be overwhelming.

There was no way he could have told Alys. She and Mother had developed a close relationship since they had met, had loved each other; for her to find out that Mother was dead – and dead in childbirth – so soon before her own confinement, and just as she was about to be left alone in a hostile place, would have been too much. No, the knowledge was a cross he would have to bear on his own for the time being.

Edwin left the town behind and followed the road that led northward to Conisbrough. By his reckoning he'd travelled about half a mile – and made no progress at all with his thoughts – when a group of riders came towards him, one moving ahead to call for him to get off the road and make way.

It was Everard. Edwin halted his wagon and waited for the sergeant to get near enough to recognise him. When he did, his surprise was great. 'Edwin! Why are you … what's happening inside Tickhill? We're on our way there.'

'I know, and I need to talk to the lord earl.'

A look of relief swept over Everard's face. 'You've sorted everything out? The lads won't need to fight?'

'Not quite – or, at least, not yet. But I might be able to persuade my lord to reconsider, or at least to wait. How far behind do you think he is?'

'Not far. So you can wait here for him to catch up, or … no, the quicker the better.' Everard called to one of the men in his party, who swapped places with Edwin. 'Now, drive carefully, you hear? Edwin's wife will be lying in the back there, and we don't want her jolted around.'

'She's not,' said Edwin, not trusting himself to say more in case his emotions got the better of him, and forcing himself to concentrate on the unfamiliar horse.

'What? But —' Everard looked at Edwin and pulled himself up short. Then a horrified expression began to dawn on his face. 'And you won't have heard the other news …'

'I have.'

'I'm so sorry,' said Everard, simply.

'We'll have time to grieve properly later. At the moment we need to prevent any more deaths.'

Everard nodded. 'Off you go, then. We're to go ahead and find the best place to set up camp, so I'll no doubt see you later.'

They parted, and Edwin rode as fast as he dared in the Conisbrough direction. It wasn't long before he could see the large armed party, the earl and some others on horseback while the rest marched in good order. He reined in so there was no chance of him being perceived as a threat – if they saw someone apparently charging towards them he might not live long enough to explain anything – and awaited their challenge.

Again a man left the main party to ride towards him, and it didn't take Edwin long to see that it was Martin.

As he got closer Martin's face broke into a huge grin. 'Edwin! You're back! Oh, I can't tell you how glad —'

Edwin cut him off. 'I need to speak with the lord earl immediately,' he said, looking past Martin rather than at him. 'May I?'

Martin's face fell. 'Of course,' he replied, stiffly. 'Go ahead.' He hesitated, but only added 'I'll tell him,' before he turned and rode back.

Edwin was soon swallowed up by the group as it reached him, the earl accompanied by his squires and a couple of knights Edwin vaguely recognised as owing service to him from somewhere nearby.

The earl saw the direction of his gaze. 'The others I've summoned will meet us there – we didn't have time to wait for them. I hope you're about to tell me that when we reach Tickhill, the gates will be open and Sir Robert will be ready to hand over the keys?'

'I'm afraid it's not quite as simple as that, my lord.'

'Why not?'

'May I explain in full?'

'Might as well – there's not much else to do until we get there. Proceed.'

As they rode Edwin ran through all that had happened and the progress he'd made, such as it was. By the time he'd nearly finished they were back in the town again, and Edwin tailed off as he saw a lone figure standing in the middle of the empty high street.

It was a priest. He was quite obviously petrified, but he stood his ground and raised one shaking hand.

The earl didn't seem perturbed; on the contrary. He leaned over in his saddle and murmured a few words to one of the knights, who moved forward.

Edwin looked on in dread. The knight was evidently a hard-bitten man, but surely he wasn't about to attack a man of the cloth?

The priest must have been wondering the same, but still he stood his ground.

The knight took a deep breath and then boomed in a startlingly loud voice, 'Let it be known that the merciful Earl Warenne intends no harm to any of the people of Tickhill. His quarrel is with Sir Robert de Vieuxpont alone. Stay in your homes and you shall be left alone.' He took another breath. 'Be it known, however, that any attempt to interfere with Earl Warenne or to prevent him taking the castle that is rightfully his will be met with severe consequences.' He lowered his voice a little, although he was still perfectly audible, and spoke directly to the priest. 'Understood?'

'Yes, Sir Knight.'

'Good. Now, get back into your church and pray that you don't have too many dead to bury before this is all over.'

Edwin expected that the priest would now retreat, but with what was incredible bravery under the circumstances, he turned and took a few paces towards the houses on the other side of the road and made the sign of the cross in the air. 'God is with you all,' he called to those who were surely listening intently behind their shuttered windows. 'I will pray ceaselessly in the church for your safety, and will come without hesitation to any house where anyone needs me.'

The knight moved a couple of paces nearer to the priest's back and loosened one foot from his stirrup, evidently preparing to kick, and Edwin saw Martin make a sudden move forward. Edwin was able to push his own horse in front of Martin's and the resulting small commotion was enough to distract the knight, giving the unsuspecting priest time to walk off towards the church with his dignity intact.

'My apologies,' said Edwin to the knight. 'I'm still not all that used to horses and I couldn't control it.'

He received a look of daggers in return, and a hoarse laugh from the second knight. This one leaned towards Edwin, allowing him a close-up view of a scarred face and an empty eye socket. 'I wouldn't try that on my brother again, if I were you.'

Then they were all in motion again, heading for the castle. Instead of making for the gatehouse they went a few hundred yards further up the Roche road and then pulled off it into an open space – the town common where animals could be grazed, though there were none there now. This afforded a clear view of the front of the castle, defended not only by its gatehouse and curtain wall but also a water-filled moat. They were, by Edwin's calculations, out of bowshot.

All was organised chaos for a while as horses were picketed and tents erected. Fortunately Martin was busy and didn't come near Edwin, who didn't want to see him. Edwin could hear Martin listening to Everard's initial report – 'moat goes about two-thirds of the way round, the rest is dry ditch but that's on the motte side; it's very steep and there's a clear line of sight down from the top of the keep for archers, so not the best place to attack, and there's a deep fishpond ...' – and then relaying the information to the earl and his knights.

Edwin, meanwhile, stood stock still in the midst of all the movement, his eyes riveted on the castle walls. It was nearing dusk, and would be full dark before too long, and Alys was hardly going to make an appearance among the row of suspicious faces on top of the gatehouse, but still he watched. She was in there. She would know by now that the earl's force had arrived, and she would know that he was with it. He would stand here so she could feel his presence even if she couldn't see it. They were joined forever by bonds of love, and those could stretch across a kingdom, never mind a wall and a moat.

Edwin kept his eyes on the battlements until he was summoned to the earl's tent. There was to be a council, which meant that Edwin was to be party to discussions on how a force of men armed with deadly weapons could best attack the castle in which the dearest objects of his life were sheltering.

Chapter Seven

Alys saw the look of horror on Prior Richard's face when he noticed her. He jumped to his feet in consternation.

'You!' began Lady Idonea, her voice rising. She took a step towards Alys, who couldn't help shrinking back with her hands protectively over her stomach, but fortunately the abbot was quicker, moving to interpose himself with his arms spread wide. Once he was sure Lady Idonea had stopped, he looked questioningly at the prior.

'Father, this is Edwin's wife.' Prior Richard addressed her directly. 'I'm sorry, mistress – I didn't know you were still here or I would have chosen my words more carefully.'

Sir Robert's face was like thunder. 'All this time you've been sitting here talking about cloth, and you were *spying* on us?' He looked just as angry as his wife, and so too did Margaret, sitting over by the wall and now staring at Alys with undisguised malevolence.

The abbot raised both his hands. 'Peace, I pray you.' He turned to Alys and motioned her to the seat he had just vacated, waiting until she had lowered herself carefully before continuing. 'Sir Robert, my lady, your anger should be directed to the proper quarter. That is, towards Edwin himself and the earl who sent him. A wife has no choice but to obey her husband, and I'm sure she would rather not have been here at all, especially in her present condition.'

Alys certainly agreed with the second part of that. She might normally have queried the first half, but just now she was grateful for his assumptions as she sought to calm her wildly beating heart. She actually felt quite faint, and hoped she wasn't about to humiliate herself by swooning.

Brother Durand now stood and offered his own stool to the abbot, who placed it next to Alys's and seated himself. His physical presence between her and Sir Robert and Lady Idonea was reassuring to a certain extent, but she still felt as though the wave of panic might overwhelm her at any moment.

The abbot was continuing. 'As such, I am placing this woman under my personal protection. Any attempt to harm her or to treat her with anything other than courtesy will incur my displeasure and that of the Church.'

There was a pause before Sir Robert nodded grimly, trying to contain his anger. 'But,' he added, 'you will at least allow me to have a guard posted on her so that she doesn't try to escape – or, indeed, to harm herself?'

After a moment's thought the abbot agreed. 'This is your right as the holder of the castle. But be aware that the same strictures apply to your guard – she is not to be touched or distressed in any way. If she is hurt and her child dies, I will consider it murder in the eyes of God.'

The word 'murder' didn't do much for Alys's state of mind.

Sir Robert went to the top of the stairs, shouted down and then issued some instructions to the man who came up in response. Alys kept her eyes on the floor while she attempted to steady her breathing and concentrated on remaining conscious. She needed to think about how she could best use the situation to her advantage, but she couldn't get her mind to work properly, nor her heart to stop pounding. The child seemed to feel her distress, squirming around in a way that made her feel even more queasy.

Around her the men continued their conversation. She let it wash over her, but tensed when she heard the abbot offer himself as a mediator between the two parties. He would go out, he said, and meet with the earl.

He was sharp, noticing the tiny movement beside him and switching smoothly to a suggestion that he would remain inside Tickhill while Prior Richard went to the earl. 'That way, one of the abbey's senior officials will be in each place.'

'I trust in your neutrality, Father,' said Sir Robert, shortly. He might already be in trouble with the crown, but he wasn't foolish enough to start a dispute with the Church at the same time. The abbot, if he stayed, was powerful enough to offer real protection, and Alys began to breathe a little more easily.

The conversation was interrupted by the arrival of two people at the chamber door. One was the man Sir Robert had given orders to earlier, and the other was Theo.

'He's the best I could come up with,' the elder of the two explained apologetically to Sir Robert. 'We need every grown man ready to defend the walls, and given that he's only being asked to guard a woman in her condition, I thought ...'

'He'll have to do.' Sir Robert addressed Theo directly, pointing at Alys. 'This woman is a liar and a spy,' he began, before catching the abbot's eye and reining himself in. 'You will not leave her side until I tell you otherwise, do you hear? She must not leave the castle, nor speak to anyone except myself, my wife and Father Abbot.'

'Yes, Sir Robert.' Theo took up a station where he could watch Alys. The poor boy looked both confused and aghast, glancing over at his sister in consternation.

The light, always dim up here, faded further as discussions continued; serving men arrived with candles. Lady Idonea instructed them to find a palliasse and blankets, so Alys at least had the relief of knowing she would be sleeping up here, and not locked in some dank cell or forced to share the floor of the hall with the castle men.

Now that she was calmer, she tried to pay more attention to the content of the men's conversation. Prior Richard and Brother Durand would shortly make their way out to where the earl and his forces were camped, with Edwin surely among them. The main gates would need to be opened in order for this to happen, or one of them at least, but it would only open wide enough for the two monks to squeeze through on foot, and then it would be shut and barred again straight away.

The monks would speak with the earl in the hope that he would send a negotiating party to deal with Sir Robert personally; both Abbot Reginald and Prior Richard would be present to help smoothe

the path of the talks. It was the abbot's fervent hope that a peaceful settlement could be reached and bloodshed avoided.

'I hope so too,' were Sir Robert's final words on the subject. 'But I fear there is no middle ground. The earl wants this castle, and I will not give it up until I receive an order from the regent to do so.'

The monks now stood, the abbot blessing the other two ahead of their mission. As they were about to leave, Alys stepped forward. In a meek voice she addressed the prior. 'If you see my husband, sir, would you be so good as to tell him that I am safe and well?'

The prior glanced at the abbot, who nodded. 'Of course, my child.'

'Thank you. When he spoke to me this afternoon he told me to look after myself, and though I can't take complete responsibility for that' – she threw a meaningful glance at Sir Robert – 'I remember and cherish the last conversation we had together.' She lowered her head, sniffed and rubbed a non-existent tear from her eye.

The prior was all sympathy as he made the sign of the cross over her. Then the men all left: Sir Robert and the abbot would see the other two off, and the abbot would then go to the chapel to pray and to hear the confession of any castle men who wished to clear their consciences in the face of imminent danger.

Lady Idonea also went out, and Alys wondered if there was any way she might be able to talk Theo and Margaret into letting her go into the curtained-off area, where she had spotted a large kist on the other side of the bed. If you were going to hide a document somewhere …

Unfortunately, however, it appeared that Lady Idonea had only accompanied the others down the stairs, and not outside. She was back almost before Alys had the chance to smile at Theo, and an extremely uncomfortable hour followed during which Alys had no chance to do anything. Lady Idonea did not let any words fall from her lips that might go against the abbot's injunctions, but she was clearly furious; Margaret attended to her stiffly while ignoring Alys; and Theo stood awkwardly at the side of the room and didn't dare to say anything. Alys remained where she was and tried to think.

Servants arrived with the evening meal, which the four of them ate separately and in silence. Shortly after that, genuinely tired and also not wanting to face Sir Robert when he returned, Alys went to lie down, pulling the blankets over her.

It only now struck Theo, she saw, that he was going to have to watch over her while she was in bed – and, indeed, sleep in the same room, given that he could hardly be expected to stay permanently awake. He stammered that he was sure it would be fine if he kept to the other side of the room, and that once Sir Robert was back he would lie across the door. It opened inwards, so Alys wouldn't be able to move it without waking him.

All of this suited Alys very well. She had no intention of trying to make a night escape, and attempted to make herself comfortable on the palliasse. She was so exhausted that she did initially fall into a light slumber, despite her best efforts. It was during this that she became vaguely aware of Sir Robert returning and of him speaking in a low tone to his wife. Alys wasn't sure whether he then stayed or went back out again; a draught played over her on the floor, but it might have been from one of the arrow slits rather than the door, and she was too sleepy to think about it. Then all noise ceased, and the candles were blown out; darkness and silence reigned.

Alys wasn't sure how long it was after that, or whether she had dozed again, but at some point during the night she became aware of a figure standing over her. She caught her breath in fright and risked opening one eye a tiny fraction before closing it again.

A glimpse had been enough to tell her that it was Lady Idonea. Alys tried to ready herself for action, should it be required, while also trying to keep her breathing deep and steady enough to feign sleep.

After a few moments Lady Idonea slipped away as quietly as she had come, and Alys was able to doze off again, thinking of Edwin and wondering whether Prior Richard had managed to speak to him.

The baby kicked, and she drowsily rubbed her belly. *God willing, little one, we'll be home and safe soon*. But that depended now on her, as well as Edwin and many others.

She knew what she must do tomorrow; she only hoped she had the courage to go through with it.

'The gates are opening!' Hugh's voice was even more high-pitched than usual as it emerged out of the gathering gloom.

Martin was instantly alert, moving forward at the same time as Sir Malvesin. They were both armed, as was nearly everyone else: they needed to guard themselves against surprise attack. Was this going to be it?

'Just two monks,' said the knight, turning his head a little to the side in that way he did. 'And the gate is closing again.'

'Are they really monks?' asked Martin, his hand on his sword as he peered into the twilight. 'Or just wearing robes?'

'Good point. But no, Roche men, I think. Yes, the shorter one's Prior Richard.'

'And the other,' added Martin with a shock of recognition, 'is their infirmarer.' *Just what I needed*, he thought, remembering the antagonistic relationship he'd experienced with Brother Durand during his time at Roche a couple of years ago.

'I'll see what they want.' His arms spread wide and away from his sword hilt, Sir Malvesin walked forward to meet the monks, who had stopped some distance from the camp.

'Go and tell my lord,' Martin instructed Hugh, who ran off.

By the time Sir Malvesin and the two monks reached the camp, Hugh was already back. 'My lord says to bring them to his tent,' he called, skidding to a halt. 'Both of you to come as well, and I'm to fetch Sir Baldwin and Edwin.' He departed at speed, skipping nimbly over the many tent ropes.

'This way, Prior.' Sir Malvesin pointed.

Brother Durand paused when he saw Martin, recognising him immediately. 'You've grown even taller.'

It was not often that Martin met anyone even close to his own size. Brother Durand was also tall, and the last time they'd seen each other there hadn't been much in it, but now Martin realised he'd gained at least another three or four inches. At their final meeting before Martin had left Roche, they had made some progress towards easing the bad blood between them, but Martin was aware that the peace might be fragile, and he didn't want to do anything to break it, especially not now with everything else being so volatile. 'Please follow me,' was therefore all he said.

Brother Durand was not afraid to be blunt. 'You've continued on your path of destruction, I see.'

Martin couldn't help at least a touch of irritation entering his tone. 'Of course I have. What other path is there? I certainly didn't want to become a monk.'

Brother Durand made no move, instead standing with his arms folded inside his sleeves and gazing intently at Martin. 'You've had many experiences since we last met, and not all of them good.'

Oh Lord, why did he have to say that? Just when Martin was trying to keep it all pushed down inside him. Then another memory of Roche struck him, further increasing the misery. 'A good knight uses his head and his heart as well as his right arm, that's what Brother Guy told me. He'll be disappointed when you tell him.' Martin couldn't keep the bitter tone out of his voice.

'Brother Guy is dead.'

'What?' Martin had only known the lay brother for a short while, but oddly he now felt that there was a gaping hole in the world, and it hurt.

Brother Durand sighed. 'He gave his life for another. A bankside tree fell on one of the younger lay brothers, trapping him under the river's surface. Brother Guy had enormous strength, as you know, and he waded in to lift it up, managing to hold it long enough for others to pull the boy out. But then a large section of the bank collapsed, and the earth and the tree crushed him, burying him under the water. It was many hours before his body could be recovered.'

Martin crossed himself. 'May his soul rest in peace.' And Brother Guy would be at peace, wouldn't he? Something Martin didn't think he'd ever know himself.

'He chose his path wisely, at least in later life, and will be judged accordingly.'

He will be judged accordingly, was the thought that filled Martin's mind as he showed Brother Durand to the earl's tent. How would the Lord judge Martin if he were to die without making sure his friends were safe? If he did not atone for his past sins?

Edwin was already there when they arrived, speaking to the prior. Once more he would not meet Martin's eye, and Martin couldn't blame him. To put both of them in danger together was bad enough, but for this to have led to Alys being left alone in hostile surroundings was appalling. He *would* get her out safely, whatever it took.

As the earl and the monks spoke, Martin eyed Brother Durand, and specifically Brother Durand's robe and hood. Those inside Tickhill would be expecting a tall monk to return from the camp, wouldn't they? But the infirmarer would never agree to such a deception, and Martin was hardly going to go up in God's estimation if he beat up a monk to steal his habit.

Edwin was saying something about a document, which didn't hold Martin's attention for long. Strategy and cleverness had failed to achieve the lord earl's aims, so it was time for force, surely. Yes, of course he understood that men of the cloth were bound to try peace efforts first; that was what they saw as their duty. Well, Martin had a duty too.

The talking went on, and the candles began to burn down. Martin indicated to Adam that he should replenish them, and tried to pay attention. As he had known would be the case, the earl was adamant that the castle was his, that Sir Robert needed to hand it over, and that he would not compromise on that point. Sir Baldwin was encouraging him towards martial action, while Sir Malvesin and a couple of other knights who had recently arrived were advising caution.

Eventually the earl lost his patience. 'I will discuss this no further tonight,' he said to the prior. 'Go back behind the walls or sleep here in the camp, whichever you prefer, but if the castle keys are not surrendered to me by noon tomorrow then Sir Robert must bear responsibility for the consequences.'

The monks left, saying they would stay and asking to see the earl again in the morning. Brother William went with them, and Martin whispered to Hugh to run and find Humphrey to tell him to make the necessary arrangements for feeding and accommodating them.

If Edwin had asked, Martin could have told him that now was not a good time to open his mouth. But he didn't ask. 'My lord …'

The earl spun round, his temper still short. 'And I don't want to hear any more from you, either, do you hear? You've failed me, failed badly. Get out.'

Edwin left without saying another word. He didn't look at Martin on his way out.

The earl scanned those remaining, who were all knights, squires and soldiers. 'Good, now let's talk about military matters. We don't have time to starve them out, so what other options do we have?'

This was more like it. Martin's attention was now fully engaged as he listened to the various merits of attacks on the gatehouse, or across the water-filled moat, or round the other side of the castle where it was steeper but the moat was only a dry ditch.

As he listened, an idea came to him, based on his earlier thoughts about Brother Durand. At first he said nothing, because if it was a good idea then surely one of the others would come up with it, and if it was a bad idea then he didn't want to make himself look stupid by suggesting it. But as time went on, the better it seemed, and nobody else said anything.

There was nothing for it. If he was going to look like an idiot, then fine. 'My lord?'

All eyes turned to him.

Martin swallowed. 'I just wondered if I might put forward a different suggestion, my lord.'

'Go on.'

'It's not completely … *honest*, my lord, but it might make things move more quickly.' *And help to get Alys out*, he added, mentally.

This brought more interest, so Martin was emboldened to continue. 'The monks want to speak to you again tomorrow morning. How about if you tell them that you're now willing to talk, and send them back along with some of your knights here as a negotiating party? They will have to open the gates to let them in, and —'

'That wouldn't work,' broke in Sir Baldwin. 'They'd have to be unarmoured and unarmed and could do nothing. Sir Robert wouldn't be foolish enough to let in armed knights who might start a fight.'

The earl motioned him into silence, seeing that Martin hadn't yet finished. 'Go on.'

'If we had a second party hidden, of men who *were* armed, then all the first group would need to do was hold the gate open long enough for them to attack. Maybe the second lot could even bring extra weapons to pass to the unarmed men.'

There were considering nods from around the tent, including from the earl. 'It would have to be quite a small group if they were to stay hidden,' he said, slowly. 'But once they attacked, the garrison would be distracted enough for us to launch a full-scale mounted assault on the gatehouse.'

Sir Baldwin, now in a more approving tone, noted that if men were armed, mounted and ready in the camp, it wouldn't take long for them to charge across the open space. 'And once we're inside the walls, we'll have them. A few might be able to retreat to the keep, but we can take that if it happens – threatening to hang a few captives will soon have them out.'

'All of this,' admitted Martin, trying to ignore Sir Baldwin's last words, 'would be dangerous for those in the first, unarmed party, but I'd be happy to volunteer for that myself.'

There were murmurs of assent and a few other offers. 'Excellent,' said the earl, clapping his hands together. 'We'll go with Martin's plan, then. Let's get to work on the details.'

Edwin wandered miserably through the camp, illuminated now only by small cooking fires and the glimmerings of a new moon. There was nobody he could trust, and it appeared that he couldn't even trust himself. He'd failed his lord, failed his mother, failed his wife … failed *everybody*. Plus he couldn't get rid of the nagging feeling that he was missing something very important. If only he could clear his mind enough to think properly then it might come to him, but he was too agonised about Alys. Fortunately, he told himself, she didn't seem to be in any immediate danger: Prior Richard had explained and apologised to Edwin for what he'd inadvertently done, and assured him that Alys was now under the abbot's personal protection. But could Edwin even trust the abbot? It pained him to suspect a churchman, but …

What Edwin really needed to do was to find a way to protect Alys from herself. If she would only sit quietly and meekly, insisting she'd acted only under duress and casting no further suspicion on herself, that would be best for her. But would she do that? Ha. While they had been in their guest chamber earlier that day, just before they went to tell Sir Robert that Edwin would take up his offer, Edwin and Alys had briefly discussed the likelihood of various scenarios and the possible ways in which they could navigate them. Fortunately, none had yet come to pass, so that was some reassurance, but she would still no doubt continue their search for the missing document as and when she could, which would be risky.

But he was *missing something*. Was it something else Alys had said earlier that day? His devastating grief at overhearing the news of his mother's death meant that he could only remember snatches of what had happened afterwards, most of them related to what Alys might or might not have to endure once he was gone.

As he wandered, Edwin found himself being hailed by Humphrey, who asked if he was hungry. Realising he hadn't eaten since the morning, Edwin accepted a bowl of stew and sat down. Once he'd finished it he felt a little less shaky, and he stared into the fire in an attempt to concentrate.

Somebody knew something. Somebody, somewhere, knew what the ordained fate of Tickhill castle was, and whoever he was, he was suppressing the information. Logically, he would only suppress it if the decision had gone against him. This very obvious idea had been at the forefront of Edwin's mind all along, but it was no use just repeating it: he needed to push himself further, to move on from the obvious, to find the correct thread in the tangled mess of the weaving and follow it.

Legally, either the lord earl or Sir Robert was going to lose this case: there was no middle ground. For Sir Robert this would mean losing his position and the place where he lived – a serious matter. For the earl it would mean only a lack of gain and a loss of face and reputation, although he might consider that just as bad or worse. Either man, therefore, might be desperate enough to kill in order to get his way, although this was surely not a long-term solution, for eventually the might of the crown would mobilise to enforce its decision.

Edwin didn't have the luxury of waiting for the crown to act. So what else was there?

Rich and powerful men, if they wanted to kill, did not have to do it themselves. But who would the earl and Sir Robert trust enough to do the deed for them? Family, of course, would always stick together, but here the available suspects were thin. The earl had no sons or brothers. Sir Robert and Lady Idonea had no children. Brothers? Lady Idonea didn't, of course; she wouldn't be an heiress otherwise. But Edwin wasn't so sure about Sir Robert, so he made a note in his mind to see if he could find out. A reckless younger brother looking out for his family's interest – maybe even acting on his own authority without direct instructions? – would be a good suspect.

Loyal retainers were the other possibility. Edwin had seen enough of Sir Geoffrey's integrity and sense of right and wrong, up to and including his recent implied criticism of the earl's actions, to be certain that he wouldn't murder a royal justice in such circumstances.

Adam and Hugh were out for reasons of size and strength, as well as conscience. Edwin's mind shied away from the very possibility that he might have to suspect Martin, but he knew he would have to consider it sometime. Sir Robert no doubt had trusted men of his own too, though Edwin didn't know them well enough to judge.

It all came back to the contents of the document. If only Edwin could find it and read it himself —

Of course. That was it! That was what he'd been missing. What a blind fool he'd been. For anyone to know which way the royal order had gone, he would need to be able to *read* the document. Well, that would certainly cut down the list. And that was what had been bothering Edwin about trying to remember something Alys had said: she would continue searching for it if she could, even though she would only recognise it as an official-looking parchment with a seal. She didn't need to read it; she only needed to pass it over to Edwin.

Reminding himself of Alys naturally made Edwin's mind fill with worry about her again. He was still wallowing in his misery when a shadow fell over him, a darker patch of night. He looked up and was able to make out the figure of Adam.

Within a moment Edwin was half up on his feet, thinking the earl had summoned him once more, but Adam motioned him to stay where he was. 'Do you mind if I sit down?'

Adam was a very different type of squire to Martin, quiet and thoughtful, and now he was clearly considering his words with care before speaking. Eventually he began with a sincere, 'I am so very sorry about your lady mother.'

Edwin fought to keep back the tears that sprang to his eyes once more, glad that they were in near darkness. 'Do you know anything about it? What happened?'

'Not much, I'm afraid. She was confined two days ago, in her and Sir Geoffrey's quarters, with Cecily and Agnes and others to look after her.'

'So it started normally?'

'Yes, no accident or fall or anything, or not that I know of. But after that … well, we just didn't hear any news. It went on and on, and the longer we waited the more worried Sir Geoffrey was – we all were.'

'How she must have suffered.'

'She was in God's grace, I know that – Father Ignatius heard her confession before it started. And she had her sister with her.'

Edwin nodded, not trusting himself to speak.

'And of course you have a sister of your own now, so that's one blessing.'

'A sister?'

'Didn't you know?'

'No. I didn't know anything about the baby, even whether it – she – was alive or dead. Is she healthy?'

'She seems likely to survive, Cecily says. She's very tiny, but then most babies are. I remember when my own little sister was born.'

'I didn't know you had one.' Edwin realised he didn't know much about Adam at all, except that he had served a very cruel lord indeed before being taken into the earl's service.

Adam's voice took on an affectionate tone. 'She's quite a lot younger than me. I don't see her very often, but whenever I do she comes running up to me with the biggest smile, and she's so pleased to see me – it makes me very happy.'

A sister. All this time, of course, Mother and Sir Geoffrey had been talking about a son, because that's what everyone did, and all parents thought of their unborn children as boys until they proved not to be. Edwin wondered if Sir Geoffrey was disappointed at not having a son and heir, and then realised what a stupid thought that was – Sir Geoffrey's grief at losing Mother would be so profound that he'd hardly have a thought to spare for anything else. But surely he would cherish his daughter. Edwin would certainly love his sister, whatever the future held.

Adam remained silent, so Edwin's mind now ran on to the possibility that he might have a daughter. He wouldn't mind at all, as long as Alys and the baby were both healthy, but he knew that her standing among the village women would be improved by having a son. Those mothers who had produced a brood of strapping boys tended to look down on those with a preponderance of daughters.

But all of this depended on Alys being in a safe place to give birth – and even that might not be 'safe', as Mother's death had shown.

He had to think of something else, or he would go mad. 'So, has the lord earl changed his mind? Or is he still determined to attack tomorrow morning?'

'Yes, he's … oh no, wait, you'd already left by then. Martin had an idea.'

Edwin's silence was frosty.

Hesitantly, Adam added, 'He is desperately sorry, you know, for what he did. And he's equally desperate to make it right.'

'I'm sure he is. But I don't think he can.'

'Well …'

Edwin fought against himself and eventually decided that he'd better find out what was going on, for Alys's sake. 'All right – what was this idea?'

'It's about what we're going to do in the morning. I came to tell you – because Martin knew you wouldn't want to speak to him – and he and Everard are going among the men now and telling them quietly. Nobody is to tell any of the monks, my lord says – not even Brother William.'

That didn't sound good. 'Tell them what?'

Edwin listened in growing horror to the details.

'So,' concluded Adam, 'the first party will only have three men in it, all dressed in civilian clothes, so Sir Robert doesn't get too suspicious.' He enumerated on his fingers. 'One, Martin himself; two, Sir Malvesin, because it would look odd if there wasn't a knight leading it; and three, Willikin, who is the most likely to be able to hold the gate open until the others can get there.'

'And they're all going to be unarmed? But then armed men will come running, and then also horses as well?'

'Yes.'

'No. No, no, no! Doesn't he realise he's just put Alys in more danger than ever?'

'How so? The fighting will be all round the gatehouse, and she'll be safe up in the keep. And they wouldn't use her to take revenge! No knight – no real man – would ever do so. And the abbot will look after her.'

But Edwin wasn't thinking of the keep, because that's not where Alys would be, if he now interpreted her words to Prior Richard correctly. One of the potential situations they had discussed, with Edwin not concentrating properly because of his grief and not really thinking it might happen, was now a distinct possibility – or at least Alys would consider it so. If Edwin was with her now he would strongly advise her against it; indeed, he would absolutely forbid her from doing something so incredibly dangerous, however much she resented him invoking husbandly authority. But he wasn't with her, was he, and he knew she would go through with it.

He jumped to his feet. 'I have to see the lord earl.'

Adam also stood. 'I'm not sure,' he said, hesitantly. 'You know what he said earlier.'

'You don't understand. Tell him it's urgent, tell him that everything might depend on it – tell him anything you like, but I have to see him and talk to anyone who's going to attack the gatehouse tomorrow morning.'

'I …'

'*Please*, Adam – Alys's life might depend on it.'

Chapter Eight

Martin awoke at dawn with a tremor of anticipation. Today was the day.

As soon as his lord was ready Martin sent Hugh to fetch the monks, who were agreeably surprised and apparently not suspicious that the earl had experienced a change of heart overnight and was now happy to negotiate. They probably put it down to God's intervention rather than Martin's, but that suited Martin's purposes.

Yes. Purposes, plural, because Martin was uncomfortably, guiltily aware that his aim for the mission differed from his lord's. The first part of it was the same: approach the castle unarmed, so that the gates would be opened, and then prevent the gates from closing again while also staying alive. But after that the earl would be expecting Martin to fight with his newly arrived reinforcements in order to secure the castle, whereas what Martin was actually going to do was find Alys and get her out, by any means necessary. Of course, he also hoped that the castle would fall easily and without too much bloodshed or loss of life, but that was not his priority. Martin could recall with burning clarity the look on Sir Geoffrey's face when he learned of the loss of his wife, and he did not intend to let Edwin experience the same devastation. He would save Alys or die trying.

What he needed to avoid, of course, was being given a direct order by the earl *not* to look for Alys. If his instructions were general, as they had been up until now, Martin reckoned he could get away with something like 'But she just appeared right there in front of me, my lord, so I thought getting her out would be better for you, as then they wouldn't have a hostage.'

He had never yet disobeyed an order from a superior, though he had to admit he'd come uncomfortably close to it a few months ago, in circumstances of a similarly challenging nature. What would he do this time, if he had to?

Prior Richard left the camp in order to get near enough to the castle to shout to those inside that they should expect a negotiating party within the hour. Wanting to get the other monks out of the tent, the earl told Brother William to take Brother Durand to the makeshift infirmary that was being set up at the rear of the camp 'in case it was needed'. The two of them departed, unaware that the area was likely to be in use rather sooner than they expected.

'Right,' began the earl, briskly. 'Is everyone in place?'

'The second party is armed and assembling, my lord,' replied Sir Baldwin, who would lead it, 'on foot and for now remaining behind the line of tents so they cannot be seen from inside the castle, or by the monks.'

'Good.'

'And there was some very useful scouting last night, my lord; we identified a few blind spots directly under the walls, so we've had four extra men posted there since before dawn, unmoving and ready to jump out. Three of them are carrying a second sword, ready to pass to Malvesin, Martin and your other man as soon as they can.'

'Excellent.'

'The third party can't mount too soon, my lord,' added another knight whose name Martin couldn't recall just now, 'lest they arouse suspicion, but they're all ready over where the horses are picketed.'

The earl nodded. 'I'll join them as soon as we've finished here and got the monks out of the way, so they don't notice. Have a lookout standing by so we know the moment the gates are open – once that's happened it doesn't matter if we're seen, so we need to make our charge straight away. Surprise might be our first weapon, but momentum is our second.'

Sounds of assent came from all around, and men began to move.

The earl bade Martin and Sir Malvesin stay for a moment. 'Your party is going to be most at risk, and I'm grateful.'

'We won't let you down, my lord,' was Sir Malvesin's only reply, but there was pride in his step as he left. Martin gazed after him almost enviously: there went a man who had a straightforward duty to do, who was going to carry it out without question or demur, and who would be praised for doing so. If only Martin's own life were that simple.

Martin and Adam now armed the earl, a task so familiar that it helped to calm everyone's nerves. There was a slight tremor in Hugh's hand as he passed each item over, and Martin gave him a reassuring pat on the shoulder. Hugh would stay here, of course, but if things went wrong it wasn't impossible that the fighting might reach the camp.

The earl swung his arms and stamped his feet to make sure that everything was in place. 'Just carry the helm, and I'll put it on at the last moment,' he instructed Hugh. Then he looked from one squire to the other. 'And we're sure, are we, about what Weaver said last night?'

'Yes, my lord.' That was Adam; Martin made no answer.

The earl noticed his silence. 'And as for you …'

'Yes, my lord?'

'You've volunteered for the riskiest part, and I don't doubt your courage. But do I need to doubt anything else?'

Those slate-grey eyes were inescapable once they locked on to you. 'I can't think what you mean, my lord.'

The earl made a derisive noise. 'You're as transparent as they come. Very well, I will speak more plainly. Your task – your *only* task – is to secure that castle for me, do you hear? No getting side-tracked by daring rescues. This is serious business, not some minstrel's tale.'

Martin watched the others leave. Yes, it was a serious business, but not in the way the earl meant. And now, if he wanted to achieve what he was determined to do, he was going to have to disobey a direct order from his lord. The man to whom he owed allegiance and absolute obedience above all others. The man who held Martin's whole future in his hand.

He, Martin, was about to risk his entire career by defying the earl.

So be it.

Alys awoke with a backache. The straw palliasse had softened the wooden floor a little, but not nearly enough for a woman in the late stages of pregnancy, and she groaned as she sat up, rubbing at the lower part of her spine.

Theo was asleep over on the other side of the room, across the doorway. Alys sat in silence for a while, trying to work out whether the breathing she could hear from the other side of the curtain meant that Lady Idonea and Margaret were still asleep, and, if so, whether she might be able to slip round and have a look in the kist without being noticed. But she could hardly 'slip' anywhere at the moment, could she? Ungainly as she was, she would knock into something and wake them up, and her presence – given what they already knew of her – would be suspicious in the extreme. She couldn't risk them deciding to confine her to the chamber.

Anyway, it was time for the inevitable trip to the garderobe, and by the time Alys emerged Lady Idonea was up and the opportunity had gone.

Alys looked warily at her hostess and braced herself for ... she didn't know what. Shouting? Name-calling? Frosty silence? Hopefully not physical violence, at least. She was already anxious about what she planned to do later that morning and exhausted and sore from her night on the floor; she didn't need any additional worries about defending herself.

But Lady Idonea seemed to have calmed down this morning, at least as far as Alys was concerned. 'I shouldn't have spoken to you that way yesterday. I was shocked to find out the truth, but of course it's not your fault – you had no choice but to obey your husband.' She looked more closely. 'You haven't slept well, have you? I did come to check on you in the night, wondering if I should invite you to share my bed seeing as Robert wasn't there, but you were fast asleep so I thought it better to leave you.'

Was this friendliness something Alys needed to be suspicious of? She was too tired to consider it properly, and she was feeling some very strange twinges. She was glad to fold into the seat at the table that Lady Idonea offered her, and to take up her suggestion of something to eat. 'Breakfast isn't a meal served generally, but someone in your condition needs food. Theo!'

Theo had by this time awoken and was standing by the door, watching Alys and yawning copiously. 'Yes, my lady?'

'Shout down for a man to come up, and I'll organise something for our guest to eat.'

It wasn't long before some bread and honey appeared, along with a cup of weak morning ale. Margaret thumped it down on the table – she hadn't forgiven Alys yet, evidently – but Lady Idonea sat with Alys as she ate, chatting away about Conisbrough, asking her if she lived in the castle or the village, wondering how well she knew the lord earl and the other members of the household and garrison. Alys tried to remain alert, finding a balance between encouraging the sociability and not giving too much away. But she was so tired.

After a while she stood up and tried to stretch. 'I wonder, my lady, if you would permit me to walk about? Outside, in the bailey? With Theo, of course. I think it would help to wear off some of this stiffness.'

Lady Idonea's expression was doubtful.

'Please, my lady. I won't get in anyone's way, and you can be sure I'm not in a state to do any harm. Just some air, and perhaps a few moments in the chapel to pray.' A sudden idea struck her. 'Or perhaps even on the roof of the keep? I'll certainly be out of harm's way there.' *And able to see over the walls and outside the castle.*

Eventually Lady Idonea nodded. 'You are to stay close to her at all times, do you understand?' she instructed Theo. 'Don't let her out of your sight, and don't let her talk to anyone.'

Theo opened the door and held it while Alys went out. Of course, her wonderful idea now meant that she would have to go up a flight of stairs, but if she took it very slowly and carefully …

After some while Alys emerged on to the roof. She paused to catch her breath, leaning back against a high part of the crenellations that was taller than she was.

'You don't need to hide behind there, mistress,' said Theo. 'We're much too far away from their camp for any arrows to reach you.' His words were reassuring, but he sounded jumpy. Although that wasn't surprising, was it? He would have plenty of nerves about the prospect of combat.

'That's good to know, thank you,' she replied. Her real reasons, of course, were a combination of fatigue and not wanting to be seen herself, just yet, by any sharp eyes from the camp. It was too early for what she wanted to do, and as she peered round the stone embrasure she could see that she was in any case far too high and too distant to attempt any kind of communication. Her heart groaned at the thought that she would have to go all the way down several flights of keep stairs, then down the motte, then across the bailey and somehow up on the outer wall. How on earth would she manage it without collapsing?

She was exhausted already, and it was so, so tempting just to stay here. This would be the furthest point away from any fighting, and she could just sit and wait for it to be over, cradling her belly and protecting her unborn child. Nobody would blame her.

Nobody except herself, that is. For she would always know that she had taken the coward's way out, that she had left Edwin and the others to face a danger that could have been lessened if she had only been brave enough to take action. And what if Edwin were to be hurt, or, God forbid, killed? She had an obligation to protect her child, yes – which, at this point, meant protecting her own body – but she also had wider responsibilities and that included making sure her child would have a father.

'Did you want to walk about a bit, mistress?' Theo sounded concerned. 'I don't know what's best for you, but you'll be in no danger, not ye— I mean, not here.'

'I find myself a little dizzy from being so high up,' Alys replied. 'Let's just take a single turn around this path – perhaps you can stay on the outside so I'm not so near the edge – and then we'll go down. Perhaps I'll be better off walking in the bailey, as I originally suggested to Lady Idonea.'

She took a first step but immediately tripped on something – a coil of rope lying on the path, she saw – and had to grab at Theo. He prevented her from falling and then, blushing, asked if he should hold her arm as they went round.

'That would be lovely.' She smiled at him. He was a polite and kind boy, and she was sorry for the deception she was going to practise on him once they got down from here, but she'd do her best to keep him, as well as herself, out of harm's way. 'So,' she continued, searching for a friendly topic of conversation that might help put him at his ease, 'it must be nice for you to have your sister here with you, at least until you get more used to being in the garrison. So many boys are sent away by themselves, away from their families. Not,' she added, 'that you need looking after, I'm sure.'

'It's my turn,' said Theo. 'It's my turn to look out for her, now I'm older – her and our mother.' His hand tightened for a moment on Alys's arm. 'It was difficult, when my father died. Mother tried to carry on his business, but it was hard, and she was sad all the time as well as being tired and busy. Margaret looked out for me, but I was too little to be much help.'

'So it was just the three of you, for a while?'

'Yes. Mother got married again, though – he's all right, our stepfather, though he doesn't have much time for us, only his own children. But Margaret and me, we can manage fine by ourselves. It feels like it's always been just us.' He paused. 'I don't know why I'm telling you all this, mistress. But I'm a man now and it's my turn to step up, however much she thinks she still needs to look out for me.'

A man. He was, what, fifteen? Maybe sixteen, but certainly no more. No wonder Margaret had trouble thinking of him as an adult, and fussed over him. And that, no doubt, was why she was so angry with Alys and Edwin; their deception had put her little brother in danger. Alys couldn't blame her.

They reached the top of the stairs. 'Now, mistress, you take it slowly. I'll go a step ahead of you, and then if you trip I'll be able to stop you falling.'

By the time they had made it down and out, Alys was shuffling even more slowly than usual. She felt that the baby had moved, somehow; she was heavier and differently balanced. Perhaps it was just all those stairs. She sincerely hoped that the night spent on the floor hadn't damaged anything, and prayed for a reassuring kick or two to set her mind at rest.

Once they were in the bailey, Alys looked as intently as she dared at the gatehouse. It was a stone building of two storeys: on the upper floor there was a chamber, and under it ran a kind of open tunnel where the gates were situated.

She glanced at the upper chamber. On this inward-facing wall there was a window, so anyone inside could look out over the bailey, but Alys didn't think there had been one on the outside. She tried to recall their arrival, which was the only time she'd seen it from that direction. They had driven up to the castle, and she had looked up from the wagon as they entered the gatehouse ... no, she was fairly sure there wasn't an opening on that side. She could recall only smooth stone. Men could still be positioned on the roof, of course, to drop things down on anyone outside the front of the gatehouse, but no archers would be positioned in the chamber itself.

Alys craned her neck to try to get a good view of the gates themselves, and then nodded in satisfaction. A pair of bulky, heavy wooden gates that opened and closed on hinges, swinging sideways rather than being hauled up and down by a rope like a portcullis. They opened inwards, so were pulled to open and pushed to close, then secured with a wooden bar that fitted across both.

Obviously the gates were shut and barred now, but judging by their size Alys reckoned that a number of men would be needed to move them, and that this would take some time – it wasn't just like shutting a light cottage door, which could be done in moments. All of which suited her purpose.

Another wave of exhaustion swept over her, and she asked Theo if they might visit the chapel. With her plan now firmly in mind, as well as her looming eventual confinement and its attendant dangers, it was time to make her confession. Just a precaution, she told herself. She wasn't really going to die today.

But just in case.

Edwin's eyes watered as he stared at the castle's outer walls, so intense was his gaze. He was shaking, he knew he was, but he didn't care. He couldn't look away in case Alys should appear, but he didn't want her to. He hoped and wished and prayed that she wasn't going to go through with her plan, even though he'd already told the earl about it; looking stupid to his lord would be a small price to pay in return for Alys's safety if she'd decided against it and stayed safely up in the keep.

Everard stood next to him, fidgeting almost as much. 'You will be careful, won't you?' asked Edwin, for what was at least the twentieth time.

'Of course. Most of the lads know what your wife looks like – and even the ones who don't are aware she's with child, which should make her easy to spot. But I've given them all the strictest instructions that no woman at all is to be touched or harmed. None. I don't know how many are in there – at least another two, from what you said – but I told them I would personally flay alive any man who harmed a woman, whoever she was.'

Edwin hoped the threat would be enough. But when they were in the heat of battle men could become wild, he knew that, and when blood lust took over …

Last night he had begged and pleaded with the earl to be allowed to join one of the parties that would move on the castle, but he had been flatly refused. He couldn't go with the first, 'negotiating' party, for his name was tainted as far as Sir Robert was concerned, and if he spotted

Edwin then he might not open the gates at all. And there was no point sending him with either of the two following groups, because they were there to fight and he would be a hindrance. Besides, although he'd failed in this instance, he was still a valuable man for the earl to have around, and the earl didn't want him killed. So all Edwin could do was watch and wait.

Over towards the earl's command tent, Edwin could see that Prior Richard was ready, and was enquiring as to why there was a delay in them setting out. They were, of course, waiting for any kind of sign from Alys, which they couldn't tell the prior, but he would eventually get suspicious if the procrastination continued. The earl knew this and had given orders that they were to go ahead anyway if they had seen nothing that could be interpreted as a signal by the middle of the morning.

Edwin's eyes flicked from the castle walls to the position of the sun and back again as he watched and waited.

'Let's go up on to the wall, so we can look out and see what's outside,' suggested Alys, once they'd left the chapel, trying to sound light-hearted and not hold her breath as she waited for the reply.

Theo was, unsurprisingly, hesitant. 'I don't think we'd be allowed …'

Alys gave him her most charming smile. 'Go on. There's no attack going on, so we'd be perfectly safe.' She remembered how keen he was to sound grown up. 'I bet you've never even seen a real army before.' She began to drift towards one of the staircases that led up to the curtain wall, between the gatehouse and the stables.

The natural belligerence and pride of a youth who wasn't really as mature as he made out showed through for a moment. 'Well, I bet you never have, either.'

Alys put one foot on the first stair, hoping nobody was going to shout out to them to stop. 'Actually, I have. I'm from Lincoln, and I was there when the city and the castle were besieged, two years ago.'

His jaw dropped. 'Really? Wait – I thought Sir Robert said you were only pretending to come from there.'

'My husband is from Conisbrough, but I was born and brought up in Lincoln before I married him.' She was three steps up.

He followed her without thinking. 'And what was it like? I mean, seeing that big French army? Were there thousands of them, all camped? With knights and banners and everything?'

'Oh, it was …' Alys rambled on, saying whatever came into her mind, as she reached the top of the stairs and the wall-walk. Here was the first moment of danger – would someone in the camp shoot an arrow or crossbow bolt as soon as they saw a head appearing over the parapet? Not if they were expecting to start a peace negotiation, surely. And were they too far away? She had no idea, but prepared to duck in any case.

No shouts were heard nor arrows loosed, and the two of them peered around one of the battlements. Theo looked down, peering intently at the base of the wall, but Alys gazed outwards. The camp was – to her eyes anyway – quite small, the earl's army nothing like the size of the one that had attacked Lincoln two years ago.

Theo was now looking at it too, and seemed quite overawed. Alys felt a pang for him and hoped he would emerge unscathed from whatever was about to happen, along with his family. None of this was his fault, after all. Indeed, none of it was the fault of any of the people who were most in danger, was it? But that was the way of the world.

She stared at the rows of tents, much more easily discernible from here than they had been from the top of the keep. Edwin would be out there, somewhere, and able to see her now. She took a brief moment to compose herself: it was time.

'Well,' she said, 'I suppose we shouldn't stay up here too long.' She stepped in front of the lower part of the crenellation, stretched her arms out wide and yawned. 'I've walked off some of my aches and pains, so perhaps we'd better go back to the keep so I can rest.'

He agreed and turned away, meaning that she could spot the sudden movement among the tents but he did not. Now, how long would it take the monks to walk from there to the gatehouse? The timing would have to be exactly right.

As they reached the top of the staircase she could see a small group leaving the camp on foot, and she paused.

Theo saw it too. 'That's the same two monks as yesterday, isn't it, coming back? With some men coming to speak to Sir R— oh my word! Is that a giant?'

Alys looked more closely at the group. 'Goodness, yes, he is tall,' she said, trying to keep her voice casual. 'I've noticed him about the place at Conisbrough.' It seemed odd to see Martin in the negotiating party along with the monks, and for one moment she was puzzled; but of course, as soon as she recognised one of the other figures as Willikin, she could guess what they were about.

A deep breath, and it was time to go. Just this one last task, this one small thing, and then she could rest.

Men were being moved into position to lift the bar, and once they had done so she would need to play her part: she intended to create enough of a diversion, both dramatically and physically, to stop the gates being shut and barred again. This was one of the ideas that she and Edwin had discussed yesterday – was it only yesterday? – before he had left. She'd been surprised that he hadn't protested about it more vociferously, but he'd seemed quite distracted while they were talking, no doubt horrified at the prospect of armed conflict.

Alys didn't intend to put herself in any more danger than was absolutely necessary. She certainly wasn't going to try to fake a fall down the stairs; no, she would simply get as close to the men with the bar as she could without being noticed, and would then play-act that her labour was starting.

As she made her way down, Theo not suspecting the true reason why she was moving so slowly, she considered the space and measured the distance carefully. What she wanted to avoid was ending up on the outer side of the gate, even when it was open, because if they needed to they could simply push it shut, taking her with it and leaving her locked out and vulnerable. No, she needed to time her intervention so that those closing the gate would be distracted and would slow down, while she tried to ensure that those holding the bar couldn't get it to the gate at all.

She had originally intended this to be something of a solo effort, hoping that those in the camp would notice and send a party up before the gate could be closed again; she wouldn't be able to keep it open for long. But what she now knew was that three strong men – discounting the monks, who were surely not in on the deception – were going to be there to hold it open themselves. So all she had to do was delay the closing long enough for them to put their shoulders to the gate, and then get herself and Theo well out of the way before the fighting started.

All. That was *all* she had to do. Easier said than done, especially now she was back on the ground and surrounded by armoured men and sharp steel. There did seem to be an awful lot of them. And were those archers on the gatehouse roof?

But it was too late to back out now. The bar was lifted, one side of the gate was opening, the monks were coming through …

'Oh! Oh!' Alys staggered, deliberately bumping into a couple of the Tickhill men. 'Help! I think the baby's coming!'

She had been imagining this moment since yesterday, and steeling herself all morning. The first part went according to plan, in that several men momentarily stopped what they were doing and looked at her. She heard a voice shouting to get her out of the way. Someone's hand was on her arm, probably Theo's.

She was in no way prepared for what happened next.

Chapter Nine

'That's it!' cried Edwin, as he saw Alys's arms spread wide. 'That will be her signal.'

Everard turned to Adam, who had been watching with them. 'Run and tell the lord earl.' Then he nodded at Edwin.

Edwin grabbed at his arm. 'Please …'

'I know. I will.' And he was gone.

Edwin watched in agony as Prior Richard, Brother Durand, Martin, Willikin and Sir Malvesin walked away from the camp and towards the castle. He had no idea how this was going to play out. Alys was going to be near the gate. None of these five men would hurt her, and the monks might even step in to protect her, but the others were there to hold the gate open and take the castle, come what may, so they might not have all that much consideration for Alys if her presence interfered with those plans. Up until recently Edwin would have trusted Martin to look after her. But now?

He was, at least, glad that it was Sir Malvesin and not his brother who was with this first group. Edwin had never met either of them before and had initially been intimidated by the horrific facial scarring – no doubt suffered during some battle or other – into thinking Sir Malvesin a hard-bitten, vicious fighter. But he'd proved to be much more even-tempered than expected, and Edwin had been forced to remind himself that he of all people should know that looks could be deceptive.

Sir Baldwin, of course, was a different matter. Edwin couldn't imagine that any other knight he'd ever met would kick a priest, and he prayed that the knight's path and Alys's would not cross.

Alys had disappeared from sight, moving away from the wall and presumably down the stairs that Edwin knew to be near the gatehouse.

She was behind that gate and in danger; he knew it, but he could do nothing.

As he watched, the gates began to open.

It was a much longer walk from the camp to the castle than he had thought; or, at least, so it appeared to Martin now. What in the Lord's name was he doing? How had he got himself into this situation? He felt so exposed as he moved towards what he knew would be a combat situation – on foot, carrying no sword and wearing no armour – that he might as well be naked.

The two monks were a few paces in front, followed by Sir Malvesin with Martin and Willikin on either side of him. Martin had hesitated about raising the subject, in case it was a point on which the knight would become touchy, but he had eventually asked straight out if Sir Malvesin would prefer to have Martin on his blind side in case of attack from that direction.

To his relief the knight had grinned. 'I manage pretty well – you compensate, you know, without even realising it – but yes, I always appreciate having a man I can trust to my left.'

Martin glanced over now, seeing no fear in Sir Malvesin's face. Was he genuinely unafraid, or just hiding it well? On the knight's far side Willikin looked a little more uneasy, but that might just be because he really was feeling discomfort. His own clothes had been deemed unsuitable for the mission: a negotiating party was always made up of men of rank, and Willikin's whole appearance screamed 'common soldier' to the world at large. He had therefore been poured into a borrowed tunic that was far too tight around his chest and shoulders, and Martin wondered if he'd even be able to move his arms properly when he needed to. He would follow his orders, though: Willikin might have something of a child's mind in a man's body, but he would always do his duty.

Their slow pace over the seemingly endless open ground continued. Martin's size made him an obvious target, he knew, and he tried not to twitch as he saw the archers on the roof of the gatehouse. Still, that was exactly where they should be – they were looking outwards from the castle and wouldn't be able to shoot directly downwards into the space under the gatehouse chamber, which is where Martin and the others would be holding the gate open. They would, of course, be able to loose their arrows as the second and third parties came storming up, but those men would be protected by mail and shields, and could take care of themselves. Martin had a rough idea of the layout of the castle, and by his calculations a group of archers would have to be very precisely positioned indeed in order to shoot at them while they were holding the gate under the archway, and this would be made all the more difficult if garrison men were milling around to spoil their clear aim.

Martin couldn't at first glance see the men he knew were hidden in various blind spots, but he hadn't expected to: if he could, then the monks would spot them too and become suspicious. The prior had been very talkative on the subjects of peace, reconciliation and all that sort of thing, so if he knew he was being used in this way he would stop the mission. He would probably even call out to Sir Robert that he'd been tricked, in some misguided notion of 'fairness', and then the game really would be up.

Wherever these men were hidden, Martin hoped they would be quick about showing themselves when it came to it, especially the one who would hand him a sword. Walking up towards a castle bristling with steel while empty handed was making him yearn for the comforting feel of his fingers around the hilt. He thought that he might have spotted one out of the corner of his eye – or a foot, at least, protruding from where the man was concealed in some undergrowth just at the point where the curtain wall met the gatehouse and the ground sloped steeply down to the moat. Sir Geoffrey would have kept that area cut short precisely in order to avoid such a security risk, but Martin was glad that the Tickhill castellan wasn't so careful.

He turned his eyes resolutely away from the spot in case anyone saw the direction of his gaze.

They reached the gatehouse and stopped. They all held their arms out wide to show that they were not armed, and Martin heard the order being given to admit them. First came the sound of the bar being lifted, and then the left-hand gate began to swing open.

This was the first moment of danger. Were they themselves about to be tricked, and overwhelmed by a horde of armed men pouring forth to attack the camp? He, Sir Malvesin and Willikin, unarmed as they were, would stand no chance of survival if that happened. Martin tried to brace himself, ready to do whatever damage he could with his fists before he went down beneath their blades.

He held his breath.

There was no charge.

The gate continued to open in silence. Breathing again, Martin waited in suspense for Sir Malvesin's order, as the timing had to be exactly right. Prior Richard and Brother Durand made ready to step inside as soon as the gap was big enough.

One moment passed. And another. The monks were through.

It was then that Martin heard a woman crying out in distress. A voice he recognised.

'Now!' roared Sir Malvesin, and all hell broke loose.

Martin was hardly aware of what happened next, not coherently, but he would recall it later in a series of flashes that enabled him to put together the whole story. He, Willikin and Sir Malvesin slammed their shoulders into the gate. They had initial success: because they'd taken the men by surprise, and because the gate was already moving in the right direction – opening, rather than being shut against them – they were able to push it wide before they felt any resistance. Willikin leaned into it with all his weight, digging his feet into the ground for extra purchase.

Martin was able to glance inside the gatehouse towards the bailey, where he noticed several things almost simultaneously.

The first was that there were many, many more Tickhill men there than he had anticipated.

The second was Alys, crying out and staggering around, surrounded by shouting men and confusion, with a red-haired boy trying to pull her away.

And the third was that there were half a dozen archers positioned in *exactly* the right place to shoot at them.

'Look out!' he yelled, grabbing Sir Malvesin to drag him downwards.

A hissing sound was followed almost immediately by a series of hard smacks as arrows hit the wooden gate.

Martin became aware of a sharp pain in his left hand, and saw it covered in red. *Blood on his hands*. But this time it was his own.

There was no time to think about it. The archers had rows of arrows stuck in the ground in front of them, and it took a good bowman mere moments to nock another. Martin and the others needed to move before another volley came; they were sitting ducks at this range.

Martin was in a crouch, with Sir Malvesin by him, both now with their backs to the gate as they continued to push against it with all their might while making themselves as small as possible. Willikin was still standing, the veins in his neck bulging as he inched the gate forward with all his huge strength against the half a dozen garrison members who were frantically trying to shut it. His eye met Martin's and the ghost of a grin played on his face, as though he was enjoying the trial of strength at which nobody could best him.

The archers had nocked again. 'Get down!' Martin began to shout, but he hadn't even finished the second word when there was a sort of wet, tearing sound, and two arrows appeared in Willikin's broad back.

Willikin gave a little grunt, as though he was mildly surprised rather than hurt, and then Martin saw the light go out of his eyes. The plain, honest face fell slack.

The gate lurched suddenly, and Martin knew that he and Sir Malvesin weren't going to be able to hold it much longer. He'd vowed that he would rescue Alys or die in the attempt, and now he was going to die before he could get anywhere near her. Where in the name of God's blood were the other men, the ones bringing swords? Martin could hardly fight off archers and men-at-arms with his bare hands, although he'd certainly give it a try if he had to.

Finally, several armed allies arrived from outside and added their weight to pushing the gate, so Martin was able to throw himself forward into the melee of Tickhill men surrounding Alys, avoiding another volley of arrows as he did so.

The red-haired lad had succeeded in dragging her further away from the gatehouse, and she was still crying out. He was shouting too, and waving a dagger dangerously close to her – Martin had no idea whether he was attacking her or whether he thought he was protecting her, but he didn't have the time to worry about it: he simply punched the boy hard, then wrested the knife off him while he was dazed. He gripped the hilt. *Where* was the sword he was supposed to have?

'Don't hurt him!' that was Alys, her voice so high it was nearly a shriek.

Martin hadn't intended to kill the boy, but he didn't waste his breath saying so. 'You have to come!' He lunged at her, grasping her arm.

But now there were more men, and everything was confusion. The second party had stormed the gate, armed knights and soldiers flailing around in the confined stone tunnel of the gatehouse in a frantic, stabbing whirlwind.

Sir Baldwin saw Martin and hacked his way through the press. 'What's going on? Why are there so many?'

'I don't know!'

'Come on – we need you! We're being pushed back!'

Two Tickhill men rushed at them from the side, but they were lightly armoured, a little hesitant, and it took Sir Baldwin no more than a moment to deal with them. He pointed at one of their dropped swords and yelled something to Martin, but then another movement caught his eye: it was the red-haired youth staggering forward again, still dazed from Martin's blow. Sir Baldwin reacted probably without thinking – or at least Martin, afterwards, would like to think so – and his sword hacked down into unarmoured flesh.

Alys screamed, and Martin suddenly felt her dead weight pulling him off balance. *Don't let her fall!* Sir Baldwin turned back towards the melee by the gate, leaving the boy, and one of the monks ran to the prone figure.

Martin swept Alys up into his arms, and saw that Brother Durand had done the same for the boy, both of them covered in bright blood.

'Out the gate!' shouted the monk. 'I'll go first – my habit might protect us!'

With astonishing courage, Brother Durand strode directly into the press of men and steel. Martin followed. He had only a dagger, still no sword, but he couldn't use it anyway as he needed both hands for Alys. Was she dead? No shield, no armour … all he could do was cradle her like a baby and hunch his body round her as best he could as he followed the monk. A blade was going to land between his shoulders any moment now, surely.

The earl's party was losing the fight. How had so many Tickhill men been ready, and why were they so well placed? No time to worry about that now, but the general momentum was that they were being pushed back out. Indeed, above the noise Martin could hear shouts about shutting the gates, and despite everyone's best efforts they were beginning to close.

Miraculously he and Brother Durand, with their burdens, emerged unscathed. The mounted party was even now cantering across the open space towards them, lances lowered, and Martin rushed to one side to get out of their path. However, before they reached him he saw the earl give the order to pull up.

Risking a glance behind him, Martin could see that the gates were almost closed; a mounted charge would be no use now. The last few blows were struck but the earl's men were beginning to stream away from the gatehouse. Two went down with arrows in the back as he watched. *You're always in the most danger when you're running away*, said Sir Geoffrey's voice in Martin's head, as he felt the unusual and humiliating sensation of having his back towards the enemy. If an arrow hit him now, he would deserve it.

But the fight was over. Nothing would be gained by attempting to turn back, so he might as well get Alys to safety and face the consequences. The earl was still wearing his helm as Martin passed him, but Martin could well imagine the expression of fury on his face behind it.

Alys seemed to have quite a lot of blood on her, although Martin thought most of it was his own, if the pain in his hand was anything to go by; either that or from the wounded boy, who had been standing close to her when he was hit. But she remained lifeless, and his heart pounded from more than just the recent action as he hurried towards the camp and the onrushing Edwin.

Edwin's instinct was to run towards the castle as soon as the gate began to open, but he knew he had to hold back. How would it help Alys if he was killed before he could even get to her? For that would be the outcome, no question.

From his position just behind the first row of tents, he actually had a fine overview of the encounter, being able to see the whole picture in a way that those caught up in it would not. The initial party of five reached the gatehouse and then passed briefly out of his sight, into the shadow of the stone arch, presumably going through the gate as planned. There had been cries of alarm – the first among them Alys's voice, which he would recognise anywhere – which must mean that they were holding the gate open.

Now, Edwin wasn't convinced that he'd completely understood the earl's plan, because he hadn't been there when the details were discussed, but he'd *thought* that there were three or four men hidden in spaces around the outside of the castle, in various tiny gaps that couldn't be seen properly from inside. They were supposed to have rushed quickly to support the three men at the gate, until the foot party led by Sir Baldwin could make it from the camp – where they'd had to be hidden while all this was going on – to the castle. Then this armed group would take the fight right inside the bailey, against the surprised men of the garrison, and the whole would be finished by a mounted charge led by the earl himself.

What had happened, as far as he could see, was that no men had leapt out of hiding, which meant that Martin, Willikin and Sir Malvesin were left alone and unarmed, trying to hold the gate for much longer than expected. In fact it was already closing again by the time Sir Baldwin got there. The impetus provided by his incoming forces had stopped it briefly, but the fight seemed to be much fiercer than anyone was expecting, and they began to be pushed out. The horses had swept past Edwin and started to pick up speed as they approached the castle, but they had stopped halfway as the earl's men began to retreat. And it was at that point that Edwin lost interest in everything, because he'd spotted Martin and seen what – *who* – he was carrying.

He ran towards them. 'What's happened? Is she all right? Is —'

Martin didn't pause, striding straight past. 'Infirmary – back of camp – that will be the best place.'

Edwin followed him, aware that a bloodied Brother Durand was there carrying another casualty, though he didn't have any attention to spare to wonder who it was.

Martin was already shouting before they reached the open-fronted tent, and Brother William and Humphrey hurried forward.

Brother William took in the situation at a glance. 'Brother, your man here, please, and we'll look at him first. Martin, lay Alys on that cot, and Edwin, you stay with her. It looks like she's just fainted but I'll be along as soon as I'm able. Humphrey, get as many helpers here as you can, and quickly, because I expect we'll have more to deal with shortly.'

They all obeyed, and Edwin was at last able to see Alys's face as Martin laid her gently down. She was breathing, but … 'There's blood! What's happened?'

'It's not hers.' Martin collapsed heavily to sit on the ground.

Forgetting, just for a moment, that he had sworn lifelong enmity, Edwin managed to drag his eyes away from Alys long enough to look Martin up and down. 'You're hurt?'

'A scratch.' Martin held up his left hand. A ragged and bloodied furrow had been ploughed across the back of it, and Edwin winced.

'An arrow. Luckily it just caught the back and didn't go right through, or it could have pinned me to the gate. And I've still got all my fingers.'

'What happened to Alys?'

'She shouted, like you said she would, and she was in the middle of it all, getting between the gate and the men with the bar for it. It was only due to her that we managed to keep it open as long as we did.'

Edwin stroked Alys's face. Was it just wishful thinking, or was a little bit of colour coming back to her cheeks?

'Edwin, I'm sorry. I'm so, so, *sorry*.'

Edwin shook his head. He had no time for Martin right now, and it had been he who had put Alys inside the castle in the first place.

'I'm sorry for everything, for what I said and did that day, for the way I've been behaving for a long time now. I've been a complete fool, and I put you both in danger, and …'

Edwin kept his eyes resolutely on Alys.

'And …' without warning, Martin burst into tears. 'I couldn't be any more ashamed of myself, I knew I had to make amends. This morning I swore I would get her safely out of there or die in the attempt —'

'And you did. You did get her out.' Edwin had to give Martin that, although he still wasn't ready to forgive him.

Martin shook his head, tears still streaming. He went to wipe them away and only succeeded in smearing blood all over his face. 'I did. But it wasn't me who died.'

Edwin didn't know if he dared ask. 'Who …?'

'Willikin. And at least two or three others. And I don't know what happened to Sir Malvesin – I lost sight of him.'

Edwin's heart tore. Poor, honest Willikin. A good man who was a friend to all the world and who would never voluntarily hurt a mouse, never mind a fellow man.

'And also this boy over here,' came Brother Durand's voice. 'He was still alive when I picked him up – just – and I was able to assure him that God loved him, but I felt his soul leave his body just as we reached safety.'

Martin looked up, his face even paler beneath the blood, sweat and tears. 'He was trying to drag Alys away. I only hit him with my fist, I swear, but Sir Baldwin didn't realise, or at least I think …' he tailed off and stared into the distance.

Edwin's heart took an even deeper dive. 'Has he got red hair?'

'See for yourself,' said the monk. 'If you know his name I can pray better for his soul.'

Edwin scrambled to his feet and moved to look at the body. Or, rather, he tried *not* to look at the poor butchered form, but only at the pale, freckled face that he knew he'd recognise. 'His name is Theo,' he said, dully. 'And if he was trying to pull Alys away, it was only to protect her.' He crossed himself.

One of Theo's arms had fallen away from his side, over the edge of the bed, the hand dangling. It had some kind of burn mark on the palm, which didn't seem to fit with his other injuries, but it made no difference now, did it? Edwin gently crossed both of Theo's arms over his chest, and looked about for a cloth to cover him with.

Brother Durand, his white robe stained crimson, began to say the prayers for the dead, but he soon had to stop as other men were brought in who needed his attention.

Edwin moved back to Alys's side and took her hand. He leaned in close. 'You can wake up now, my love. You're safe. You're safe and I'm here with you.'

Alys stirred. She could hear Edwin's voice, but she was imagining it, wasn't she? Because she was in the castle and he'd gone.

She was still lying on the uncomfortable palliasse she'd been on all night, and it was hurting her back. In fact she ached all over. She'd better get up, hadn't she? There was something very important she had to do.

No, wait. She *had* got up, and she'd gone up to the top of the castle wall. Then there had been the gate, and screaming, and violence, and terror. She'd tried to curl up, to wrap herself around the precious burden in her belly, but there had been pushing and pulling, and so many sharp blades flashing. Theo's voice, his hand, and then …

Alys woke up with a shriek, the fear and horror striking at her heart and the shock nearly making her fall out of bed.

And then arms were around her and the voice she loved best in the world was speaking to her, comforting her. 'I'm here. I'm here, you're safe, and everything is going to be all right.'

He repeated it over and over again as she allowed herself to be soothed, to be pressed back and settled. She wasn't on the palliasse; it was some kind of narrow bed. But she could still hear cries and groans.

'There are men who are wounded,' murmured Edwin in her ear. 'Nothing for you to worry about, my love – Brother William and Brother Durand are seeing to them. I'll get you away from here as soon as I can, but we'll wait until they say you're fine to move.'

She nodded and mumbled something, though she wasn't sure what. She felt his arms about her and a cup pressed to her lips. 'It's just a little watered wine. Try to drink some, if you can. Then you can rest, but don't worry – I won't leave your side, not for a moment.'

Alys managed to get some of the liquid down her throat, though she could also feel it trickling down her chin. The drops were wiped gently away as her surroundings faded once more.

When she woke again, her head felt clearer, though she was still in pain. She said a brief prayer for the safety of the child, and then opened her eyes properly. She was lying on her back, with the roof of a tent above her and the afternoon sun casting bright rays as it slanted in through the open wall. A fresh breeze played across her face, and her hand was in Edwin's as he sat beside her.

Alys felt a brief moment of peace. Then it all came crashing back: her heart began to pound again, and her breath to come in sharp gasps.

Edwin was looking down on her. 'How are you, my love?'

She tried to calm herself, for his sake as much as her own. 'Well, I think. Not injured. And glad to be here with you.'

'Could you manage something to eat? You need to keep your strength up.'

She thought about this for a moment. 'Actually, yes. Yes, I could.'

'I'll see what I can find.' Edwin made as if to move away, but she clutched at his fingers, unwilling to let go of him even if it meant going hungry.

'I've brought you something.' That was another voice – Adam's, coming from somewhere behind her head. He appeared in her eyeline, carrying a bowl and a spoon. 'I thought you might like something from my lord's own meal, and Humphrey said it would be all right to bring it.'

Alys blessed them both in her mind, and Edwin smiled and thanked him.

'It's only fish, I'm afraid,' continued Adam, 'because of it being Friday, but it's soft and it's nicely cooked in this sauce.'

Edwin froze in the very act of reaching out for the bowl, so suddenly that Alys knew that something had just occurred to him. But then he shook his head and brought himself back. 'Sorry.'

With some assistance, Alys was able to assume more of a seated posture, though the pain was becoming more noticeable. Perhaps a warm meal would help.

Adam disappeared as quietly as he had arrived. Alys felt recovered enough to be perfectly capable of feeding herself, but Edwin insisted on doing it for her, spooning tiny amounts of delicately poached white fish into her mouth. She made no objection, enjoying the sensation of being safe and looked after. It didn't matter where they were or what else was going on – only that they were out of immediate danger and together.

The bowl was almost empty when Alys felt an altogether different sensation, followed by a gush of wetness under her skirts.

'What is it?' Edwin was poised with the last spoonful, but stopped with it in mid-air when he saw the expression on her face. 'Are you all right?'

It was not something Alys had ever experienced before, but she'd had enough advice on pregnancy from older women in the village to know exactly what was happening.

She tried to keep her voice steady, but couldn't stop an audible tremor. Indeed, her hands were shaking as she reached out to him. 'Edwin, I think the baby is coming.'

Chapter Ten

'*Please*, my lord.'

Martin heard Edwin's voice as he entered the earl's tent. 'What's going on?' he asked Adam under his breath as he took up a position next to him.

'Mistress Alys's labour pains have started, and Edwin wants to take her back to Conisbrough,' came the whispered reply.

Thank *God*, thank the Lord and all His saints, that he'd managed to get her out of the castle before this happened. That was Martin's first thought. But his second was that the earl was in no mood to offer concessions to anybody, so he might have to go into battle for Edwin and Alys in a different way.

He'd missed the first part of the conversation because he'd been sent out to attend to his wound. Earlier he'd left Edwin and Alys together in the infirmary tent, not bothering to ask either Brother William or Brother Durand to look at his hand as they were taken up with the men being brought in with more serious injuries. He'd taken a few moments to compose himself and wipe his face, and then gone to find the earl – to help him dismount and disarm, as usual, and then to face the fury he knew was coming. Best to get it over with, and if he was going to be out of a position by the end of the day he might as well know now.

It hadn't *quite* got that far, but he'd certainly been on the end of one of his lord's more legendary rages. Strangely, though, it hadn't bothered Martin nearly as much as he had feared it would. He'd got Alys out of the castle and seen her reunited with Edwin, and he'd apologised to Edwin. He hadn't been forgiven, of course, but he had some hope that his penitence was taken seriously and that their friendship might eventually be repaired. What else could matter when set beside all that?

The pain had also been a distraction from the earl's wrath. He'd been lucky, as he'd already said to Edwin, that the arrow had only hit the back of his hand; if it had gone right through it or damaged any of his fingers then he might have had permanent trouble in future holding his shield, which would be a disaster. But they were still in place and he flexed them occasionally to make sure he could feel and control them. This, of course, stretched the gaping wound open again and started the bleeding afresh, making the edges of it all red and angry, and that was what had eventually curtailed the earl's ranting. Martin had been told bluntly to stop dripping all over the place and go and have it seen to before he came back.

Still not wishing to disturb the monks in the infirmary tent, and afraid of looking like a weakling before the men if he turned up begging to have such a small wound treated, Martin found a bucket of water and a spare rag. He dipped it and wiped off the recent blood, then gingerly poked it into the wound itself; the blood there was congealing, going black and starting to scab over, which would be better. Tearing the wet rag into strips, he bound it tightly round his hand to stop any further dripping, and considered the job done. He'd have a scar on the back of his hand for the rest of his life, he supposed, but that was no bad thing for a fighting man, and it would give him a tale to tell around the fire in the evenings.

Now he stood at the side of the earl's tent, wondering if he dared intervene on Edwin's behalf. He was perfectly willing to take another bout of fury, to direct it away from Edwin and towards himself, if it would help; he was hesitating only on the grounds that any intervention from him at this point might actually make things worse. He looked around at the various knights, trying to gauge whether any help would be forthcoming, but their expressions ranged from apathy to eye-rolling disbelief at such a minor matter being canvassed when there were more important things to be discussed. If Sir Geoffrey or Brother William were present, there might have been some potential, but it looked like Martin was going to be the only hope for an increasingly desperate Edwin.

Martin prepared to speak, but was forestalled from an unexpected quarter as he heard the words 'Pardon me, my lord,' from beside him.

Adam, taking his life – or at least his future career – in his hands, was stepping forward with a mild yet determined expression as all eyes turned towards him. The earl, unused to being interrupted in such a way, was too surprised even to bellow at him to be silent, so Adam was able to continue. 'If you please, my lord, is it not the case that having a labouring woman in the siege camp will be a great distraction for everyone, and may harm our purpose?'

That was the way to do it. Never mind Edwin pleading for compassion, asking the earl to take pity. Positioning the situation as an inconvenience to the earl himself, a threat to his own interests, was far more likely to get results. Indeed, he was pausing now, and instead of shouting at Adam he merely turned to Edwin and snapped, 'Very well. She can go, but not you. You need to stay here and sort out the mess you've made.' Edwin began stammering out thanks, but the earl cut him off with a baleful glance that encompassed Martin as well. 'Besides, after what happened this morning there will be carts leaving the camp anyway, to carry away the bodies.'

Edwin left, and Martin sent up a heartfelt prayer. That Alys shouldn't suffer unduly during the birth, that her child would be healthy and that Edwin shouldn't have to endure the wrenching loss that Sir Geoffrey had.

There was no time to think on the subject further, however, because now came the close analysis of what had happened earlier in the day, and how it had all gone so wrong.

The general agreement among the experienced heads was that there had been nothing wrong with the *idea* of Martin's plan – for which he was profoundly grateful – but rather that the execution of it had gone awry. The earl had been hoping to take the castle by surprise in an almost bloodless fashion, but now they had a casualty list much more extensive than anticipated. Five men were confirmed dead: Willikin, three of those who had been of the second party under Sir Baldwin, and one of those who had been hidden. Four were missing and might be alive or dead inside the castle: the other three who had been concealed, plus Sir Malvesin. And on top of that there were seven men in the infirmary tent being treated, at least one of whom was not expected to survive.

And in return for this they had *nothing*. In fact they were probably worse off than they had been to start with, for they had tried a ruse that had not worked, which would make Sir Robert both more determined to resist and more suspicious of them in future. Any further trickery was out of the question. Moreover, Abbot Reginald and Prior Richard were both locked inside the castle and presumably also furious at being deceived into an action that had ended in such violence. This would make further negotiation all but impossible, which left only one option if the castle were to be taken.

Sir Baldwin was already agitating for a full-on assault, regardless of the cost in lives, and Martin looked at him in some distaste. He could allow for the knight being anxious for his brother's safety – just as he himself had been for Edwin and Alys – but Martin had been unimpressed with the way Sir Baldwin had dealt with the priest upon their arrival, and he could not forget the totally unnecessary killing of the boy inside the gatehouse, who had been unmistakeably both young and unarmed.

He brought himself up short. What was the matter with him? Normally he would be the first man in the room to support the idea of direct action, of winning via force and combat. Was he going soft, the same accusation the earl had levelled at Sir Geoffrey?

The sound of his own name cut through these horrified thoughts and he forced himself to pay attention. As the only one of the three who had returned alive, he was being asked to describe exactly what had happened as his party had approached the gate. Martin cast his mind back so he could give an accurate report, picturing everything as he had seen it. His audience was made up of other military men, so he concentrated on the technical aspects and omitted mentioning what he had felt, either about Alys or about watching Willikin at the exact moment he died.

After he had finished, there was a fair amount of head-shaking and muttering.

'Archers on the gatehouse roof is no surprise, of course,' said a knight. 'A perfectly normal precaution. But you say there were more already stationed in precisely the right spot in the bailey?'

'Yes.'

There was another murmur. 'And,' added another man, 'they had their arrows already lined up and pushed into the ground in front of them?'

Martin hadn't considered that before, and berated himself for his stupidity. This detail meant that the archers had been in place for some while; they had not just taken up their station in a hurry as the danger by the gate became apparent.

'You also say,' barked Sir Baldwin, 'that you thought you saw the foot of one of the men and considered that he was not well hidden?' He looked about him. 'Do we know, or can we confirm, whether this is the one we know was killed? He might have been dead already, not slain in the action?'

Again Martin wished he was thinking straighter. If the hidden man was dead *before* they approached the castle – and perhaps the other three as well, although they had no bodies to be sure either way – then it indicated that their ruse had been discovered in advance.

'And that,' concluded Sir Baldwin, who was still speaking, 'can only mean one thing.' He turned to address the earl directly. 'We were betrayed, my lord – and somewhere in your ranks there is a traitor.'

Edwin rushed from the earl's tent and hurried to the infirmary. Alys was still lying where he had left her, though he noted that someone had hung a blanket from one of the roof struts in order to give her some semblance of privacy away from the wounded men.

He threw himself on his knees by the cot and took her hand. 'My lord says you can go home. I'll organise a wagon and make sure it's comfortable.' He kissed her fingers.

'What about you?'

'I'm sorry, he won't let me come with you – I have to stay here. But you'll be safe and comfortable at home, so that's the main thing. And I wouldn't be in the house with you anyway – what you need is women about you.'

She nodded and made a brave attempt at a smile. 'Your mother will take good care of me.'

Edwin's eyes began to sting. He felt his face screw up, knowing full well that it was happening, but he couldn't stop himself.

He turned away, but it was too late.

'Edwin?'

He kept his face carefully averted. 'You'll be fine once you get home.'

Her voice took on a different tone, though he couldn't place it exactly – worried, anxious, panicky, cross? 'Tell me.'

He shook his head.

This time it was definitely verging on anger. 'You tell me right now what's going on, husband, or I'm not moving anywhere. We promised to have no secrets from each other.'

'I can't.'

He was aware that his voice sounded full of the weeping he was hoping to hold in, and her own softened. 'Edwin, has something happened? To your mother? Or … to her baby?'

It was no use. Besides, the tears were falling in earnest now. 'I'm so sorry to tell you, my love, but Mother has died. She went to God yesterday morning.'

Alys was so shocked that she attempted to sit up. 'What? How did it – how did you – and why didn't you tell me?'

She was going to say more but he saw her face crease in pain and she collapsed back on the cot. 'Please, please, don't think about it too much now,' he pleaded. 'Just concentrate on yourself and the baby, and getting home. I'll go and sort it out, and at least when you get back you'll have Cecily, and Agnes, and Rosa as well if she can be fetched. And any of the other women who know best about these things.'

She was sweating and gritting her teeth now, in an effort not to cry out, and merely nodded without speaking.

Edwin didn't want to leave her, but the quicker he could get her back to Conisbrough, the better. He went back outside to find that a couple of carts were already there, shrouded bodies being placed into them.

He recoiled. 'You can't put Alys in there!'

Humphrey, who was directing, came to lay a comforting hand on Edwin's arm. 'I know. These two are for the lads, and there's a third coming for your wife. I've set one of my best and steadiest men to drive it, and he'll get her home safely, never fear.'

Four of the bodies were now loaded, and the men now stood uncertainly looking at the fifth, still on the ground. By its size, it could only be Willikin's.

Edwin crossed himself. 'He was a good man.'

Humphrey did likewise. 'He's the only one for Conisbrough, thanks be to God – the rest are from my lord's other estates. Did he have family there?'

Edwin shook his head. 'An orphan, or so I believe; he's been in the garrison almost as long as I can remember, since he was quite young.'

Humphrey sighed. 'Nobody to mourn him, then.'

'No,' said a man of the Conisbrough garrison who was one of those waiting. 'That's not true. He'll have plenty to mourn him, don't you worry. All of us counted him a brother.'

Edwin nodded at the man. 'He'll probably already be buried by the time I get back, but I'll pray over his grave and pay for Masses for his soul.'

In order to lift Willikin with some dignity he had by now been placed on a board, and Edwin and Humphrey joined with the other men in picking it up. One end was safely placed on the tailgate, and then the body was slid into the cart ready for Willikin to begin his final journey. As they departed, Edwin remembered how easily those strong but gentle arms had placed Alys in their own wagon on the way here, and he sighed.

With both vehicles now gone the third was able to pull up, and Humphrey busied himself finding whatever he could to make it comfortable, while Edwin went to fetch Alys.

She had recovered a little from her earlier pain, and with his help was able to sit up. Both the monks were hovering; Brother Durand was hesitant about approaching and touching her, but Brother William had no such qualms, taking one arm and helping her to rise. Between him and Edwin she was able to make her way out. The same board that had just conveyed Willikin's body was now used to form a ramp, and before long Alys was settled as comfortably as the wagon would allow. Humphrey gave yet more flustered instructions to the driver, who listened patiently, nodded at Edwin, and set off at a steady pace.

Edwin waved, choking back his emotions and hoping desperately that this wasn't the last time he would ever see Alys alive.

What he needed was some quiet time to think, to compose himself and to get back to solving the problem that would get them all out of here, but it wasn't long before a commotion caught his attention and he followed a group of others over towards the side of the camp that was nearest the castle.

The earl emerged from his tent just as Edwin passed it, followed by his knights and their sergeants, and Edwin joined Martin, Adam and Everard as the party moved to where they had a clear sight of the walls. Figures were appearing on the battlements. Abbot Reginald and Prior Richard were easily recognisable in their white robes, and Edwin was able to point out Sir Robert and his garrison commander, Anselm. There were also two women: Lady Idonea and Margaret.

Sir Robert was speaking to Anselm, who listened, nodded and then turned before bracing himself and letting his voice boom out across the open space. 'Sir Robert deplores the unprovoked attack on the castle, and still more the underhand way in which this morning's assault took place.'

Edwin winced. He knew, just as everyone else around him did, that this sort of language was guaranteed to infuriate the earl. He glanced over to see his lord speaking in a low tone to Sir Baldwin, who stepped forward and bellowed in his turn. 'My lord Earl Warenne is the rightful holder of this castle and orders you to surrender it to him. Despite the loss of his men, which resulted from Sir Robert's refusal, he will seek no reprisals. Surrender now and you may all leave with your lives and possessions intact.'

The dialogue continued in the same way, each principal speaking to his own man in order to have his words relayed at a loud volume. 'As Earl Warenne well knows, Sir Robert holds this castle directly from the crown. He has pledged to defend it with his life, and will surrender it only if commanded to do so by the king and his regent.'

'The lord earl is a loyal servant of the crown, so in handing over the keys Sir Robert would be acting in the king's interest.'

'Earl Warenne has not always acted in …' here Anselm tailed off as he was interrupted by the abbot. Sir Robert joined in and for some moments they seemed to be having a heated discussion. Edwin sincerely hoped that no serious accusation was about to be made, no reference to the lord earl's multiple swapping of sides during the late war. If anyone in Tickhill said the word 'turncoat' out loud, the castle and the town would both be in smoking ruins before sunset.

Fortunately, this seemed to have been the gist of the abbot's interruption, and when Anselm spoke again he began anew. 'If Earl Warenne can produce a written order from the regent, over the royal seal, instructing Sir Robert to hand the castle over, he will do so with a good heart. Until that time he stands for the king against all who would seek to gain personal advantage.'

Edwin thought that the speech was over, and Sir Baldwin was already taking in a breath preparatory to shouting again when Anselm continued. 'As a mark of good faith, Sir Robert is happy to show you that your men have not been harmed.'

More figures appeared on the battlements: some of the Tickhill garrison shepherding the four missing men from the earl's host. Their hands were tied, but they looked unhurt.

Sir Baldwin stiffened at the sight of his younger brother, screwing his eyes up as though he wanted to observe him closely despite the distance.

Anselm's voice came again. 'You have a man of ours – where is he? Can we expect similar good faith?'

At first Sir Baldwin looked puzzled, but then someone murmured to him and he gave a thin smile before calling out. 'The boy with the red hair? He's dead.'

A wail came from the battlements, and Edwin knew that it came from Margaret. The poor girl. She must have been worried almost out of her mind about her brother, and perhaps suspected the worst, but to find out in such a way …

Sir Baldwin belatedly realised what should have been obvious, which was that crowing in such a way while his brother was captive inside the castle probably wasn't the best idea. 'He was dead already,' he added, in a marginally more conciliatory tone. 'The monk brought him down thinking he might be able to save him, but nothing could be done. His body shall be returned, if you wish.'

Edwin heard Margaret's sobbing, as the sound drifted across the space, and knew that he wouldn't be able to get it out of his head. So much grief, everywhere. She was being supported by Lady Idonea, who was looking outwards, scanning the faces staring back at her across the space. Edwin had the uncomfortable feeling that she was looking straight at him, and he felt a pang of guilt. If only he'd done his duty better, if he'd been able to solve the mystery, all of this could have been avoided. Theo's death, Willikin's, the agony of those men still lying wounded … it was all his fault.

Sir Baldwin was now cursing under his breath, calling Sir Robert every name under the sun. Edwin winced when he got to 'bastard son of a whore' – not due to the profanity, but because one did not generally use the word 'bastard' around the lord earl, who was occasionally still touchy about his father's illegitimacy.

The earl was losing his patience. 'Surrender!' called Sir Baldwin, again.

'Not until Sir Robert has the royal order to do so,' came the predictable reply, and there was no point in continuing after that.

The figures on the battlement began to disappear as they made their way down the stairs, and Edwin turned away. As he did so he met the eye of the earl, who was throwing him a look so malevolent that he would have been frightened if he hadn't already had so many terrible experiences in the past couple of days. Edwin realised that, just for a few moments as he'd been concentrating on the exchange, he'd stopped thinking about Alys, and guilt overwhelmed him once more.

He couldn't face the earl, not now, and not when he still didn't have any answers, so he joined a group of men drifting away and hoped to avoid a direct summons. What he really needed was some quiet time on his own to think properly, but there was little prospect of that in a siege camp, so he wandered back to the infirmary. He might be useful there, he supposed, and it was better than sitting with raucous fighting men.

As he entered, Brother Durand and Brother William were saying prayers over a body with its face covered, so Edwin paused. This must be an additional death, because the corpse he knew to be Theo's was over to one side. He went over to it in order to pray there, not just for Theo but for everyone who was stuck in this situation not of their own making, who would only get out of it if he, Edwin, could get his mind to work properly and stop letting everyone down. How many people were now dead because of him?

It was getting dark, and it was some moments before he realised that the shadow that fell over him was not either of the monks but the priest he had seen in the street when the earl's host had arrived.

'Father?'

'I've come to collect Theo's body, if this is it.'

'It is. And I'm sorry.'

'You are? Sorry about the death of a man who was your enemy?'

'He wasn't my enemy, Father – nobody is, and I certainly had no quarrel with Theo. I was inside the castle for a few days before all this started, and I got to know him a little. Him and his sister.'

The priest sighed. 'Ah, poor Margaret. I baptised them both, you know, and it seems like only yesterday.'

Edwin felt the need to talk, the need for some human contact while he was surrounded by so much death and loss. 'I didn't realise they were related, to start with. They didn't look much alike, did they? I mean, of course I didn't see Margaret's hair, but she didn't have that same freckled face as him, so I wasn't sure it was red like his.'

The ghost of a smile played across the priest's face in the dim light. 'No, it wasn't. Hers was – and still is, I suppose – the colour of wheat. But although they didn't resemble each other physically, they were alike in character, both such sweet children, and keen to look out for each other. Both with the same smile. And now …' he tailed off as he looked down at the shrouded form.

He had such a deep sadness, such a simple dignity about him. Edwin remembered his courage when he'd stood alone in front of an armed host – had that only been yesterday? – and faced down one of the most powerful men in the realm. 'I'm going to make all of this stop, as soon as I can,' he said, to the priest's evident bemusement. 'So that nobody else needs to die.'

'I don't know how you're going to achieve that,' came the sombre reply, 'but I'll pray for your success. Now, I have a handcart outside, if you would be kind enough to assist me?'

For the second time that day, Edwin helped to load a body on to a cart. Theo's death would cause immense sorrow for his family, but at least he had them to mourn him and pray for his soul, unlike poor Willikin.

That reminded him of something. 'Father, may I ask you a question?'

The priest made sure that Theo's body was lying straight and dignified before he answered. 'Yes, of course.'

'Do you know if Sir Robert has any brothers?'

If the priest was surprised by such a random topic, he didn't show it. 'Let me think. I've certainly never met any … no, I'm sure I heard him mention once that he did not.' He paused. 'Nor any living sisters, either, if I recall correctly. Why do you ask?'

'Just … I had an idea about something, but it doesn't matter.'

Edwin walked with the priest to the edge of the camp and then returned, thinking of Theo and Margaret, and of Sir Robert, like himself, having no siblings.

He pulled himself up short. He *did*. He now had a sister himself, thanks be to God. A half-sister, of course, at least officially, but that didn't matter: he would love her as though they were full-blood siblings.

Theo had loved and protected his sister, and now Theo was dead. Edwin was not going to let anyone else suffer such a loss, he was determined. And that meant he needed to work past all his own cares, to put them to one side for now, and really *think*.

The camp was still crowded, but by now it was full dark so it might be easier to find a quiet corner. It was getting chilly, the spring warmth not lasting after sunset, so he fetched his cloak from where he'd left it in the infirmary tent. The monks probably wouldn't mind if he crept into a corner and went to sleep, but he knew he wouldn't be able to concentrate properly in there, so instead he made his way around the outside and sat down on the side furthest from the camp. The ground was relatively dry and his cloak was warm, so it wouldn't hurt him to stay out late, or all night if necessary. He pulled the fur-lined wool around himself and looked up at the stars as he prepared to sink deep into his own thoughts, to find and follow the one golden thread that would lead him to an answer.

Martin awoke the next morning feeling odd in a way he couldn't quite define. Brittle, confused images of the previous day's events played through his head, not in the right order, and he was shivering. In fact, his teeth were chattering. Why was it so cold in here? And what was that strange smell?

He sat up too quickly and was almost overcome by a combination of dizziness and the pain in his hand. He looked at it, noting in an almost detached manner that it was so swollen that the bandage was cutting into the soft, puffy flesh, and that the rag itself was soaked through. A fly landed on it as he watched, and he tried to flick it away, causing a wave of almost unbearable agony. Honestly, was he a child, to make such a fuss about such a minor injury? It just needed washing again, he supposed, but he'd deal with all his morning duties first.

Something was definitely wrong with him. He was clumsy as he roused the others, and then he tripped as he was laying out his lord's clothes, narrowly avoiding sending Hugh flying along with the jug of water he was carrying. And he was so *cold*. He wondered if the weather was turning wintry again, and where his cloak was.

As the earl was washing, he stopped and sniffed the air. 'What is that Godawful stench?'

Adam and Hugh were also wrinkling their noses, and for some reason they were staring at Martin. What could they mean by it? Adam pointed at him and whispered something to the earl.

'Show me your hand.'

Still confused, Martin held out his right hand.

'The other one.' The earl's voice sounded different; less impatient than he might have expected. There was a hiss, and then, 'I thought I told you to get that seen to?'

'I did, my lord. I washed it and tied it up so it wouldn't bleed.'

'I meant to go to the infirmary tent and see them there – it should have been washed out with wine, or had a poultice put on it, so it wouldn't go bad like that. Get over there now and have Brother William or that other one look at it for you.'

'Yes, my lord.'

There was a brief silence as Martin swayed more or less in the direction of the tent entrance, which seemed strangely far away.

'Adam, go with him, make sure he gets there, then come back and tell me what the monks say.'

Martin felt Adam take his arm, and they went outside. How strange! It looked like a sunny spring morning, but it felt like a freezing midwinter day.

They reached the infirmary tent without mishap, and Brother William came forward to greet them.

'My lord said I needed to see you, to get this cleaned out,' said Martin, managing to hold up his hand and wondering why the monk's expression changed so quickly. 'I didn't like to bother you with it yesterday, as you had so much else to do.' He paused. 'Actually, do you mind if I sit down while you look at it? I'm feeling quite dizzy. Perhaps I ate something bad.'

He folded himself down on to the edge of a cot. There were a couple of blankets on it, so he pulled them up round his shoulders in an effort to stop the shivering.

Both the monks now came over to him, Brother Durand leaving the prone man he'd been tending. He supported Martin's arm while Brother William unwrapped the bandage, making Martin almost cry out with the pain as it came away from the sticky mess on his hand, taking some of his flesh with it.

Brother Durand manoeuvred so it was in the best light, and they all peered closely, trying not to breathe in the foul stink.

'Should it be that colour?' asked Martin, hazily, looking at the unrecognisable mass of soft, fetid flesh. He peered more closely, in a disconnected way, as though the hand wasn't his at all. Yesterday the edges of the wound had been red, but now the angry shade stained his whole hand and was spreading up his wrist, and all of his fingers had turned purple. There was a large oozing wet patch where the skin had lifted away when the bandage had been removed. And the *smell* …

Strangely, instead of answering, the monks looked at one another and then retreated some distance across the tent, where they engaged in an earnest discussion. He caught a few snippets of it as he huddled, shivering, in the blankets: 'putrid … that colour and smell … fever …

yes, back when I was in … only yesterday … less than a day … might be able to … if we …?' Then they seemed to come to some kind of decision, and Martin heard Brother William say, 'I'll tell him.'

Martin knew that he should be getting back to his lord, to his duties, instead of wasting all this time here. Why was it taking them so long to decide that his wound needed to be cleaned? Surely that was obvious to anyone with eyes. Or a nose.

The two monks approached once more, and exchanged a glance. Then Brother William spoke. 'Martin. I will be frank and honest with you, because you deserve no less. Your wound has festered.'

Martin looked at his hand again. 'Even I can tell that. Can't you just clean it out, so I can get back to work?'

The faces of both monks were pained as Brother William continued. 'That won't be possible, I'm afraid.' He took a deep breath. 'If we take it off now, I think we can do it above the wrist and save your elbow. If we wait more than a few hours, it will have to be up nearer your shoulder, and if we do nothing by tomorrow then you'll die.'

Martin had almost forgotten that Adam was in the tent, hovering somewhere near the entrance, but now he heard him cry out. He fought to get his mind to work, but everything was so confusing, and it was so *cold* – why couldn't he stop shaking? He needed to find somewhere warm and rest for a while. 'I don't understand. Take it off? My tunic isn't that dirty.'

Brother Durand knelt so that his eyes were on a level with Martin's, and grasped both his shoulders. His voice was firm. 'I've criticised you before for being a man of violence, but now we need you to be as brave as you've ever been in battle. It's not your tunic that we're talking about, do you understand? It's your hand. The wound. The damage is too far gone, and the only way to save your life is to cut your hand off. Right now.'

Chapter Eleven

The thoughts and threads were beginning to assemble themselves in the right order, but they weren't quite untangled yet and some were still missing. Still, it was a start, and Edwin now had a better idea of what he wanted to look out for. A suspicion was not proof, but it was better than no idea at all.

He was just getting up from his place behind the infirmary tent when the shouting broke out inside. Was it some kind of attack? Did he need to raise an alarm? As he rounded the corner towards the entrance he could see a couple of men running in, but there was no clash of weapons, only the continued yelling of several voices, one of which was Martin's.

Adam came hurtling out and Edwin grabbed him. 'What's happening?'

'It's Martin,' he gasped. 'You'd better go in, but I have to go and tell my lord.' And then he was gone.

A scene of chaos confronted Edwin as he entered: Martin was laying about him like a raging bull, kicking and knocking things over in an apparent bid to leave, while the monks and newly arrived men fought to stop him and the wounded cowered in their beds.

Normally Edwin would have backed Martin to see off four men, but he didn't seem to be himself, while the monks were burly and the soldiers strong. Eventually he was restrained, although he still struggled desperately.

As Martin fought to free himself from their grasp, he saw Edwin. 'Help me!'

Edwin advanced. 'What in the Lord's name is going on?'

'Help me, Edwin – get them off me. They want to cut off my hand!'

The shock was so great that at first Edwin couldn't answer. As he stood stupefied, Brother William managed to wrestle Martin towards a stool and force him down on to it. 'Just. Sit. Down.'

He knelt behind Martin and clamped his arms round him, which made Martin cry out in pain. 'Nobody,' continued the monk, in a steady tone, 'is going to do anything to you without your permission. But you must calm down before you hurt yourself or someone else.'

Edwin shook his head to clear it. Martin had hurt his hand yesterday, hadn't he? But he'd said it was only a scratch. How had he possibly got the idea that —

'Perhaps,' said Brother Durand, 'you might be able to help.'

'How?' Was Martin having some kind of fit, Edwin wondered? Was he possessed?

'Sit with him, calm him, and let us explain. It has been a great shock to him, of course, and he hasn't grasped it yet.'

Edwin stumbled. 'You mean – you really *do* want to cut off his hand?' It was no wonder that Martin had reacted as he had; Edwin felt a dizziness coming over himself.

Brother Durand procured another stool. 'You look like you'd better sit down too.'

Edwin obeyed. Beside him Martin was swaying in Brother William's restraining grip, while the two soldiers stood warily to one side.

'Edwin,' said Martin, in a voice that was now puzzled and hurt rather than angry, 'what's happening? Make it stop, please, and get me out of here.'

Brother William began to murmur into his ear in a comforting tone, and Edwin turned questioningly to Brother Durand.

'He was hit by an arrow yesterday, as you probably know,' began the monk. 'But sometimes even a small wound can fester terribly, and once it gets bad you can't stop it. Indeed, it will spread and the rest of his flesh will go rotten until it kills him.'

Edwin opened his mouth, but no words came out. He rubbed his hands over his face and tried again, trying to make sense of what he was hearing, and hoping he would wake up any moment now. 'So, his hand needs to be taken off in order to stop the spread, is that what you're saying?'

'Yes.'

'And if you don't . . .?'

'He will die.'

'Die?' Edwin still couldn't take this in properly.

'Within days. And it will not be an easy death.'

'And cutting it off will save him?'

Brother Durand hesitated. 'I can't lie to you, my son, there is also a good chance that the surgery will kill him. But it is his only chance of life, do you understand? The procedure will give him a half-and-half chance of survival, but if it is not carried out he has none at all.'

Edwin turned to his friend, who was now rocking back and forth in distress. 'I don't want to lose my hand. How will I hold my shield? How will I fight?'

He seemed to have stopped being violent, so Edwin motioned to Brother William to let go of him. The monk obliged, but it turned out he was the only thing keeping Martin upright.

They just about managed to catch him before he hit the ground. 'Perhaps we'd better get him to a cot,' suggested Edwin.

Once Martin was lying down, Edwin took up a position on his right, so he could safely touch the good arm. It was burning hot, as was the rest of Martin's body, radiating a heat so intense that Edwin could feel it striking his own skin. 'Can I see your hand?' he asked, gently.

The stench hit him before the sight, shocking even amid the fetid smell of the infirmary tent. He forced himself to look. He knew nothing of medical matters but he could see at one horrified glance that Brother Durand was right, and his heart cracked and bled for Martin's plight and the impossible choice facing him.

'Your hand,' he continued in the same tone, as though talking to a small child, 'is very badly hurt.' He laid it down as gently as he could on Martin's chest.

Martin stared at it. 'A poultice, my lord said. Or get one of them to wash it with wine.'

'I think it's too late for that.' Edwin paused to gather his wits. 'What we need to concentrate on now is keeping you alive, do you understand?'

'Alive?'

'Yes. I'm sorry, but your hand is so badly damaged that it will poison the rest of you, and if we do nothing, you will die.'

Martin stared straight up at the tent roof.

'So,' continued Edwin, carefully, 'Brother William and Brother Durand want to save your life.'

Martin's eyes, as they met Edwin's, were like nothing he had ever seen. He couldn't even begin to describe the pain and confusion they held. 'But what,' said Martin, 'if I don't want to live without my hand? What if I'd rather die?'

Edwin considered, as quickly as he could manage under the circumstances. 'Only you can decide that, of course. But think also of those around you. We all want you to live.'

Martin made a sound that might have been a hoarse laugh. 'Do you? Nobody does. Everybody hates me.'

'Nobody hates you.'

'She didn't want me, did she? Sent me away. My family? My father doesn't care, he's got all those brats to worry about. And my lord won't forgive me for what I did, nor Sir Geoffrey for what I said.' He paused and swallowed before continuing. 'And then there's you.'

'Me?'

'You hate me for what I said and did, and you're right.'

Edwin felt cold, despite the waves of heat still emanating from Martin's body. Perhaps it was only now that Alys was away from here that he could see past his own panic, but he suddenly realised how deeply Martin had been wounded by the rupture between them, and by his own refusal to accept an apology or attempt a reconciliation, even after the lengths Martin had gone to in order to make amends.

Martin was clutching at him with his good hand. 'Forgive me, please, Edwin. I'm sorry, and I'm ashamed, and I'd do anything to take it back, but please say you forgive me. Don't let me die without hearing it.'

Edwin shook his head. 'There's nothing to forgive.' The hold on his sleeve grew stronger. 'All right! If it's what you need to hear, then I forgive you with all my heart. But I also need to ask you to forgive me. I was stubborn and pig-headed, and I wouldn't listen to your apology, and I'm sorry.' He looked his friend in the eye. 'I'm truly sorry.'

A tired smile played briefly on Martin's face. 'So we're friends again?'

'Always.'

'Good. I can die happy now.' Martin lay back and closed his eyes. The grip on Edwin's arm slackened.

Panicking, Edwin shook him, concerned about the pain he might cause but also hoping it would help to waken him. 'You're not going to die. Please don't let me lose another friend. Open your eyes! You need to live.'

'Yes, you do,' came the earl's voice, 'and that's an order.'

Edwin turned to see that his lord was standing a little way off, his arms folded. How long had he been there?

'If this surgery will or might save your life, then I'm telling you to have it.'

Brother Durand, who had been watching in silence all this time, shook his head. 'No. It has to be his own decision.'

The earl started to make an angry retort, but the monk cut him off and thundered in the way Edwin remembered from his time at Roche. 'You may have earthly power, but a man's death is between him and God. God will guide him, and it is His will now whether he lives or dies.'

'My lord,' began Martin. 'I …'

The earl took a swift step forward. 'Even I can't defeat God. But if you choose …' his voice cracked. 'Damn it, man!' he burst out. 'You're far too good to lose, and I won't stand by and watch it happen.'

The shock of hearing such words brought Martin out of his daze, and Edwin could feel his own jaw sagging. That the earl should betray such emotion about anyone was almost beyond belief.

He was continuing now, quickly recovered, in a voice that held more of his usual brusque tone. 'And if victory is not possible, at least influence must be tried.' He said something Edwin didn't catch to Adam and Hugh, who were both hovering near the tent entrance, and they ran out.

Edwin pressed the advantage. 'You see? My lord wants you to live, as well as I do. And there are many others.'

He kept on in the same vein for a short while, hardly aware of what he was saying, until Adam and Hugh returned with Sir Baldwin and several other knights.

Brother Durand started to bristle. 'If you think that bringing more fighting men in here is going to —'

The earl interrupted. 'That's not why they're here.' He turned to the newcomers. 'You will all bear witness.' Then he addressed the monk again. 'Can he get out of that bed? Not to stand, but to kneel?'

Brother Durand looked puzzled. So, for a moment, was Edwin, but then he realised what was about to happen. So did Brother William, who moved forward with alacrity to help.

Between them they got Martin out of the cot and on to his knees before the earl, who didn't have to stoop all that much to meet his gaze on the level. 'This was always my intention, though it was going to wait a while. But, given the circumstances …' he stood upright again and assumed a more formal tone. 'You have been my good and faithful squire and have proved yourself a brave and loyal man in battle. On this day, Saturday in the octave of Easter in the third year of the reign of our sovereign lord King Henry, I dub thee knight.' He raised his right hand towards his left ear and then brought the back of it down hard, striking Martin at the place where his neck met his shoulder. 'Arise, Sir Martin.'

Martin was frozen, just staring at the earl with tears starting to well up. Edwin's own eyes felt hot as he watched the two of them gazing at each other. Then the earl bent to Martin's ear. His voice was low, but Edwin was so close that he heard it all. 'Whether you accept the surgery or not is between you and God. And we will speak of manors and estates another time. But know now that you will be a knight for the rest of your life, however long that is.'

He walked out without saying anything further, taking Hugh with him.

Most of the knights followed, but Sir Baldwin hesitated. 'You saved my brother,' he said, abruptly. 'I saw you pull him down as I came towards the gate. I'm not one for soft talk, but know this – if you live, you'll find a way to fight again. He thought all was over when he lost his eye, that he wouldn't be able to do it without a proper line of sight. But he learned to live with it and he's as good a knight as any. You'll do the same.' He nodded and left.

There was a long moment of silence, and then Martin – *Sir* Martin – somehow managed to struggle to his feet. 'All right.'

Brother William gave him a piercing look. 'You're sure?'

'Yes.' And then, without a tremor, 'I should confess first. Just in case.'

'I'm not a priest, my son, though Brother Durand is. He hears the confession of the dy– of the sick all the time. Let him be the one, while I get everything prepared. There is no time to lose.' He addressed Edwin. 'Can you help?'

'Yes, of course.' Edwin helped Martin to lie down again. 'I'll be back ready for when it happens – I won't leave you until it's done.'

'Nor I.' That was Adam, who was still standing over by the tent entrance, looking very pale.

'No,' said Martin. 'Who's going to look after my lord earl if I'm not there? You're the senior squire until I get back. You have to do your duty.'

Adam came forward to grasp Martin's good hand. 'All right. I'll serve him well until you get back – but remember, you're not his squire any longer, are you? You're one of his household knights.'

They left Martin with Brother Durand, and Adam departed while Edwin moved to assist Brother William. The preparations were complex, involving not only a set of knives and a saw that made Edwin feel sick when he looked at it, but also bandages, leather straps, a heated brazier and 'the strongest wine or spirit that Humphrey can come up with', as the monk instructed him to fetch.

By the time everything was ready, the confession was over.

Brother Durand beckoned to Edwin. 'I have one more thing to say, and you can hear it too.'

Edwin knelt by Martin, who was by now somehow managing to look both pale and flushed with fever at the same time.

'Now that you are absolved, you are without sin. And on top of that, you need to remember that you sustained this wound in saving a life – a woman's life. If you die, you will have given your life for another, which will smoothe your path to heaven.' He paused. 'Brother Guy, of blessed memory, would be proud of you.'

Martin only nodded and swallowed.

Brother Durand cleared his throat and addressed Edwin. 'Brother William and I will carry out the procedure, but we will need several other men to hold him down.'

'I'm not going to run away, Brother,' began Martin, sounding rather slurred now, but the monk shook his head.

'I know that, my son, but it's a natural human reaction to seek to avoid pain. Once we begin you will not be able to help struggling, and if the surgery is to succeed then we need you to be as still as possible.' Then, to Edwin, 'The strongest you can find.'

'I'll fetch Willik—' Edwin brought himself up short.

'I was right next to him when he died,' said Martin, in a dreamy voice. 'I was looking into his eyes. It was … peaceful. He didn't look like he even knew anything about it.' He held up both his hands at looked at them in puzzlement. 'I think he was the lucky one.'

As Edwin stood to leave, Martin suddenly clutched at him. 'I have to die so Alys can live, don't you understand?'

'No, no you don't.'

'It was supposed to be quick. Get her out or die trying, that was it. Or *and* die trying. But where is she? Oh, Edwin, I've dropped her somewhere, and I have to go back. She's not here.'

Edwin looked at Brother Durand in confusion.

'Delirium,' said the monk, quietly. 'We need to get on with this as soon as possible.'

Edwin made another attempt to leave, but Martin had a fistful of his tunic in his good hand. 'Is she coming? Joanna?'

'Martin, I …'

'Mother? Where's my mother? She should be here, shouldn't she? Can you fetch her?'

Edwin's tears pricked again, for he was well aware that Martin had never known his mother at all; she had died bearing him.

'Oh, *there* she is – I can see her at the end of my bed. I knew she'd come. Everything will be all right now.'

Edwin untangled Martin's fingers as best he could. 'She'll look after you until I get back. I won't be long.'

Brother Durand picked up the jug of fortified wine. He poured a generous measure into a cup and then slipped one arm behind Martin's neck to raise him. 'There's more here than we need for cleaning. Drink this, and then the same again, before we start.'

All too soon, it was time.

Martin looked dazedly at the men surrounding him, and then directly at Edwin. 'You should go. You've got a weak stomach, you won't like it.'

Edwin shook his head. 'I'm not leaving you.' He took up a position at the top of the bed so he could cradle Martin's head – his poor, burning hot head – and speak in his ear, while the rest braced themselves. Sir Baldwin, wearing his mail for additional weight, knelt on Martin's left shoulder, his body thankfully screening the sight of the outstretched arm on its board, around which Brother William was tightening straps. A second man held Martin's right arm, while a third leaned over his torso and two more sat on his legs.

Brother Durand loomed. 'Are you ready?'

Martin closed his eyes for a moment and then opened them again. He stared through the men restraining him at a point just above the end of the bed. 'Yes.'

As gently as he could, the monk put a piece of wood in Martin's mouth. 'Keep your tongue out of the way, and bite into this with your teeth. It will soon be over.'

Edwin held Martin's head firmly and bent his own, so they were touching, as Brother Durand reached into the brazier and took up a knife.

Alys screamed.

She couldn't help herself. Of course, she knew that women shrieked and cried out during childbirth, because everybody knew that and she'd heard it herself on numerous occasions. But somehow she had never really associated that with the fact that she would do it herself; she had never thought that she would lose control in such a way, like the lowest beast of the field.

When the pains had begun, back at Tickhill, they had been awful, but they had come and gone in a manner that was just about bearable. Then, on the way back, they had become stronger and she had gritted her teeth and then finally chewed on a piece of sacking in order to stop herself from crying out. Surely, she had thought, as the waves rolled over her, nothing could be worse than this? The baby might even be born in the cart and she could present it to Moth— to Cecily and the others when she got back.

The driver had shouted out his errand to someone as soon as they had neared Conisbrough, and had then called back to her that a boy was running ahead to warn them in the village. By the time he pulled up outside the cottage, therefore, Cecily and Agnes were already there. They had taken her inside so that she was in her own bed, and Alys had thought and hoped and prayed that it would all be over soon. But then Cecily had examined her and announced that the early stages were going well so far.

Early stages? Alys came as near to swearing as she ever had. She was barely able to keep herself composed as she confessed to Father Ignatius, who had arrived in order to shrive her and pray to the saints who protected labouring women before beating a hasty retreat and leaving her in the all-female company that was so necessary.

Then it was decreed that she shouldn't be lying in bed at all, and they had made her walk up and down, eat, drink ... hours had passed, and more women had arrived, including Rosa, but there was still no baby. Or, at least, no baby of her own. There were others – indeed, the cottage seemed to be full of them. Rosa's son; Joan's daughter; and over to one side of the main room was a cradle in which lay the tiny bundle that was Mother and Sir Geoffrey's child. Edwin's half-sister had survived, and Alys gave thanks for it, but she had been able to do little else for the new member of the family other than leave her safely with the nurse while she concentrated on what was happening to her own body.

The night had been endless, waves of searing agony crashing over her as she moaned and panted, gripping the hands of each woman staying awake with her in turn. She sought to keep sipping whenever they put a cup to her lips, and prayed and prayed that the darkness and the labour would soon be over.

By the time dawn broke she was exhausted. How much longer was this going to go on for? Was something wrong? Was the baby stuck? Was it going to die? Was she? She begged Cecily to tell her, to speak the truth, but Cecily only kept answering that everything was fine and that it wouldn't be long now.

Then a swell of pain struck that was even greater than any yet, tearing her in half. Delirious as she was, trapped inside the agony, screaming without being able to help it, Alys wasn't sure whether she had heard or merely imagined that Cecily had added under her breath the words 'one way or the other'.

There was silence in the infirmary tent. Sir Baldwin and the other men had gone, Brother William and Brother Durand were attending to their other patients, and Edwin was sitting beside Martin's cot.

Edwin had hoped that Martin might fall unconscious during the surgery, thus sparing himself some of the pain, but he had remained awake all the way through, screwing up his eyes with the effort of trying not to scream or to buck too much against those who were holding him still. It was only after everything was over, and the monks had managed to force some kind of herbal concoction down his throat, that he had finally fallen asleep. Edwin had removed the stick from his mouth to see that it had been bitten almost all the way through. Martin lay now on his back, with his right arm by his side tucked under the blankets and his shortened and bandaged left arm lying on top, across his chest. There had been a great deal of blood, but most of that had been cleaned up, and all that remained were the droplets sprayed across both of them. Edwin wiped Martin's face, gently so as not to wake him, and then scrubbed his own.

Brother Durand had declared the immediate surgery to be a success, in that the cut had been made far up enough above the wrist for it all to be 'clean', and all the rotten flesh removed. And Martin was still breathing after this had been achieved, which was another victory; he might have bled to death, or apparently some people with less strength would die during the procedure, their hearts simply stopping. So this was all good. He was still not certain of survival, however: the dangers now were of further poisoning to the flesh, in the event that it spread because some of the rotten part had not been successfully removed; or that the new wound caused by the procedure itself might bleed too much or become putrid. The monks had cauterised the stump before they bandaged it, which had caused poor Martin even more agony – and Edwin nearly to pass out from the smell – but it was necessary.

So now they needed to keep checking that the bandage over the stump did not suddenly become bright red with new blood, or yellowy-green with pus, and that the remaining arm above it did not turn black. This was not a difficult exercise, so Edwin was able to keep his eyes on it while he let his mind wander a little. It was Alys, of course, who filled his thoughts, and he wished he knew what was happening back in Conisbrough. He could be a father or a widower by now, for all he knew, but he would keep hoping for the former until he was informed of anything to the contrary. He had to be rational about it, and not let his fears take over. Just because Mother had died in childbirth, it did not mean Alys would. Plenty of women – the majority – delivered their babies and survived. But if only he *knew*.

The only way he was going to find out was by getting back to Conisbrough, and the only way that was going to happen was if the situation here at Tickhill was resolved before the lord earl had to set off for London, which wouldn't be long now. Which meant that the same seemingly impossible problem had to be solved.

This morning, in the half-doze before waking, things had started to make a little bit more sense, but he still wasn't sure enough to proceed with any action. He'd come to wrong conclusions before, and the stakes here were just too high to allow for him making even the slightest mistake. He had his suspicions, but he needed to be sure, and he needed proof.

Edwin kept his gaze on Martin's bandage while all this was playing through his head. *Please, please, live.* Live to fight another day. If there was one tiny sliver of hope, it was that Martin had lost his left hand, not his right; he would still be able to hold his sword, and perhaps something could be done that would enable him to use his shield as well? Edwin recalled the man he'd once known who had a wooden leg. Could some kind of implement be devised that Martin could use? Or what was it that Sir Baldwin had said? That he would learn to compensate for the injury. After all, Sir Malvesin managed to fight with one eye, even though he had lost his line of —

Of course.

Yet again, Edwin had failed to see something that should have been glaringly obvious to him. He'd been so anxious and worried about everything that he just hadn't been able to think straight and put everything together. But there was Sir Baldwin's insult about bastards, Theo and Margaret not looking much alike, Adam's mention of fish, and of course the line of sight.

Edwin stood up as quietly as he could. It was a wrench to leave Martin – *Sir* Martin, he reminded himself – but he now knew enough to move forward and hopefully to get all of them out of this mess before anyone else had to die.

He slipped over to Brother William and explained that he needed to go and see the lord earl. The monk gave him a sharp look and went to sit by Sir Martin himself.

Edwin was tiptoeing out of the tent when he heard his name being called from across the camp. 'In the sick tent, I think,' came a voice, 'over that way.'

Thudding footsteps sounded and Edwin found himself faced with the wholly unexpected sight of a gasping Hal. Immediately his heart plummeted. There could be only one reason for …

'Have you just run all the way from Conisbrough?'

The boy nodded, unable to speak, his hands on his knees.

'What's happened? Tell me!'

Hal stood up and took in a huge, gasping breath.

He wasn't smiling.

'This is just an excuse to go home, isn't it?'

'No, my lord, I assure you it isn't. I really do need to go to Conisbrough, because the answer to everything is there.' *And has been all along*, Edwin added to himself, *only I didn't see it*.

'Well …'

'And I need to bring Everard with me, if you please, because I will need his authority with the garrison when I get there.'

The earl looked surprised. 'Geoffrey is there. That's more than enough authority.'

'From what I hear, my lord,' said Edwin, carefully, 'Sir Geoffrey is … unwell, and not quite himself.'

The earl grunted. 'That's true enough. Very well, go.' He turned to Hugh. 'Run and find Everard and tell him.' After the boy had scampered off, the earl looked out at the sun, already well on its way down. 'You won't have time to get there and back before nightfall, but I want you to return here as soon as dawn breaks tomorrow, you hear? Another letter has arrived and I'll need to set off for London on Monday. I want Tickhill in my hands before I go.'

'I'll set off at first light tomorrow, my lord,' replied Edwin, not wishing to guarantee any of the rest of it. Things could still go awry.

He left the tent with his mind in turmoil, unsure which of his many conflicting emotions were uppermost. He was about to do something both dangerous and upsetting, which was going to change the lives of many people. But this could be balanced out by the sheer joy of the news Hal had brought.

The eight-mile run had been tiring, even for a youth who was used to working in the fields all day, and at first Hal had been unable to speak until he got his breath back. He was also wary of what Edwin's reaction would be when he told him that he had a daughter, not the son he must have been hoping for; there were a number of men in the village who would have been either disappointed or angry at receiving such news.

Edwin recalled the worry he had felt on first seeing Hal and his expression, and how his feelings had turned from anxiety to jubilation. He would remember the moment for all his life. Alys was safe, their child was healthy, and he felt as though he could float several feet in the air. And now he would be able to see them! Before today ended, he would embrace his beautiful wife and meet his daughter.

He went to enquire about being allocated a horse, and to see if he could get one that would carry both him and Hal; the boy deserved a ride home after all his efforts, and Edwin was now a competent enough rider to be able to control a steady mount even with the additional passenger.

Everard arrived at the horse picket while Edwin was in negotiations with the head groom. 'What's all this about?' He looked strained: the deaths of a number of men under his command, in a conflict he hadn't wanted in the first place, had hit him hard.

'I need you to come to Conisbrough with me,' said Edwin, simply, unwilling at this point to explain further. 'I'm going to need you when I get there.'

Everard's face creased in puzzlement, but he was used to following orders without question, so he merely began to check the girth on the horse that was brought to him.

They took the road at a steady pace, Edwin with Hal sitting behind him and holding on to his belt.

When they got to within sight of Conisbrough, Edwin pulled up. 'Hal,' he said, 'why don't you run ahead and let my wife know we're coming? Tell her I'll only be able to stop briefly to start with, but after I've been up to the castle I'll come home and be there all night.'

Hal slid down and nodded. 'Of course.'

They watched him depart, and Everard was about to urge his horse into motion again when he noticed that Edwin was making no effort to move. 'What's the matter? I'd have thought you were keen to get going. Or did you want to give her a good chance to tidy herself up before you get there?'

'Do you remember,' replied Edwin, staring into the middle distance, 'about a year and a half ago, when I was accused of … you know?'

'Yes, of course I do,' came the bemused reply. 'What of it?'

'We were on horseback, like this, you and I, on our way back to Conisbrough.'

'Yes?'

'And you stopped, and you gave me the opportunity to run away. I could flee, you said, and you wouldn't chase after me, you'd make an excuse as to why I got away.'

'Yes, I did. And you refused, because you'd rather face up to it all. It worked out all right for you in the end, of course, but I still stand by what I said that day. It might have saved your life.'

'Well, I want to give you the same opportunity.'

'What?' Everard sounded shocked. 'What do you mean? Why?'

Edwin turned to look him full in the face. 'Because I know what you did.'

Chapter Twelve

Martin stirred and found himself in a heaving sea of pain.

Pain was barely even the right word for it. Pain was when you had toothache, or when you'd taken a fall from your horse – it wasn't this overwhelming sensation of screaming agony that suffused your whole being and made you want to dive back into the depths of unconsciousness so you could get away from it.

'The worst is over now, my son,' came a voice from somewhere nearby.

Martin managed to open his eyes, but the effort of trying to turn his head was too much.

'You have survived, Martin, do you understand?' It was Brother Durand's voice. 'You have lived.'

Some kind of groan escaped Martin's lips, but he couldn't even *think* words, never mind say them out loud.

He heard the familiar sound of a Latin prayer of thanksgiving, and was ready to doze off to it again when the monk finished and spoke directly to him once more. 'And now, I wish to give you some reasons to continue living.'

Martin said nothing, but he did find this interesting enough to try to stay conscious.

'Firstly, you will wish to know that Edwin's wife was safely delivered this morning, and that they have a healthy daughter. And, make no mistake, you were instrumental in ensuring that she was able to do this in the comfort of her own home, with her own women about her, rather than inside an enemy castle. You brought her out, and you may have saved the baby's life, for who knows whether it would have survived had it been born under different circumstances.'

Martin came nearer to wakefulness, able to feel the first stirrings of feeling. Maybe surviving all this wasn't completely bad? He managed to turn his head a little so he could meet the monk's eye.

'Ah, good, well done. Now, another small drink, if you can.'

Martin realised how thirsty he was. He felt his head being lifted and a cup being put to his lips. He couldn't seem to control his movements, and most of the watered wine went over his chin; but enough made it down his throat for him to feel a little refreshed in spite of the agony that was still imprisoning his body.

'Now, another thing. I heard you say earlier that everyone hated you. This is not true.'

Martin rolled his eyes. The monk was going to tell him that God loved him, wasn't he?

He must have somehow said or mouthed the word 'God', because Brother Durand smiled. 'Of course God loves you, my son, but I was speaking of another. You knew him for only a short time, but Brother Benedict prays for you every day.'

Martin allowed his mind to wander back to those days at Roche. He remembered Benedict, the novice he'd befriended. He'd been a very intense young man, and it was no surprise that … oh.

A sudden memory came back to him. When they'd parted, Martin had promised to pray for Benedict the following Easter, because that was when he would be taking his final vows. And that hadn't been the Easter just gone, but the one last year. And not only had Martin not said those prayers, but he couldn't honestly say that he'd given Benedict one thought in all the intervening while. And yet Benedict had remembered him through all those months and was praying for him still.

Tears of shame sprang to Martin's eyes.

Brother Durand saw them and misunderstood. 'There, now. You see? Those around you care for you, as Edwin and the lord earl said earlier, and now you know that there are those further afield who are concerned for your welfare.' He paused. 'I've been harsh on you in the past, I know, and I hope you'll forgive me for it. But believe me when

I say that if you don't want to feel hated, Martin, you have to stop hating yourself.'

After that Martin must have slept a little more, because when he came to himself again it was Brother William, not Brother Durand, who was kneeling in prayer by the side of his bed.

This time the agony was more localised, centred on his left arm. Resolutely not looking at it, Martin roused himself and attempted speech. 'Brother?'

The murmuring paused. 'Martin? Sir Martin? You're awake? How do you feel?'

He licked his lips. 'Hurts.'

'Yes, it will do. But, thanks be to God, the surgery was a success and the early signs are good – so far there is no festering or severe bleeding.'

He still wouldn't look. 'Edwin?'

'He left earlier, but not before he knew that you were out of your initial danger.'

'Ah. Baby.'

'Yes – what wonderful news for him.' There was a pause. 'Although, come to think of it – no, he was already on his way out to see the lord earl when Hal arrived to tell him.'

What Martin wanted to be able to say was, 'Oh dear – and did he have that look on his face, the one that means he's just solved something and is about to dive head first into danger?' but the most he could manage was 'See my lord?'

'Yes. He'd been sitting by your bed, watching over you, and then he came to me and said he had to go. He had that look – you know the one.'

Was Brother William possessed of supernatural powers? Or perhaps they both just knew Edwin too well. But this was not good. If he, Martin, wasn't there to protect Edwin, he would no doubt go and do something stupid.

'Danger!' So strong was this thought that Martin even tried to move, his mind forgetting for one moment where he was, and why. But he didn't get anywhere near sitting up – the mere act of attempting it shot a pain up through his arm greater than any he'd ever known, and he immediately collapsed back with a hastily swallowed cry and tears of pain and frustration. He had to try very hard not to whimper like a child.

Brother William placed one large hand flat on his chest. 'You need to remain still. Please. As I said, the initial signs are good, but too much activity, or any sudden movement, might damage everything beyond repair again. I'm sorry, but whatever trouble Edwin has got himself into, this time he's going to have to manage it without you.'

Everard's reaction was so abrupt that his horse shied, and it took a few moments before he could bring it under control again.

'I can't think what you mean,' he began.

'Can't you?'

'Are you trying to accuse me of murder?'

'Actually, no, but the fact that your first thought was of the dead man is certainly illuminating.'

Everard's face was white. 'Well, what then?'

'I think you found him, and he was already dead, but you didn't raise the alarm.'

The tiny hint of relaxation dispelled any remaining doubts Edwin might have had. 'Well … what if I did? It might not have been right, but it isn't a serious crime. I certainly didn't kill him; it looked like an accident.' He paused. 'I can show you the place if you like – it's not far.'

'Please do.'

They retraced their steps for a short while, and then left the Conisbrough–Tickhill road to take the less well-defined shortcut that led to the Great North Road. This was the way that the royal justice would have taken on his journey from London, if he was familiar with the less-travelled path that would cut several miles off the trip compared with staying on the main road for longer. Edwin recalled that Prior Richard had said that the justice had been in this part of the county on numerous occasions, so Everard's story was plausible so far.

'Here,' Everard said, eventually. 'He was lying dead here, looking like he'd fallen from his horse.'

Edwin dismounted, noting that the ground was rocky and uneven. It hadn't rained at all since the body had been found, so perhaps if he looked closely … 'That's blood.'

Everard also dismounted and came closer. 'Looks like it.'

The stain was on the top of a stone that was embedded in the ground and had clearly not moved for years. Edwin tried to picture the scene to himself. The justice was riding along this path, perhaps confidently because he'd been this way before, when something had befallen his horse – it had stumbled, or perhaps a small animal had run out and startled it. He had fallen, breaking his wrist as he landed awkwardly and hitting his head on the stone. The horse had run away. The man had died either immediately or shortly afterwards from the head wound, the one Edwin had seen when he examined the body.

'You see?' asked Everard. 'An accident.'

'Oh, I believe you.'

'Then why did you want to offer me the chance to run away? There will be some consequences for me not reporting the death, now it's known that I found him first, but nothing worth becoming an outlaw for, especially as he was discovered not long afterwards anyway.'

'That's not why I said it. I said it because I know you are not a murderer, and that you acted – to start with, anyway – with good intentions, but despite that, I might not be able to save you from the lord earl's wrath when he finds out what else you did.'

'And what did I do?'

'You robbed the dead man's belt pouch, stole the royal order and hid it. And then, when we were at Tickhill, you told those inside what our plans were.'

Everard was shaking his head. 'It wasn't like that. You don't understand.' He paced away and then back. 'Why are you saying this? Why are you telling me all this now, while we're out here on our own? If you really think I did all this, why aren't you scared that I'll kill you?'

Unsurprisingly, this was a thought that had already crossed Edwin's mind. All this time he'd been telling himself that he could trust nobody, and now he was about to put his life into the hands of a man he was accusing of a crime. Was he mad? But he had to be able to trust himself, to trust in his own instincts, because if he did not, then what was left?

He tried to keep his voice steady. 'Because you're not a murderer. You're a loyal and honest man who got wildly out of his depth. You started something, and then it got away from you, leading to many deaths that you already feel a great guilt for. And all of that might result in your execution once the earl hears of it, but none of it was your intention. If this comes to trial – either private or public – I will do everything I can to stand up for you, to speak the truth, but it might not be enough.' Edwin rubbed a hand over his face. 'Which is why you might prefer simply to run. It would be very easy for me to say that you overpowered me once Hal was out of sight, and stole my horse.'

The sergeant was clearly in an agony of indecision. Edwin watched as a variety of emotions played out across his face and as he considered what he ought best to do. Did he think Edwin was bluffing?

'Tell me one thing,' burst out Everard, at last. 'You seem to have all these ideas about what I've done, but none of it would make sense to anyone else. Can you tell me – or the lord earl, or any other man, for that matter – *why* I would have done all this? Because they surely wouldn't believe you otherwise.'

'Oh yes,' replied Edwin, calmly. 'I know this isn't what you want to hear, but I can explain it all. I know why, and I know *who*.'

Alys looked down at her baby daughter. Did she most resemble herself, or Edwin? Edwin, she thought, but it didn't matter. The important thing was that their beautiful girl was here, she was alive, and she was in her own home. And the ordeal was over. Alys shuddered when she thought of the pain she'd endured, and felt a deep guilt because she knew that, at the height of it, if she had been offered a choice between its continuance and instant death, she would have chosen the latter without hesitation. This must be a great sin, surely.

But, oddly, as time went by and as Alys became more and more besotted with the tiny bundle, somehow the pain and the memory of the labour receded. Had it really been that bad? Or had she just been making an unnecessary fuss? She could almost blush when she recalled how she'd screamed and shouted out loud like that.

She heard the knock at the door and some kind of subsequent conversation, though she didn't know who and what until Rosa came in to let her know that Edwin was on his way. 'Hal says he's not far behind, won't be long at all. He gave Hal a ride nearly all the way back from Tickhill on a horse, fancy that!'

Alys's joy was complete, but she had only a moment to contemplate it before she realised that she must look a complete mess; her hair was like a bird's nest after all the sweating and tossing about, and her shift and the bed clothes were —

'Calm down, my dear,' said Cecily, who was with her in the room. 'I was just thinking it was time to get you changed and a little more comfortable now you've had some time to rest. We'll do it now before he gets here. Now, just pass her to me to lay in the cradle, and we'll sort everything out …'

Alys felt she should make haste, but she found herself unhurriedly changed into a clean shift, lying upon clean bedding and with the baby once more in her arms while Cecily combed her hair … and still Edwin had not come. 'He must be leaving me enough time to make myself presentable,' she joked. 'Did you say Hal had said Everard was with him? He'll be telling him all about how he shouldn't go into a chamber too early following a birth.' She wasn't worried; it wouldn't be long.

The first pangs of anxiety began as more time passed. Alys fed the baby for what felt like quite some while, and took a little broth herself, and still Edwin had not arrived. What could be keeping him? He'd apparently been within sight of the village when he sent Hal on ahead. Surely there was nothing to be frightened of, but the experiences of the past couple of weeks had left Alys feeling so much on edge that she couldn't help thinking that something tragically poignant had happened. What if Edwin had been worried about Alys's safety all this time, and had finally succeeded in getting her home, only to fall himself at the last stage before meeting his child? Maybe he was even now lying injured on the road! Although – she checked herself – if Everard was with him then that was unlikely. She needed to calm down.

Alys's nerves experienced a short reprieve when Cecily pointed out that if Edwin was returning to Conisbrough on the lord earl's business, he had probably been instructed to go straight up to the castle without calling in at home first, and had obeyed. But it only took a few moments for her to overturn that comfort: he'd sent word with Hal that he would come here first, hadn't he?

A knocking sounded.

'There you are,' said Cecily, soothingly, without stopping to think that Edwin wouldn't knock at his own door.

Alys was not surprised, therefore, when the newcomer turned out not to be Edwin.

Rosa put her head round the bedroom door. 'It's Sir Geoffrey, come to enquire,' she said. 'He says he won't come in while you're resting, but he asks are you all right, and the child.'

Alys knew perfectly well why he wouldn't enter the cottage, but she was in no fit state to remonstrate with him about it. 'Please tell him we're fine,' she replied. 'And … could you ask whether he's seen Edwin up at the castle?'

She waited while this was relayed.

'He says not, and should he be expecting him?'

Alys felt cold. Something terrible had happened to Edwin. On this of all days! What was she to do?

Rosa had been out and in again. 'He says, if you're sure Edwin was on the way, he'll send out after them. Probably just dawdling, he says, and nothing for you to worry about.'

Alys heard the cottage door shut, and then she had nothing to do but fret. Where could Edwin possibly be?

Everard started, visibly, at Edwin's last words. Then an expression of acute misery flooded over him. His shoulders slumped and he looked at the ground. He still made no attempt to get away, and Edwin knew that he wasn't going to, not now that he would be leaving someone else to face the storm.

'And so my only questions to you now are: what did you do with the royal order, and what did it say? Given what you've done, I can only assume —'

'I can show you where it is, but as to what it says, I have no idea.'

'What?'

'I can't read, you know that.'

'But then how did you know what it was? Or why to steal it?'

'It's a parchment thing with a big seal on it, looks pretty royal to me. Besides, I sort of know what the word "Tickhill" looks like – the shape of it. It was obvious what it was, what with people talking about the castle all the time, so I took it and hid it until I could give it to – I mean, until I could find someone to read it and tell me what it said.'

'So,' said Edwin, with some incredulity, 'you've caused all of this, or at least inadvertently allowed it to happen, and you don't even know what the decision was? You don't know whether the castle is to stay with Sir Robert or to be handed over to the lord earl?'

Everard merely shrugged.

It was at that point that they heard themselves being hailed, and Edwin turned to see Sir Geoffrey riding towards them. 'Say nothing,' he cautioned Everard, before the knight was within earshot. 'I'm still thinking, and if I can, I'll find a way out of this without any further bloodshed or violence.'

'There you are,' called Sir Geoffrey as he approached. 'Alys has been worried about you – Hal told her you were coming, and she thought you were hard on the boy's heels.'

He reined in, and Edwin had to stop himself exclaiming at the change in his appearance. Sir Geoffrey was, by any measure, an old man, but he'd always been so fit and active that nobody really noticed, and it was just assumed that he'd go on forever. But he seemed to have aged twenty years in the short time since Edwin had last seen him, and now looked haggard to the point of being three steps away from the grave.

Edwin attempted to recover himself so as not to make his shock evident. 'I'm on my way now,' he managed. 'But we stopped here because it was important. This seems to be where the royal justice met his death, and I'm fairly sure it was an accident.' He outlined his reasons for thinking so, and Sir Geoffrey agreed, fortunately not thinking to ask how Edwin and Everard had happened upon the exact spot when it was not actually on their road between Tickhill and Conisbrough.

They all mounted and rode at a steady pace, Edwin and Sir Geoffrey slightly ahead and Everard trailing behind.

'The bodies came yesterday,' began the knight without preamble, choosing this subject ahead of family matters. 'Willikin's was left and then they went on with the others to their own villages.' He sighed. 'Tell me of the engagement.'

Edwin recounted what he'd seen.

'And Martin disobeyed the lord earl? Deliberately? In order to get Alys out of the castle and away from danger?' He expelled a breath. 'In normal circumstances I'd have him cleaning the latrines from now until midsummer, if not worse, but in this case I'll let it pass.'

'I'm grateful to him, more grateful than I can say.' Edwin hesitated over how to break both pieces of news. Perhaps it would be best just to dive in. 'Sir Martin acted with great bravery, but I'm afraid he's paid a heavy price.'

Sir Geoffrey was already reacting to the first part before he grasped the second. 'Sir Martin! Well, it was always going to happen, especially after – wait, what sort of price?' His tone changed. 'He's not …'

'He's alive,' said Edwin, 'but I have to tell you that he's lost a hand.'

There was a sharp intake of breath. 'Left, or right?'

'Left. About halfway between his wrist and elbow. An arrow hit him during the fight, and at first he thought it wasn't too serious, but the wound went bad and Brother William and Brother Durand – the infirmarer from Roche, he's there – said it was the only way to save his life.'

'No doubt they were right. I've seen such injuries go putrid before. If you leave them it's a death sentence, but sometimes the poor souls don't survive having it cut off anyway.'

'Well, Martin has, at least so far, and they think it's hopeful.'

There was silence for a while, other than the sound of the horses' hooves.

'When he gets back,' said Sir Geoffrey, thoughtfully, 'he'll need action rather than sympathy. It won't help if we all keep saying what a shame it is and feeling sorry for him. We'll need to concentrate on what he *can* do, how he can work round it. I'll devise some new training exercises for him.'

Edwin agreed. Then there was another lengthy silence, and he could stand it no more. 'Sir Geoffrey,' he began, 'I know you don't want to talk about it – and neither do I, really – but perhaps we can go over it this once and then have done.'

The knight stared in the opposite direction.

'It's about my mother.'

Sir Geoffrey tensed. Then he nodded and, with infinite sadness, turned. 'It's my fault, Edwin. At her age – and mine – we should have made it a marriage in name only. But after so many years … and then she found she was with child, and it was too late, so all I could do was pray. And now look! I'm responsible for her death, and I'll carry that burden until the end of my days.'

'It wasn't your fault,' replied Edwin, gently. 'She was pleased and happy to be carrying your child, and talked to me many times of how she'd always wished I had a brother or sister.' He paused. 'If anything, it was me going away at this time and taking Alys with me into danger that caused it all to go wrong.' The grief and frustration that he'd been trying to hide for the last few days bubbled up again. 'If only I'd been here!'

'You wouldn't have been able to do anything.' Sir Geoffrey shook his head. 'Once a woman goes into the birthing chamber it's simply down to God's will whether she lives or dies. And He decided that she was better with your father in heaven than with me on earth.'

Edwin let go of the reins long enough to cross himself. '*Requiescat in pace*. She's in the best place now, and it's just up to those of us who are left behind to continue living without her.'

'But what if —' Sir Geoffrey bit off the rest before he could say it out loud.

Edwin knew what he'd been about to say. *What if I don't want to live without her*. Just as he wouldn't want to go on without Alys, and Martin didn't want to survive an injury that would prevent him from following the path in life that was his heart's desire.

'Well,' continued Edwin, with an effort. 'One of Mother's wishes has come true: I have a sister. Please, tell me of her. Does she look like Mother, or like you? Or even like me?'

'I haven't seen her.'

'What?'

'I couldn't face … I just couldn't.'

'But she's your daughter!'

'I know. And she's also the only part of my wife I have left, but still …' Sir Geoffrey looked older than ever.

Another thought struck Edwin. 'If you haven't seen her, who took her to church to be baptised?'

He received no reply, but the aura of guilt in the air increased considerably.

'She … she has been baptised?'

'Not yet.'

Edwin was aghast. Babies, even healthy ones, could sicken and die with frightening speed, and making sure they were in a state of God's grace was almost the first thing any parent did. Many were taken to church on the actual day of their birth, and most or all within a few days or certainly the first Sunday following.

Edwin took a deep breath. 'I have no right to overrule your decision as a father,' he said. 'And I have too much respect for you to ever normally speak to you in this way. But I must insist that she be baptised. Why, they can both be taken together. Does she even have a name?'

'Not yet,' said Sir Geoffrey, again.

They were by now entering Conisbrough itself, and Edwin waved at a couple of men returning from the fields who called out to him with congratulations.

They reached the cottage. 'Will you come inside with me now?' He had to get Sir Geoffrey to snap out of this.

Sir Geoffrey shook his head. 'I need to get back to the castle. I told them I wouldn't be long as I was only coming down to enquire about Alys, but now I've had to chase after you for miles I've been gone some time.' He paused. 'You come up after you've seen them, to tell me more of what's happened at Tickhill, and then we'll both return here together later on.'

He and the still-silent Everard moved off, taking Edwin's horse with them, and he faced his own door for the first time in what felt like years.

Bizarrely, he was nervous.

He took a breath, pushed open the door and called out.

It was busy and noisy inside; very different from the usual peace when only the two of them were home. The fire was burning, something was cooking and he could make out a number of female figures bustling about.

'There you are!' Cecily ran to embrace him.

He held her for a few moments, aware of how difficult the last week must have been for her, then stood back to look at her from arm's length. 'I am so grateful to you, aunt, for everything you've done for us. Everything.'

She wiped one eye. 'That's what family's for. Now, never mind me, you have to see Alys and meet the new arrivals.'

There was a large baby making quite a noise over in one corner, and for a moment Edwin was bemused, until he saw Rosa picking it up. Her own, of course; she was still feeding him herself and so couldn't leave him anywhere while she was tending to Alys. Joan was also there with hers.

Cecily led him over towards Alys's loom, the last piece she'd been working on before they left for Tickhill still on it. It was to be a blanket for the baby, made of the softest-spun of her wool, and Edwin gave thanks once more that it would be needed to serve its intended purpose.

Next to the loom was a cradle, and lying in it was a swaddled infant, fast asleep. 'Your sister,' whispered Cecily.

Edwin looked down and was overwhelmed with love. His *sister*. The first sibling he had ever known, in almost twenty-two years on God's earth. 'She's beautiful.'

'She doesn't yet have a name. We wondered if Sir Geoffrey would want to call her Anne, but until he says so there's nothing we can do.'

'I'll bring him back with me later, and we can discuss it.'

'And now …'

Cecily pushed open the bedroom door, and Edwin followed her inside almost shyly. It was Agnes who first caught his eye, sitting on the near side of the bed, but when Edwin moved to see past her he was able to feast his eyes on the most beautiful sight he'd ever seen: Alys, sitting up, smiling, and cradling a baby in her arms.

Cecily and Agnes slipped out, Edwin barely noticing as he came to sit on the edge of the bed.

'Oh, my love! How wonderfully you've done.'

Alys leaned forward to kiss him, and the movement made the baby open her eyes. They were blue, and they stared into Edwin's with what appeared to be ferocious determination.

'Little one,' whispered Alys, 'meet your father.'

Hesitantly – she was so small! – Edwin put out a finger and gently stroked his daughter's face. 'Hello, my sweet one,' he said, almost choking. 'I'm here now, and I'll look after you forever.'

Alys kissed him again, and Edwin was the luckiest, happiest man in the world.

'We'll need to decide on a name for her,' he said, trying to remain in the room instead of drifting away on a cloud of joy.

'I had wondered if we should call her Anne, after your mother, but then I thought we'd better check with Sir Geoffrey, in case that was what he wanted. They can't both be called Anne, or life will get very confusing.'

Edwin had already given this matter some thought. 'I agree. And, much as I would love to call her Alys, that might be confusing too. So I wondered – what do you think to naming her after *your* mother? After all, you're the one who did all the work to bring her into the world.'

Alys gave a soft cry. 'Oh, Edwin! That would be wonderful.'

'Well then, let's do that.' He gazed again in besotted wonder at the baby. 'Edith, welcome to your family.'

He and Alys spoke together for a short while, enjoying this special time with their firstborn that would never happen again. But eventually she had to ask. 'Didn't you say you had to do something up at the castle?'

Edwin sighed. Duty always reappeared, didn't it? 'Yes, yes I do. But I won't be long, and then I'm to come back here for the night, because the lord earl isn't expecting me back at Tickhill until tomorrow morning.'

She couldn't help grasping at his sleeve. 'And then ...?'

'If I'm right, which I'm almost certain I am, then this is all going to be over quite quickly now, and God willing with no more bloodshed.' Reluctantly, he stood up. 'I'll see you very shortly.'

He tiptoed out of the cottage and made his way up the village street towards the castle. It was now full dark, but he was home and he knew every turn and bump in the path, so he reached the outer gatehouse without mishap. The main gate was closed, but the guard on it was expecting him and knew him by sight, so he was admitted. The same process followed at the gatehouse to the inner ward, and soon Edwin was in the hall; here he had the opposite experience to the one he'd had at home, in that it was significantly emptier and quieter than usual.

Everard was sitting alone at the end of one of the long tables, and he got up as soon as he saw Edwin. 'Well?'

'Let's fetch the document, and then we can see what's what. I think I know where I'm going, don't I?'

They left the hall and Everard, as Edwin had expected, led him to the armoury. Lighting a torch from one of the braziers that stood in the inner ward, they entered. This was the only logical place that Everard could have hidden it, Edwin knew. He didn't spend much time in the keep, so wouldn't be able to conceal anything there; and, like virtually everyone in the castle, he had no private space of his own. He slept in the hall with dozens of others and kept his spare clothes under one of the side benches, in a box that he shared with several others. The armoury was likewise a communal space, but he was in charge of it and the furthest reaches were not much used, so Edwin was unsurprised when Everard dragged out a stool and stood on it to fumble around at the back of the top shelf.

He turned. 'Here.'

He was holding out a folded piece of parchment that had a large seal appended to it. Edwin looked at it in the dim and smoky light: the royal sigil.

This, then, was it. This is what all the death had been about, all the violence that could have been avoided if it had been delivered straight to its intended recipient.

'What does it say?' Everard's voice was urgent. 'Tell me, please – what is the future of Tickhill, and everyone in it?'

Edwin unrolled the parchment and began to read.

Chapter Thirteen

How to keep the precious royal command safe overnight was Edwin's next concern. Given all that had passed, he didn't think that Everard would make any attempt to steal it back, but the suspicious part of him couldn't rule out that someone might somehow have divined that the document was at Conisbrough and would send armed men after it.

This left Edwin in a terrible dilemma. The safest place for the order overnight would be in the keep, behind two gates and three sets of walls. But as Edwin didn't want to let it out of his sight, that would mean him staying there as well, rather than going home as he had promised. But if he took it home with him, was he potentially putting his family in danger? The agony of his duty versus his desire had never been so apparent; he knew exactly what the earl would say, if he were here, but he also knew that the earl had very little regard for anything except his own wishes.

For once, Edwin's heart won out and he decided to go home. The chances of either the earl or Sir Robert having worked anything out were remote, and armed men were not going to appear on the village green. All the same, when Edwin met with Sir Geoffrey in order to walk down to the cottage, he asked if he might be able to bring his sword and stay all night.

That shook the knight out of his stupor more than anything else Edwin had seen so far, and he was almost as alert as usual on the way. He accepted Edwin's decision not to tell him why this was necessary other than that it was on the earl's business, and followed him down the empty, moonlit village street.

When they reached the cottage Sir Geoffrey hesitated. 'Here I am, about to meet my daughter for the first time, and I've brought my sword,' he said. 'I had thought that peace had come to the land, and that my days of violence were over, but evidently not.' He sounded old and tired.

Edwin put one hand on his arm. 'Any violence is not of your making, and your sword is as ready now as it was half a century ago to defend the weak.' He tried to sound a little more cheerful. 'Now, are you ready?' Remembering his own experience of a couple of hours earlier, he was secretly excited and hoped with all his heart that Sir Geoffrey would feel something similar.

They went in. This time it was Agnes who was in the main room, simultaneously stirring a pot of what smelt like broth and keeping an eye on a smaller container of something herbal that was quite pungent.

She looked up. 'You've finally forced yourself to come, then?' she asked Sir Geoffrey. Nobody else in the village would think of addressing the knight in such a tone, but extreme age brought with it certain privileges.

Sir Geoffrey looked uncertainly around him. 'Yes. Is ...?'

'You sit yourself down,' she replied, unfolding herself like a bundle of gnarled sticks, 'and I'll bring her over.'

Edwin moved towards the bedchamber, partly as he didn't want to waste a single moment that he could be spending with Alys and Edith, and partly as he wanted to give Sir Geoffrey some privacy at this special moment. But he couldn't help himself; he lingered in the shadow by the door.

Sir Geoffrey was facing the fire, and his face was illuminated as Agnes gently placed the baby into his arms. 'She's properly swaddled so she can't wriggle, so no need to worry about dropping her.'

Edwin watched the old warrior's face grow still, then soften, then take on an expression of love and joy. He smiled to himself and slipped through to the bedchamber.

It was some while later when he came back out. He and Alys had spoken for a while, not only of their love for each other and their daughter, but also catching up on what had happened while they'd been apart. But now she and Edith were both asleep, so he thought he'd leave them to rest, knowing they'd have to wake in the night for a feed. He'd heard from other parents that day and night, time itself, had no meaning when you had a new baby, and he was already beginning to see that they were right.

Sir Geoffrey was still sitting in the same place with his daughter, but she was becoming fretful and soon let out a wail of startling intensity. He jumped, unsure what to do and perhaps thinking that he'd done something himself to cause it. But Joan hurried over, assured him it was just because she was hungry, and took her away. Soon the noise ceased and was replaced by sounds of suckling.

Edwin, who couldn't remember the last time he'd eaten anything, ladled out a couple of bowls of broth, found some bread and sat down facing Sir Geoffrey across the table.

They ate in silence for a few moments before the knight spoke. 'I've been a fool. Not wanting to come here, not wanting to see her – and I've missed the first few days of her life!'

'She won't mind,' replied Edwin. 'It's what you do from now on that counts.'

'I'll have her baptised first thing tomorrow morning; it's Sunday tomorrow anyway.'

'Us too. I told my lord I'd set off at first light, but if we go to see Father Ignatius very early, just as dawn is breaking, or even a little before, we should be able to get it done before I leave. I won't let Edith be baptised without me being there, and I won't go away and leave her before it's done.'

'Edith?'

'Yes, that's what we've decided. It was Alys's mother's name.'

'I did wonder if you might want to call her … you know.' Sir Geoffrey's expression was sad again.

'And you? Will you?'

There was a pause before Sir Geoffrey replied in a considered tone. 'No, I don't think so. Anne was Anne, and I don't want her memory to fade because it gets mixed up with the name of her daughter. I'll have to think of something else.'

'Your own mother's name?'

'She was called Matilda. She's been dead these forty years, God rest her.'

'Matilda it is, then, and we'll go to church just before dawn.' Edwin let out a large yawn. 'In the meantime, we'd better get some rest.'

'You sleep. If I can have that chair instead of this stool, I'll put it by the door and stay up to watch, just in case.' He made a rueful face. 'I'm not sleeping much anyway, at the moment. And you've got more to face tomorrow.'

Edwin didn't argue. He decided against disturbing Alys and instead unrolled a palliasse and laid it on the floor, just as he had slept all his life until he got married. The precious document was tucked in between his shirt and his tunic, and he kept one hand on it as he let the room fade around him.

He didn't sleep very well, because all four babies cried either separately or together for most of the night, but they were otherwise undisturbed, and the parchment was still safe when he rose.

Alys, of course, was not able to go to the church – Edwin had never considered it before, but actually it was a shame that mothers could never attend their babies' baptisms – and Agnes stayed with her, but the rest set off together. A child needed three godparents, two of the same sex and one of the other, and at least two of them had to be present in church. They could be friends or family as long as they were not the child's own parents, so after some quick calculations Edwin was able to work out that he, Alys and Cecily could stand for Matilda, and Cecily, Rosa and Sir Geoffrey for Edith. Edwin suffered a pang that Martin – *Sir* Martin, he would have to get used to that – was not able to be with them, nor any of Alys's own family, but it was the children's souls that were most important, and this needed to be done now.

Father Ignatius was already up, saying the early morning office, and he welcomed them all. The babies were prayed over, dipped in the font and anointed with oil, and then their Christian status was forever assured.

It was still not completely light when they all emerged from the church, wreathed in smiles, and Edwin was sure he could still get to

Tickhill without anyone realising that he had delayed. But when he and Sir Geoffrey had bid their farewells to the others and were nearing the castle, they became aware of a disturbance. Some men inside were calling out. The outer gates were just opening; before the gap was much more than a foot wide, a man of the garrison shot out.

He started to run but stumbled to a halt when he saw them. 'I was just coming to find you, Sir Geoffrey.'

'Why? What's happened?' The knight already had one hand on his sword.

'It's Everard, Sir Geoffrey.'

The knight looked puzzled, but Edwin's heart began to pound and he could feel it in his throat. Had he made a dreadful mistake? Had he been wrong to trust his instincts, after all? He'd told Everard last night that he did not intend to have him put in custody, that he'd try to minimise any danger to him, but that some things were bound to come out and that he should prepare himself for the consequences. Had Edwin misjudged the sergeant and his motives? Perhaps the events of the previous week weren't as inadvertent as Edwin had thought, and now Everard had committed some terrible crime. Visions of dead men lying on the hall floor swam before his eyes.

'Well?' Sir Geoffrey was snapping, unaware of what was going on in Edwin's mind.

'We're not quite sure how it happened, sir, but there's been a terrible accident. He's fallen from the roof of the keep.'

It was much later than anticipated when Edwin finally left Conisbrough. He'd felt obliged to go up to the ward with Sir Geoffrey, though he'd balked at going anywhere near the broken corpse that had thankfully already been covered with a blanket. He didn't need to examine it to determine the cause of Everard's death.

His conscience told him that he should tell the truth straight away, and air his suspicions that Everard had jumped. But that was a very,

very serious accusation: if it was decided that Everard had committed self-murder, he would be denied burial in consecrated ground and his soul would suffer in torment forever. And it would raise very awkward questions as to *why* he had done it, which would result in more information becoming public than Edwin wanted.

Sir Geoffrey – who might have been tired but who certainly wasn't a fool – had asked him why Everard had accompanied him back to Conisbrough, and had looked distinctly sceptical when Edwin had tried to get away with 'apparently I need looking after on the road', which might have been true but certainly didn't explain why his companion had to be the sergeant-at-arms himself. It hurt Edwin deeply to deceive Sir Geoffrey, to deceive anyone, but this was a complicated situation and it was better to keep his mouth shut until he had worked out the best way to deal with it.

His primary thought now, as he rode morosely towards Tickhill with an armed member of the garrison for company, was to find a way forward that was as honest as possible while preventing any more deaths. And that was the rub. If the earl learned that Everard had conspired with those inside – or rather, as he would see it, that they had subverted one of his most loyal men – he might wreak terrible revenge even if Sir Robert surrendered the castle to him when he saw the royal order to do so.

For that was what the document said: Tickhill castle was to pass from the crown to Lady Alice, countess of Eu, and custody of it was therefore to be relinquished by the crown's representative to hers. Sir Robert, as it happened, was commended in the document for his loyal service and promised a castellanship of equal value, so if Edwin could make them all see sense – *if* Sir Robert kept to his word to surrender peacefully, *if* the earl could be persuaded to accept that surrender without any hangings or destruction – this could all be over by the end of the day. The earl could set off for London ready to jostle for position in the new regime once a replacement regent was appointed, and the rest of them could bury their dead and mourn in peace.

The problem with all of this, of course, was that it would require Edwin to lie. And not even merely to blur the edges of the truth, but to tell deliberate falsehoods in a steady voice that everyone would believe. Probably, at some stage, in front of the abbot as well as the earl and Sir Robert.

Despite the cool spring morning, Edwin felt sweat beginning to form on his brow.

They rode through Tickhill town on their way to the camp, and Edwin looked at the church as they passed it. The priest would have buried Theo by now, perhaps with some members of his family in attendance but certainly without his sister, trapped inside the castle and with her own fate depending on Edwin's actions. He thought of her grief, viewed at a distance on the battlements, and all the sorrowing men and women he'd seen at closer quarters. There was such misery in the world, and he had the chance to stop more being created, as long as he didn't mind imperilling his own soul.

They were halted by a guard as they neared the camp, but they were both easily recognisable and Edwin was expected, so the garrison man bid him farewell and turned back straight away, while Edwin was led to the earl's tent. As soon as he got there Edwin managed to attract Adam's attention to ask him how Sir Martin was, and received the heartening news that although he was in great pain, he was alive and coherent, and his survival seemed more certain.

Thanking God and feeling more confident, Edwin was admitted to see his lord and give him the good news. This was the easy part. The earl was jubilant, checking the seal and ordering Edwin to read the Latin aloud and translate it.

'There is no doubt about it,' he said, when Edwin had finished, 'Sir Robert will have no choice but to submit.' Then his face began to darken. 'If only he had done so when I first told him, this could all have been avoided.'

'My lord,' said Edwin, carefully, 'Please recall that Sir Robert has not yet seen this document. As far as he is concerned, he holds

Tickhill for the king until ordered to do otherwise, and he has received no such command.'

The earl was in too good a mood to resent this interjection. To Edwin's relief, his only reply was, 'Very well. If he surrenders the moment he sees it, I will consider the matter closed.'

Unfortunately, Edwin's respite didn't last long. 'But I would dearly like to know,' continued the earl, 'how and why he has not seen it yet. No doubt you can explain this.'

Here we go, thought Edwin. 'When I was inside Tickhill castle, my lord,' he began, hoping he wasn't shaking too much, 'a body was found, which turned out to be that of a royal justice.'

'Yes. The news reached us at Conisbrough too.'

'I initially wondered if he had been murdered. His bags were empty, so he could have been killed either by footpads, or by somebody with … another motive.'

'Somebody who wanted to stop the order getting through.'

'Precisely, my lord. And naturally my suspicion was that Sir Robert had ordered this, and that when he saw the document he would seek to destroy it.'

'So that's it! Why —'

'Pardon me for interrupting, my lord, but that is definitely not it. In fact, Sir Robert is completely innocent in all of this.' Well, at least he'd said *one* true thing.

'Weaver, don't try my patience. Just tell me what happened.'

'It just didn't make sense, my lord. Firstly, why *hide* the document when it would be safer simply to burn it? And why hide or destroy one order at all, when another would surely follow as soon as it became known he had not obeyed? And if he was expecting such a thing, why not start to prepare the castle for a long siege? He could surely anticipate a royal army turning up sooner or later. Furthermore, I could find no evidence at all that the document was actually in the castle, or ever had been. The only logical explanation was that Sir Robert was holding out because he was genuinely awaiting a command.'

'So what happened? Out with it, man.' The tone was becoming a little more clipped, and Edwin knew he didn't have long.

'I began to wonder, my lord, whether my own suspicious mind was inventing crimes where there were none. The reason I wanted to take the Conisbrough road yesterday was because I had found out from the men inside Tickhill roughly where the body was found, and I wanted to examine the spot.'

Understanding began to dawn. 'Ah. And you needed Everard – while Geoffrey is incapacitated – to raise the garrison to help you look.'

That will do, thought Edwin. *And Everard can't contradict it now*. 'As you say, my lord. And what I discovered was that the man died in an accident.'

'You're sure?' The earl's tone was hopeful. 'You know this will make a great difference when the lord regent or his successor hears what happened?'

'Yes, my lord. He died in a fall from his horse, and then his bags were robbed after that, by someone who came across the body. They took everything and ran, but later presumably considered the document of no worth to them and discarded it while they kept the money, or clothes, or whatever else he was carrying.'

'And you found the document.'

'Yes, my lord.' *Please don't ask exactly where*.

But the earl seemed satisfied. 'All right. Now, we will send a delegation towards the castle.'

His mind was already moving forward and Edwin should presumably consider himself dismissed, but he held his ground. 'If I may, my lord?'

'Is there something else?'

'After … what happened the other day, Sir Robert will naturally be suspicious. He won't want to open his gates to any sort of party. Might I suggest that I approach the castle alone, holding up the order, and ask him to send the abbot or the prior out to meet me, in the middle of the open space, so he can read the document himself and confirm to Sir Robert what it says?'

The earl considered this. 'Yes. Let it be so. Or maybe Everard should go with you so he can confirm all this about finding it.'

Edwin winced. 'I really do think that no fighting men at all should be near, my lord. I, as an unarmed civilian, talking to a monk, can pose no possible threat to anyone.' He took a deep breath. 'And besides, my lord, I'm afraid Everard is dead.'

'*What*?'

This was a dangerous moment, and all Edwin's web might be about to unravel, but once the earl had mentioned the name the truth had to come out, or he would wonder later why Edwin had not told him, which would be much worse in the long run. 'I'm sorry to be the bearer of the news, my lord, but I can confirm it was another accident, and no possibility of murder.' No need to mention the third option. 'He'd been upset about the deaths of some of those under his command, and it made him absent-minded. He was on the roof of the keep, maybe leaning out to look over the churchyard, or maybe just deep in thought and not really paying attention, and he fell. There was nobody else up there at the time and no way that he could have been pushed.'

The earl shook his head. 'He was a good man.' Then, as Edwin had correctly predicted to himself, his lord returned immediately to his own concerns. 'Let's get this organised, then. The sooner the better.'

Edwin left the tent, still feeling edgy and nervous but a little more confident that the first stage of his plan had worked. He was a liar and would go to hell if he died before he was able to confess, but lives would be saved if he could just keep going. And he had the slight comfort that there was one other person who was going to know the whole truth, if only he could get safely inside the castle.

Edwin was accompanied to the edge of the camp by a group of knights and interested hangers-on, and then he set forward alone. Feeling incredibly exposed, he held the document, its seal dangling, high in the air as he walked. When he reached what he judged was the halfway point he stopped and called out. 'I need to speak with Sir Robert.'

It was at that moment that an arrow hit the ground next to him.

He should have jumped back, but he was so shocked that for a moment his feet seemed rooted in the earth, and he was still in the same place when he heard the telltale whistling of a second arrow.

The pain had not subsided, but at least now it was one that could be recognised, fought against, controlled, rather than the all-consuming agony that had clouded Martin's mind as well as capturing his body.

Brother Durand came over and helped him to drink. It was more of that foul-tasting potion, but if it took the edge off the torment for a little while then Martin would down as much of it as he could get.

'Can I get up?' He couldn't stay here, just lying in bed; it would drive him mad.

The monk considered. 'Let's try something a little less drastic to start with, shall we? Maybe sitting up.'

'All right.'

'But before we do that, there is something very important I need you to do.'

'What's that?'

'I want you to look at it.'

Martin stared over the monk's shoulder and said nothing.

'This is going to be with you for the rest of your life, my son, and the sooner you face it, the better. You're not frightened of an armed enemy – why should you be afraid of this?'

'I'm not afr—' began Martin, and realised straight away how he'd been tricked.

'Well then, you'll have no problem looking, will you?'

Maybe it was better to get it over with. Martin had spent his waking hours trying to ignore it, trying to pretend that the whole thing hadn't happened, but deep down he knew that couldn't last. He gritted his teeth and looked down at where his left arm lay on his chest.

The tent began to spin as he contemplated the space where his hand used to be. His mind almost failed to grasp it – why, he could feel himself flexing his fingers! But he couldn't see that happening because he had no fingers, did he. Never again would he curl them around the strap of his shield, or his horse's reins. How would he ride? How would he fight? It was all …

'If you're going to vomit,' came Brother Durand's voice from somewhere far away, 'try to turn your head so that you don't do it lying flat on your back. The last thing we need is you choking.'

'I am not going to vomit.' The words came out from between clenched teeth as, with a huge effort of will, Martin controlled both the bile in his throat and the dizziness in his head.

He forced himself to look again. The hand and wrist were gone, but the rest of his arm was still there. He poked it above the elbow, relieved that he could feel the touch. Then he forced his eyes down again. The … the *stump* was covered by a bandage that was weeping a little but not soaked. 'What does it look like under that?'

Brother Durand began talking about cauterisation and flaps of skin and tying and stitching; the tent lurched again and Martin's head fell back, which thankfully caused the litany of details to stop.

'In short, once it's healed it should just look like smooth skin with a few scars. Don't worry, there will be no bone or inner flesh to see.'

Martin lay still for a few more moments. 'All right,' he said, when he was sure the tent roof had stopped moving, 'I'm ready. How do I do this? I can't lean on it to push myself up.'

'We'll help you.'

Brother William came over, carrying a square of linen that he folded in half to make a triangular shape. 'I'm going to use this to support your injured arm. Until the wound is fully healed, it is very important that you keep it raised, do you understand? You must not allow your arm to fall down by your side, or the weight of the blood in it will be too heavy and the wound might reopen.'

Martin nodded. The linen was slipped under his arm and tied behind his neck, and then both monks helped to lift him into a sitting position.

The dizziness came again, but this time it was more fleeting.

'Sit still for a moment, to get used to your head being upright, before you try anything else,' said Brother Durand. 'You're doing very well.'

The next step was to turn sideways so that Martin could put his feet on the floor. This was achieved, but again with an odd sensation, a sort of tingling in his feet. The monks explained it was because he had been lying down for some while, which he supposed made sense.

One of the other two remaining patients in the tent gave a groan and a whimper, and Brother William went to tend to him. This man had also been struck by an arrow, but in the back, meaning that when the wound went bad it could only be cut and bled and cauterised, as there was nothing that could be removed. It had festered still, and he was clearly dying, but it was a slow and agonising process. Martin looked at him with pity, and the realisation dawned on him that he should be thanking God for his own good fortune, not cursing his ill luck.

The third patient had sustained a sword cut to his thigh, and thanks to the monks' care he looked likely to survive, but he was under orders to lie completely still and not attempt to leave his bed in case the wound burst open and he bled to death. Even when he recovered he might walk with a limp for the rest of his days, another fate Martin had avoided. *Praise the Lord, and be grateful to Brother Benedict for his prayers.*

'I'm ready to stand,' he said, suddenly, to Brother Durand. He could bear the pain if he felt that he was on the road to doing something, rather than just lying sick and helpless.

'I'm not sure …'

'Please, Brother. It will help me.'

'All right. Perhaps for a few moments. But keep that arm tied up and the wound raised, do you hear?'

With his good arm draped over Brother Durand's shoulders, and the monk's around his waist for support, Martin slowly raised himself to his feet. He swayed for a moment, leaning heavily, and then took his own weight. 'There.'

Brother Durand looked at the bandage, which had not darkened with any sudden flow of anything. 'Good man.'

Hugh appeared in the entrance to the tent, looking like he was in a tearing hurry. 'Brother Durand, you're —' he stopped dead at the sight of Martin, and his eyes grew round.

'Hugh? What is it?' Martin's mind leapt to all sorts of potential troubles.

'I'm to fetch Brother Durand. He's … wanted.'

The monk was instantly alert. 'Someone's hurt? I'll get my bag.' He was still holding on to Martin. 'Let's sit you down again first.'

'I'd prefer to stand, just for a few moments. I can manage.'

Warily, Brother Durand released him, staying close until he was sure Martin wasn't going to fall. Then he took up his bag of herbs and bandages and left the tent.

Hugh lingered for a moment, staring in a kind of petrified horror up at Martin and at what was left of his arm in its support.

'Hugh,' said Martin, again, 'What's the matter? Who's hurt?'

'Sir Martin …' stammered the boy. 'Are you … I mean …'

'Is Edwin back? Is that what it is?'

'I have to go.' Hugh turned and fled.

Some moments later, when Brother William looked up from his patient, he saw that Martin was gone.

Chapter Fourteen

Belatedly, Edwin came to his senses and skipped backwards, but fortunately the second arrow fell well short.

There was uproar both behind and ahead of him. The earl's men were crying betrayal, while there was some kind of struggle going on atop the battlements. Edwin scanned them and saw that nobody now appeared to be drawing a bow, and that a single figure was in the process of being restrained and disarmed by others. He therefore stood his ground and motioned to those in the camp to do the same.

After a short while, Sir Robert appeared. This time he called out himself, rather than having Anselm do it for him. 'Are you all right?'

'I am,' shouted Edwin. 'What happened?'

'It was Margaret. I'm sorry, we never thought she would be a danger or she wouldn't have been up here. She picked up a bow without anyone noticing. I had no idea she knew how to use one.' He took a breath before continuing. 'I'm sorry – it was certainly not my intention to attack you.'

Edwin reflected on the madness of extreme grief. 'It's fine. No harm done. Please, be kind to her.'

He could see Sir Robert nodding in acknowledgement, and then his voice came again. 'Do you seek further negotiations?'

Edwin held up the document. 'I have here the royal command for you to hand the castle over to the lord earl.'

There was silence.

'The seal is that of the king and his regent,' Edwin continued, 'and it has not been tampered with.' He wasn't used to bellowing like this, and was going to run out of breath soon. 'I suggest you ask Abbot Reginald or Prior Richard to come out and see it. I will stay right here, and nobody else will approach.'

It was uncomfortable standing out in the open between two groups of armed men, but Edwin was now relatively confident that nobody else in the castle was going to shoot at him, and he reminded himself once more that this was all in the cause of preventing further suffering.

The gates opened a crack, and Prior Richard emerged. Edwin now prayed that nobody *behind* him was going to do anything stupid. Surely they wouldn't – that was why he'd asked for one of the monks, not Sir Robert himself or any of his armed men – but his shoulders itched all the same.

The prior reached his position. 'Edwin.'

'Brother. Please, accept my apologies for any deception I practised, but please also understand that my aim was always – and remains now – to avoid violence.'

'In due course I will ask you to explain all this to me more fully, but for now, may I see the document?'

Edwin handed it over. 'It's dated some time ago, from London, and was … mislaid on its way here. I only found it last night.'

'Mmm hmm,' said the prior, as he scanned the text and seal, then went back to read it more closely.

'There seems to be no doubt,' he said, finally, refolding the parchment. 'And this was supposed to be sent directly to Sir Robert?'

Edwin explained once more that the royal justice had died in an accident and that his bags had subsequently been robbed, causing a delay until the document could be located.

'So, what now?' asked the prior. 'Shall I take this inside for Sir Robert to see?'

'Only if I can come too,' replied Edwin. 'My lord wouldn't like me to let it out of my sight, for all that several of us can now vouch for its contents.'

Prior Richard nodded. 'Very well. Our task, then, is to make sure that this stand-off ends peacefully.' He looked about him. 'We are far enough away from both sides that nobody can hear us, so we may speak freely as two men who trust each other. Let us confer now on what we think we can achieve.'

'I have the lord earl's promise that if Sir Robert keeps to his word and surrenders the castle immediately, now he has the order to do so, everything will be done in an orderly fashion and there will be no bloodshed.'

'I have no reason to doubt that Sir Robert will do so. I suspect that he will want it confirmed to the lord earl that this is the first he has heard of the order, and he was not holding out either against the earl or contrary to the wishes of the crown.'

'I have already said as much to my lord, and will happily stand up and say it again in front of witnesses.' *And lie about how that actually happened*. 'My lord will want to know that his captured men are safe.'

'They are. I have seen them every day, including this morning. They have been fed and well cared for.' The prior paused. 'However, Sir Robert has men of his own who have been lying wounded since the day of the engagement. Father Abbot and I have done our best to tend to them, but we are no substitute for our infirmarer. I take it that Brother Durand is still with you?'

'He is, and he has saved more than one life, including Sir Martin's.'

The prior noticed the new honorific. 'I neither approve nor condone the methods by which he gained entrance to the castle, but I am glad he was able to take your wife away. Is she …?'

'Safe at home, Brother, and with a healthy baby girl.'

'Praise the Lord. Now, I suggest that you return briefly to your lines to put this to the earl and have Brother Durand summoned, while I call up to Sir Robert. Then we will walk together from here into the castle.'

Edwin's face must have betrayed some of the apprehension he felt, because the prior patted him on the shoulder. 'Have faith, my son. The same faith that helped you to save my life two years ago, so that I could stand here with you now. We are nearly at the end of a long road, and we will reach it in peace.' He passed the document back to Edwin. 'Hold on to this as you go, so the earl can see that I have not taken it from you.'

Edwin returned and relayed the information, then waited as Hugh was dispatched to find Brother Durand.

The monk arrived, but Edwin had hardly started explaining everything to him when a familiar but somewhat slurred voice was heard from the camp. 'Let me through! And pass me a sword! If he's in danger …'

Sir Martin appeared, his injured arm bound up, staggering past men who melted out of his way.

'Don't stop him!' exclaimed Brother Durand. 'And whatever you do, don't touch his wound.'

Everyone appeared keen to keep out of the way, and he reached Edwin unopposed only to collapse into his arms. Edwin was extremely glad that Brother Durand was there to help him take the weight, and between them they were able to keep him upright.

'What,' asked the monk, with some asperity, 'do you think you're doing?'

'Edwin was in trouble,' explained Sir Martin. His face creased in puzzlement. 'Aren't you?'

'No,' said Edwin, wondering how many pain-deadening herbal concoctions his friend had ingested recently. 'I'm fine. Look.'

A heavy hand landed on Edwin's shoulder. 'You are, aren't you?'

'Yes. And you need to get back to bed.'

'Do I? Yes, I suppose I do. But you were in danger, so I had to come.'

The words were so simple, and so honest. Edwin felt tears coming to his eyes as he looked at his giant friend, the man who would remain his friend for the rest of their lives, no matter what happened.

Sir Martin bent his head so he could speak in Edwin's ear. 'I will *always* come,' he said, as firmly as he could, 'if you're in trouble. You or any of your family.'

Edwin's eyes were stinging now with the effort of keeping it all in. He had work to do. 'I know you will. But now, go back to bed and rest, so that you're well enough to meet my family when we get home. Sir Martin.'

'*Sir* Martin. Yes, I am, aren't I? I haven't started thinking of myself as that yet, but perhaps I should.'

Brother William had by this time arrived, and he and Sir Baldwin were able to move Sir Martin away. The normally irritable knight even spoke in a tone of admiration – 'Nothing stops you, does it? Good man,' – as they moved off, which only served to confirm Edwin's long-held belief that knights would always admire the physical courage of other knights, no matter how foolishly they were behaving.

But now it was time for the final act. The weaving was finished, and the fabric needed to be cut from the loom.

Edwin heard the castle gates shut behind him.

Sir Robert came forward to greet him. 'Master Thomas.' He shook his head. 'Edwin.'

Edwin thought he'd better get off on the right footing. 'I apologise for coming here originally under false pretences, Sir Robert.'

He didn't want to make excuses or lay the blame anywhere else, but he was nonetheless glad when the knight replied that he could understand that Edwin was only following orders. 'As was I,' he sighed. He pointed to the parchment. 'Is that it?'

'Yes. Shall we go up into the keep to discuss the details?'

'Very well. Brother Prior, you'll accompany us? The abbot is already there. And Brother Durand, thank you for coming. One of my men will take you to our wounded.'

For what he sincerely hoped was the last time, Edwin took the winding path up the motte. *There's a good line of sight from the top of the keep*, he remembered Everard reporting on that first evening, when the earl's camp was set up. *A deep fishpond*. You might just about be able to guess that a fishpond was deep without having seen it before, but nobody could know what the line of sight was from the top of a keep unless he'd been there, unless he was familiar with the view.

To Edwin's great relief, Sir Robert recognised straight away that the royal order was genuine. 'So I've been holding out for nothing, and Theo and the others have died for no reason.' There were dark smudges under his eyes and he looked haggard.

Edwin attempted to reassure him that there was nothing else he could have done, and repeated again the story of the mislaid document.

'And,' added the abbot, pointing at the relevant passage, 'see how the king and the regent commend your loyal service. This is no light matter.'

Sir Robert replied in a bitter tone. 'Well, at least my wife and I will have somewhere to live.'

Edwin glanced over at Lady Idonea, who was evidently struggling to keep her composure, both at what she was hearing from the men and also because Margaret was sitting with her, weeping inconsolably.

'Well then,' said Sir Robert, forcing himself to sound businesslike. 'I'd better go and do what's necessary – any delay and the lord earl might decide to attack again. I'll go out myself with the keys and lay them down, that should be obvious enough. And release the earl's men that we have here, of course.' He reflected for a moment, rubbing his face. 'I suppose I should give thanks that our losses all round were not even greater. If one of my men hadn't been alert enough to spot those spies creeping under the castle walls, I might never have realised the trick that was about to be pulled, and we might have been overrun and slaughtered.'

He departed, accompanied by the prior, leaving Edwin, Abbot Reginald, Lady Idonea and Margaret in the room. The only sound was Margaret's continued sobbing, and Edwin realised that this could be the opportunity he'd been seeking for an important private conversation.

He went to Margaret and knelt by her side. 'I'm truly, deeply sorry about Theo,' he said, gently. 'He was fine young man and he didn't deserve to die. He was only doing his duty.'

The girl's ravaged face was raised. 'He's still dead, though, isn't he?'

'Yes.' Edwin paused. 'I wonder if it might comfort you to know ... Brother Durand took him out of the castle to our camp in an attempt to save his life, but his injuries were too grave and he died before reaching it. But the last thing he heard was the good brother telling him that God loved him. And then his body was laid out with respect, and your own priest came to collect it. So he will be buried and at peace in your own churchyard.'

'There now,' urged Lady Idonea. 'This is some comfort, at least. You must try to calm yourself.'

'Perhaps,' said Edwin, addressing Margaret but turning to look questioningly at the abbot, 'Abbot Reginald would be good enough to accompany you to the chapel, so you can pray for Theo's soul?'

'Gladly,' replied the abbot, his face full of sympathy. 'We will pray together, and I will implore God's grace for you and your brother.'

Margaret assented, and she stood to follow him out of the room.

Lady Idonea also made as if to rise, but Edwin muttered to her under his breath. 'I need to speak to you alone for a moment.'

She looked puzzled, but then called out, 'I will follow directly. I must just ask Master Thomas about his wife.'

When the footsteps had receded down the stairs, she eyed him. 'And?'

'If you mean Alys, she is well and delivered of a daughter, safe in our own home.' He placed a slight emphasis on the word *safe*. 'But that's not what I wanted to say. I need to talk to you about Everard.'

She *almost* managed to cover up her shock, but Edwin had been looking out for the tiny flash of panic in her eyes. 'I can't think who you mean. I don't know anyone of that name.'

Edwin's voice took on a harder edge. 'Please don't take me for a fool. You know who I mean: Everard, your brother.'

She gasped as if he'd struck her, but said nothing, so Edwin went on. 'All of this had to have been done by someone who was outside the castle, but who had a strong loyalty to someone in it. Sir Robert has no brothers, and of course I thought you didn't, either, or you wouldn't have been the heiress to the castellanship. So I couldn't think of anyone who might fit. But to be an heiress you only need to have no *legitimate* brothers. And Everard's a bastard, isn't he? He's mentioned it several times in the past.'

Lady Idonea clamped her lips firmly shut.

Edwin took her lack of denial as an admission, and ploughed on. 'He must be – what, twenty years older than you? The product of an early liaison of your father, before he married? And brought up here, in this castle, before he left for better prospects in the earl's service. And he settled in Conisbrough so long ago – and married, and had children and grandchildren – that most people have no idea it wasn't his birthplace.'

She made an attempt to head him off. 'And why would a man who had made a good life for himself, despite his origins, want to put himself in danger for a half-sister so much his junior?'

Edwin almost laughed. 'I can tell you that I'm the wrong person to be asking that question to, if you want bafflement, because I can understand his motives completely.' He sobered again. 'He knew you as a little girl, I expect, and always felt protective of you. His patrols and rides often brought him in this direction, and of course nobody needed to keep track of what he did whenever he had time to himself. So there must have been ample opportunity, since January, for you to tell him of your troubles, and the possibility that you might lose your home. And so he decided to do something about it.'

She was half on her feet. 'Everard would never —'

Edwin waved her back down. 'He didn't murder the justice. But he was on the lookout for such a man appearing, because you told him to be. I suspect that you'd already had one letter, delivered by a normal messenger with little fanfare. How did you keep that from Sir Robert? Was it brought to you, rather than to him, as I know sometimes happens with letters? And I know you can read.' He pointed to the psalter that he'd seen her consult previously. 'So, what did you do – see the seal, open it, read it and throw it on the fire before he could ever know of it?'

Her expression told Edwin he was right.

'But you knew it could only be a temporary reprieve. The regent would wonder why his order hadn't been obeyed and send another, by the hand of a man with greater authority. You were worried and you conferred with your brother, telling him to look out for such a person. He then came across the body, guessed who it must be, and stole the document. He couldn't read, but he recognised the shape of the word "Tickhill", no doubt having seen it before when he was younger. So, crucially, he couldn't destroy it: he must have suspected that it contained bad news, but what if it was by some chance a reprieve? He couldn't be sure until you'd seen it, so instead of burning the order, he hid it. Once you'd read it and confirmed the contents, the two of you could decide what to do.'

She didn't say anything, but Edwin didn't need her to. 'And where this all went very wrong was that he didn't bring the document with him when the lord earl's host came to Tickhill. Perhaps he never had the chance to take it out of its hiding place without being seen, or he thought it was too dangerous to have about his person, or he just didn't realise he'd be able to get close enough to you to hand it over. But he didn't bring it, so the whole engagement took place without anyone being exactly sure of what the true situation was.'

There was a long moment of silence.

Edwin let it stretch out.

Finally, she gave in. 'If I confess, can you guarantee that Everard won't face a charge of murder?'

'I swear it.'

'All right, then.' She twisted her fingers together. 'Everything you've said is true. When the body was brought in, I knew who it must be, and when his belt pouch proved to be empty I hoped Everard had the order. Indeed, I felt sure he would, because he would never let me down. But, of course, once the castle gates were shut there was no possibility of us meeting, so neither of us could know for sure what it said.' She paused. 'And neither could Robert, of course – he was speaking the truth when he said he'd received no command to surrender.'

Edwin inclined his head. 'I know.'

He waited for her to continue, but she appeared to think the conversation was finished.

'Carry on,' he said, eventually.

'Carry on what? There's nothing else to tell.'

'As I said earlier, I'm not a fool.'

She said nothing.

'All right, then – if you won't tell me, I'll tell you. We both know it's the truth.'

Now she began to look properly frightened.

'When the earl's host arrived, you knew Everard must be in it. I'd already noticed that he was unusually nervous, but I put it down to him worrying about the younger members of the garrison – an easy mistake to make when you knew his devotion to duty and that there are many family connections between the manors of Conisbrough and Tickhill.'

'Of course I knew he was there! What of it?'

'He was out scouting in the dark on the night before the attack on the castle. Which gave you time to communicate.'

She made a derisive noise. 'Really? And how did I do that?'

'On the far side of the castle from the camp, the moat is dry, and there's a break in the wall where the motte sits. It's far too steep for anyone to go directly up and down it – not without risking a dangerous fall, anyway – but someone who was secured by a rope at the top could let themselves down and then use it get back up.'

Now she laughed. 'Are you seriously suggesting that *I* –'

'Not you,' continued Edwin, cutting her off. 'Theo.'

Once more, she was stunned into silence.

'He would be the ideal person: small, light, agile, eager to please. You should know, Lady Idonea, that I've spoken to my wife about the night she spent up here in the keep. Theo was lying across the door, so you couldn't have gone out without waking him. But what if you *did* rouse him, deliberately, to tell him that Sir Robert, when he visited the room earlier, had told you to give him an order? What if you then both went out? You would have been noticed if you'd left the keep by the main door, so my assumption is that you went up to the roof, tied the rope to something solid, and then Theo let himself down. You were confident that this would be the place Everard would be waiting, because anyone who knew the castle well would know that it was the only potential viable spot.'

She tried to interrupt him. 'You can have no possible —'

He waved her away. 'Alys saw the rope, the morning afterwards, a rope that hadn't been on the roof when I'd been up there previously. And I saw poor Theo's body: I thought at the time that the mark on his hand didn't fit with his other injuries, but now I see it was a rope burn.'

Edwin could see that every word he spoke was lying more heavily on her. But he was nearly done, and it would soon be over, although the greatest blow was yet to come. 'Everard told Theo to tell you about the planned ruse. You didn't want to tell Sir Robert about it directly, in case he was suspicious of where you got your information from, but you were able to get a member of the garrison to watch specifically for any movement towards those exact spots. It would have been all but impossible to notice unless they knew precisely what they were looking for. And that resulted in the death of one of the earl's men there and then, the capture of the others, and the bloodshed at the gate in the morning when the surprise assault failed.'

She reacted angrily. 'Well, what if I did do all that? Was it not my duty to protect this castle – which my father protected before me – against an unjust attack?'

'That might have been your duty if you were sure the attack was unjust. If you hadn't conspired in destroying and hiding the orders to surrender it. And this is why you've been so upset about Theo's death, and so solicitous to Margaret, isn't it? Theo wasn't supposed to get mixed up in what you knew would be a vicious encounter, but he did and he lost his life as a result.'

That made her hang her head. 'So young – just a child, really.' She sat in silence for a few moments before pulling herself together and looking directly at Edwin. 'So, what are you going to do now? For myself I don't care, not now I've lost my home. "Another castellanship", indeed. I've lived here all my life and I don't particularly care to leave.' Then her defiance faltered. 'But Everard. Once you tell the earl all this, if you haven't already, he won't see anything except a traitor. He won't stand for it, he'll have him executed ...' she started to cry.

'I'm not going to tell the earl, or at least not if we can come to an agreement.'

'What?'

'He's got what he wanted, and he doesn't need to know all the details. If he did, he might end up doing something ... unwise, and more innocents would suffer along with everyone else.' Edwin paused. 'And I have to consider Everard's terrible dilemma. He never wanted to betray his lord – he just wanted to keep his family – keep *you* – safe. In order to help you, he was willing to give up his good name and even his soul.' Edwin found his voice becoming less steady. 'He just wanted to protect his little sister, and then it all got terribly, horrifyingly, out of hand. He felt the guilt of it, I assure you.'

'Please, save him. Save him if you can. What agreement do we have to come to?'

'It's two things, both of them simple. One: make sure Margaret is looked after. Find out from her whether she'd rather go with you to wherever you end up, or whether she'd rather stay in Tickhill. Let her choose, and in either case make sure she's safe and comfortable.'

'But she shot at you this morning! Why would you care?'

'I know she did. I might have been tempted to do the same if, like her, I thought I was aiming at the person responsible for the death of a beloved brother.'

'Very well. Agreed. I would have done this anyway.'

'I know. While I was here I could see how you cared for them both, and other young people about the place. But sometimes this took a sinister turn, as my wife could detect in your behaviour towards her. So my second condition is: stop coveting the children of others because you have none of your own. You may or may not go on to have any – that's God's will. But if you don't, then making other women afraid that you'll steal their babies is not the answer.'

She did not speak, but after a while she gave a tight nod.

'Good.' Edwin breathed a sigh of relief.

'And so,' she managed. 'Everard will keep his position? The earl will know nothing of this and he won't be punished?'

Edwin turned away for a moment to compose himself before he faced her again. Then, as kindly and gently as he could, he said, 'I'm afraid I have some very bad news for you.'

Epilogue

Six months later

The cottage was full of laughter as the fire crackled and the smell of good food filled the air.

Edwin looked around him in contentment. The harvest was safely gathered for another year, and yesterday the whole village had rejoiced together. This evening he and Alys were hosting a family celebration. Cecily's children were excited at the thought of the treats to come, and were rushing in and out of the house playing noisy games. Alys, Cecily and Joan were cooking, though Alys kept pausing to cast loving glances over to Edwin where he sat at the table with Sir Geoffrey and Sir Martin. Each of the knights was dandling a baby on his knee in an expert fashion, having by now had plenty of practice.

Sir Geoffrey should, by rights, have sent Matilda back to his own manor to be raised, so that she could grow up on the estate she would one day inherit. But as his duties kept him at Conisbrough and allowed him to visit his home only twice a year, he'd decided that he couldn't bear the separation. Matilda, Joan and Joan's own daughter – for she seemed to have no trouble feeding both babies – had therefore remained at the cottage. Once Matilda was weaned Joan would go home, her purse heavy in recognition of her service and the money very welcome to her family. Edwin and Alys would foster Matilda and bring her up alongside Edith for the time being.

It was Edith who was being held by Sir Martin, as he bounced her up and down and pulled faces to make her chuckle, cheerful in a way Edwin would have considered impossible half a year or a year ago. The stump of his arm had healed well, and now hardly pained him at all. The journey back to Conisbrough from Tickhill, undertaken so soon after his surgery, had been a trying one and his recovery had been set back a little, but as soon as he was able he was up and about. For reasons Edwin couldn't quite fathom – he assumed it was to give thanks for his recovery – Sir Martin had travelled to Roche Abbey as soon as he could, staying overnight and returning in a much calmer state of mind.

Sir Geoffrey had, as promised, devised new exercises, and Sir Martin had thrown himself into them with gusto, working and pushing himself almost beyond endurance as he trained and learned and sought to convince everyone – including himself – that he was just as good as he used to be. Now that he was a household knight his duties had changed, but he remained at Conisbrough for the present and was content to do so rather than being sent away to a manor. Whether his long-suffering sparring partners felt the same was another question.

Sir Martin now began to give Sir Geoffrey a long and very technical-sounding description of some sort of sword manoeuvre, but he did not forget Edith and held her safely. Now that she and Matilda were beginning to move and sit, they were taken out of their swaddling for large parts of each day, and she was wriggling. But his huge hand kept her steady while her pudgy little ones drummed merrily on his arm.

Edwin had regretted, over and over again, the trouble that had set him and Sir Martin against each other, and which had led indirectly to his injury. He swore to himself that it would never happen again, and that their very different paths in life would not stop them being friends. He could sometimes wish that the knight – and they'd all got used to that by now – had *something* else in his head other than military pursuits, but that was Sir Martin, and always would be. Indeed, recognition of this difference was why Edwin had been keeping a little secret for the past couple of weeks.

Edwin's contentment extended to the state of peace that had existed in the region since the conclusion of the business at Tickhill. Sir Robert and Lady Idonea had moved out, and the earl had given Sir Malvesin charge of the castle. The garrison, of course, owed service to the place rather than to their previous castellan in person, so they had remained and were content under the new leadership, or so Sir Geoffrey had said. Edwin privately considered that Sir Malvesin was a much better choice for the post than Sir Baldwin, who would no doubt have gone about everything in an abrasive way, so he was glad for all concerned.

Edwin had, in earthly terms at least, got away with the lies he'd told back in the spring. There had been no repercussions for Sir Robert or Lady Idonea, nor even for Everard, whose body had been laid to rest in consecrated ground after his 'accidental' demise. He would have to face God's judgement, of course, for the future of his soul, but that was between him and the Lord, and at least Edwin had not prevented him even from starting on that journey.

He'd been to the churchyard that morning. After Mother's death, Sir Geoffrey had ordered that she be buried next to Father rather than having her conveyed to the church on his own manor, and Edwin was grateful to have the opportunity to pray over them both. Everard's grave and Willikin's had also cut savage new scars in the earth, but time had by now softened them a little, as it did everything.

Making his peace with God had been a little more difficult. Edwin knew that if he confessed his sins to Father Ignatius, the priest was bound to everlasting silence, and so no word of them would ever get abroad. But Edwin had not confessed. In order to receive absolution he would have to be truly penitent for what he'd done, and he wasn't. He wasn't sorry that he'd lied, because those untruths had saved lives. He knew the earl well enough by now to be confident that he wouldn't have taken the betrayal of his sergeant-at-arms, nor the involvement of those at Tickhill, quietly. His pride and his reputation among his peers would have demanded that he take reprisals, and if Edwin's soul had to carry a permanent stain in order to avoid that, then so be it. The fact that Edwin now knew that he didn't trust his lord enough to tell him the truth did not really bode well for their future relationship, but he tried not to think about that too much.

The earl had made it to London ahead of the regent's death, which had occurred in mid-May. He'd been there while discussions had taken place on what to do next; the king was still only eleven and thus far from able to take control of the realm himself. In the end it had been decided that there would be no appointment of a new single regent, but rather that a group of three men should act together: Pandulf, the papal legate who was in England; Peter des Roches, the bishop of Winchester; and Hubert de Burgh, England's justiciar. As it happened, the earl did not particularly like any of these men, so that was bound to cause trouble in due course, but Edwin resolutely refused to dwell on that just now.

There was a knock at the open door. 'Can I come in?' It was Crispin, the only other member of the family they were waiting for before they ate. He was carrying a sack, which he put down in one corner with a wink at Edwin.

The meal was superb – not the sort of fancy fare served at the earl's table, of course, but good, honest food prepared well and with love – and after it Edwin sat back with a sigh of satisfaction. 'You are wonderful,' he said to Alys. And she was: she ran the house, the children and her business with seeming effortlessness, and loved them all.

'Flatterer,' she said, indulgently. 'Pass me those empty dishes, and then why don't you show Sir Martin what you've got for him?'

Sir Martin looked up from his latest attempt to make Edith laugh. He'd enjoyed his meal too, judging by the amount of it he'd put away, and he was now much less shy and awkward about eating in front of them, needing to cut his food and then spoon it with the same hand while he tried to hold the bowl steady with his shortened arm.

Edwin fetched the sack. 'Now,' he began, 'I don't want you to think this means I particularly approve of you knocking the living daylights out of anyone who dares to challenge you, but it's what makes you happiest, so I thought I'd find a way to help. Crispin has made these, and they're our gift to you.'

He pulled out the first item, a short leather sleeve ending in a beautifully crafted metal left hand, the fingers fixed in a bent position.

'He made it exactly the right size and shape to fit around the strap of a shield, so you don't necessarily have to use that special one you've adapted. It should also work for reins. You put your arm in here and it straps on – now the wound has healed you should be able to manage that, or so Brother William said.'

Sir Martin took it, looking as pleased as Edwin hoped he would.

'And,' continued Edwin, with a combined flourish and eye-roll, 'because you're sometimes in a more warlike mood …' he revealed a similar sleeve, but this one ending in a solid, heavy ball, like the head of a mace. 'Don't thump anyone with this if you want them to get up again.'

Sir Martin's smile was even wider. 'My, my.'

'And finally …' Edwin reached into the sack a little more carefully to remove the remaining item. Then he pulled off a scabbard to reveal that the third sleeve was tipped with a sharp, vicious-looking knife blade.

'It's your life,' he said under his breath to the now almost overcome Sir Martin, 'and I have to respect that.'

'They will only ever be used to defend the weak,' promised Sir Martin. 'Never unjustly.' He wiped his eye on his sleeve. 'But now I feel that I should have something to give you.'

'You've done that already,' replied Edwin. 'You gave me back my wife, and allowed our daughter to be born safely in her own home. No gift could be better than that.'

The dead were dead and must be mourned, and their blessed memory honoured, but the living needed to go on living, in the best way they could. Edwin leaned back in perfect happiness as he contemplated his friends and his family.

Historical Note

Earl William de Warenne's entry in the *Oxford Dictionary of National Biography* notes that, in 1219:

> He obtained the restoration of her estates to Alice, countess of Eu, his niece [...] Acting as custodian on Alice's behalf, Warenne henceforth enjoyed custody of the honour and castle of Tickhill in Yorkshire [...] His possession of Tickhill was vigorously resisted by a local magnate, Robert de Vieuxpont, leading for a time to the threat of violent unrest.

Further information about exactly how the earl went about gaining possession of Tickhill is sparse, so this was the ideal opportunity for a fictional story to fill in the gaps and speculate on how this 'threat of violent unrest' might have played out in the local area – and how Edwin might have become involved.

Strange as it may seem now, especially to those familiar with the large city of Sheffield, Tickhill was actually the second-most important town in South Yorkshire in the thirteenth century, after Doncaster; it was a thriving centre of trade with shops and a marketplace. Its castle had originally been built in the 1080s, but it was expensively restyled a century later, at which point an eleven-sided polygonal keep was constructed on top of the original and very steep motte (the 'hill' that gave the settlement its name), along with stone curtain walls, a chapel in the bailey and a two-storey gatehouse.

The holder of Tickhill in early 1219 was Robert de Vieuxpont (sometimes spelled Vipont), who had inherited the castellanship from his father-in-law. He contested the rights of Alice of Eu, as put forward by Earl Warenne, but was eventually obliged to give up the custody of Tickhill; he then held various other crown positions before he died sometime around 1228, leaving a widow, Idonea, and a son who was still a minor.

Earl Warenne held Tickhill in his niece's name, awarding the castellanship to Sir Malvesin de Hersey (whose brother Sir Baldwin was also in the earl's service). The castle returned to royal custody in 1244 and remained under direct crown control from then onwards, its importance gradually waning. By the mid-sixteenth century it was noted to be in 'decayed' condition, and most of it, including the keep, was demolished in the mid-seventeenth century. All that remains today is the motte, the gatehouse and some portions of the wall, with a newer house inside the bailey. The site is privately owned and not open to visitors, although the outside of the gatehouse can be viewed from the road.

The nearby Roche Abbey, which Edwin and Martin visited in an earlier book in this series, *Brother's Blood*, had been founded in 1147. By 1219 it was a flourishing foundation under its abbot, Reginald, who would be succeeded in 1229 by Abbot Richard. The Cistercian Order was international and well connected, its senior officers keeping in regular touch with each other, and monasteries would have been in receipt of important news just as promptly as any local noblemen.

All we know about the real individuals mentioned above are their names and a few of their documented actions; I have invented the details of their looks and personalities. All the other characters are completely fictional, although their occupations are plausible and based on thirteenth-century evidence.

Medieval combat was generally carried out with weapons that were sharp and none too clean. This meant that open wounds and cuts were very common, as were blood poisoning and gangrene, and that even minor injuries could turn out to be fatal. Both Richard the Lionheart and William Clito (the eldest son of the eldest son of William the

Conqueror, and therefore at one time a candidate for the English throne) died of seemingly inconsequential wounds to arm and hand, respectively, after they festered. Clito, we are told by a contemporary, made what he thought was a temporary withdrawal from a fight outside a castle when his hand was cut by a spear, but he was later forced to retire to bed where 'his whole arm up to the shoulder turned as black as coal' from the infection and he died in agony days later.

Martin is more fortunate, due to a combination of luck, his own strength and the presence of two well-read monks, one of whom is an experienced healer. The only option available to stop the wet gangrene afflicting him was amputation; even this would only succeed if it was done with skill, before the infection spread too far, and if the patient was fortunate enough to avoid further infection and strong enough to survive the blood loss and shock. Many such operations no doubt ended in death, but we do know from archaeological evidence that some patients did manage to survive, and that they might make use of prosthetic limbs afterwards.

Medical texts had been written and circulated for some time, and a monastery was the most likely place to find one. The procedure that Martin undergoes is based on that described by Henri de Mondeville, a French surgeon who lived in the later thirteenth and early fourteenth century, in his treatise *Cyrurgia* (*Surgery*). On amputation he writes:

> Encircle the limb with two tightly wrapped cords or towels. Place one just below the join and the other on the healthy side of the site amputation. Two aides must grasp the limb securely, above and below, to enable the surgeon to do his work in a stable field. The tight bindings will reduce the patient's sensibility. The limb should be elevated to lessen the loss of blood [...] Make a circular incision between the two bindings. Cut right down to the bone with a hot iron or gold cautery, as broad and as slim as a knife blade. Then cover both surfaces of the soft tissues with damp cloths to spare them injury by the saw. Use the correct tool and saw through the bone with deft, light and smooth strokes.

This sort of operation could be carried out in the thirteenth century, but unfortunately it would be hundreds of years before an effective anaesthetic was developed.

Childbirth was marginally less dangerous than amputation, but it was still a remarkably hazardous activity: a woman in labour had a greater chance of dying than an armoured knight in battle, and expectant mothers were advised to make their confession before their labour started, in case they died in the course of it. As many as one in eight mothers would not leave the birthing chamber alive, and nor would one in six newborns.

Official medical care was non-existent, but as ever, the informal networks of women were what kept society alive and functioning. An expectant mother would be 'confined' – literally shut in a room, her bedchamber if she was lucky enough to have one – and would be surrounded by experienced women who had already given birth themselves and who had attended on others. A safe, natural labour was always the goal, but unfortunately (again, as ever) this was something that could only be diagnosed retrospectively, so those in the birthing chamber had to be ready for anything. Those shut outside, including the father, could only hope and pray.

As and when a baby was born alive it needed to be baptised: unbaptised children who died were denied burial in consecrated ground and would never reach heaven. In an emergency this could be done by the midwife in the chamber, but if the baby survived its first hours and days the normal process was for the ceremony to take place in church. This meant that the mother could not attend, as she was confined to bed for a lying-in period to avoid the dangers of infection and bleeding after the birth. She would re-emerge after about a month for a 'churching' ceremony, after which she resumed her place in normal society, hopefully with a thriving infant to care for.

Although the civil war that had divided the kingdom was over, this was still a time of unrest and upheaval. William Marshal, the aged regent, died in May 1219. His death was due to natural causes, but it was still something of a shock and it left a gaping hole in the realm's governance: he had served Henry III's father, uncles and grandparents for decades. Earl Warenne did make it to London, and he was one of the noblemen who formed Marshal's funeral procession.

The triumvirate that replaced Marshal's regency did not function smoothly, and there was to be yet more trouble and lawlessness in England in the years to come, as Edwin and his friends and family will find out.

Further Reading

Bennett Connolly, Sharon, *Defenders of the Norman Crown: Rise and Fall of the Warenne Earls of Surrey* (Barnsley: Pen & Sword, 2021).

The Gatehouse record for Tickhill castle, online at www.gatehouse-gazetteer.info/English%20sites/915.html

Hey, David, *Medieval South Yorkshire* (Ashbourne: Landmark Publishing, 2003).

Mitchell, Piers D., *Medicine in the Crusades: Warfare, Wounds and the Medieval Surgeon* (Cambridge: Cambridge University Press, 2004).

Leyser, Henrietta, *Medieval Women: A Social History of Women in England 450–1500* (London: Weidenfeld & Nicolson, 1995).

Vincent, Nicholas, 'Warenne, William de, fifth earl of Surrey [Earl Warenne]', *Oxford Dictionary of National Biography*, online edition, oxforddnb.com